The Lowest Healer
and the
Highest Mage

HIYODORI

Contents

CHAPTER ONE

30 Days Left

AFTER SEVEN YEARS, I had grown somewhat fond of my cell. This was a coping mechanism, obviously—I knew I would never be free.

The cell really could've been much worse, though. It had a round window that let in a stingy circle of sunlight, and a mostly-accurate black clock on the marbled concrete wall, and a floor bed with insulated padding. It had a white ceramic sink, and a partially walled-off toilet, and a desk equipped with cheap pens and notepads, and a solid steel door with a reverse peephole. And it would be home forever, unless the Osmanthian government felt inspired to transfer me elsewhere.

I'd made my share of escape attempts early on, back when I was still in my mid-twenties, armed with baseless optimism and disgusting amounts of energy. At some point, though, I realized I had no idea what I'd do after escaping. I could hardly expect to get away with hiding anywhere in Osmanthus. Leave the country, then? Even if I made it across the border, I'd have to avoid most of our neighbors. Osmanthus had few true allies; most countries on the continent preferred to maintain an attitude of perfect neutrality. And an enemy nation didn't seem like a much more inviting prospect.

Granted, I was a convicted traitor to Osmanthus. You might think certain other countries would welcome the infamous Asa Clematis with open arms. Celebrate her as a hero, even. But my furtive attempts at rebellion had ended in humiliating failure, and I'd frankly outgrown any interest in overthrowing (much less reforming) oppressive governments.

Pathetic though it may sound, I was now more or less content to be alive and mostly free of the worst kinds of suffering. I just didn't think I was cut out for a lifelong career as a fugitive. More than anything, I dreaded being dragged back here. I could tolerate it now, but what if life in my cell became unbearable after the adrenaline of the chase? Either way, cooperating with my captors saved me from anything resembling full-blown torture. It also kept me too busy and tired to spare much time for philosophical agonizing.

I had every reason to expect that this chilly fall morning would lead to another day of working to hobble convicted mages (my own peculiar form of prison labor, since I was the only one who could do it). That assumption turned out to be terribly wrong, but no one was kind enough to enlighten me at the time.

So, ignorant of what lay in wait for me, I went through my usual routine. Around sunrise I splashed icy water on my face from the sink in my cell, gargled mouthwash, and quickly changed from one off-white prison jumpsuit to another, which was hopefully a bit cleaner. I gnawed on an energy bar while waiting for my kettle to heat up to make instant coffee.

The raisin-studded bar was still sticking halfway out of my mouth when someone rapped at the cell door. It couldn't even be 6:30 yet. Guess I had a lot of mage-hobbling to get done today.

The steel door swung partway open. A masked guard stuck his head in. "Visitors for you, Magebreaker."

"Visitors?" I echoed, muffled by my energy bar. For a stupid second I pictured my parents, blurry faces trapped in time. They either hadn't tried or hadn't been allowed to visit me, not once in all these seven years. I had no idea what they looked like nowadays, come to think of it. I'd branded them the family that produced a traitor, so I couldn't cultivate too much in the way of resentment.

"They're from Public Security," said the guard. "Nothing else on your schedule today."

"Wha—"

He promptly withdrew, pretending not to hear me, and held the door open wider for my mystery guests. In walked two strangers and one all-too-familiar face.

I choked on my remaining mouthful. I came dangerously close to spitting raisins all over the visitors. The cell door clanked shut at their backs. I flapped my hands for them to wait. Just wait. Please.

I swigged water and swallowed and wiped my mouth and stared feverishly up at the small round porthole of a window cut high in the wall above my floor bed. I turned back around once I'd stopped coughing, and my eyes were done watering, and my expression hopefully looked more or less human.

The three visitors stood there unchanged. For the sake of preserving my composure, I focused on the two of them I'd never seen before. One was a young man—barely college-age?—buried in an oversized cardigan made from some kind of quilted material. No aura of magic. No bond thread around his neck. An unbonded healer, then. Just like me. In contrast, the uniform-clad woman at his side had to be at least a few decades older and was clearly a mage. A military-trained one at that.

I cleared my throat, which still smacked of raisins. "Sorry," I said to the pair of them. "I only have one chair. If you'd like to play rock-scissors-paper for it, I'd be happy to—"

"We have a problem," said the mage. She had dark waist-length locs and better posture than all the rest of us in the room combined.

I eyed the chair by my wood-veneer desk. Yellow stuffing had begun to leak out of its seat cushion.

"Prison furniture, you know," I said. "This is about as good as it gets."

The mage wasted little time on my blather. I was only a few syllables in when she turned to touch the gray wall. An iridescent ripple like a heat mirage flowed from her palm to cover all four cell walls, the ceiling, the floor. The magic faded from sight within seconds, but I could still sense it there, a kind of invisible force-field closing off the room. I recognized this particular magical skill—a seal to protect classified information. Claustrophobia crawled with little prickly feet up the back of my neck.

The mage pivoted to face me again. Thus far, she seemed to be the one in charge here. "I'm Manatree," she said. "PubSec. Class—"

"9-2?" I guessed.

The mage called Manatree returned my gaze without blinking. Her companion—the healer in the cardigan—did a double-take at me.

"Correct," Manatree said after a moment. "You seem to be as described, Magebreaker."

"Call me Clematis," I said. "What'd they tell you about me?"

"You strive to annoy. But you have gifts unlike any other healer."

Well, couldn't argue with that.

"We came here to get your professional opinion," she continued.

"My opinion as what? A prison lifer? A traitor to the nation?" The subliminal hum of Manatree's magic sealing the walls was starting to get to me. I wanted desperately to dig something in my ears, but I was all out of cotton swabs. "Or as the so-called Magebreaker?"

"As a healer of mages."

I snorted. "You know I got that Magebreaker nickname for a reason. I haven't actually *healed* a single stinking mage since—"

"Examine her first. Then tell us what you think," Manatree told me, unfazed. "This is a direct order from the Board of Magi."

Manatree and the young healer both turned to contemplate the third visitor they'd brought along with them. And now, despite my ferocious efforts to ignore her existence, I too had little choice left but to look at her.

She hadn't uttered a word since the now-departed prison guard closed my cell door behind her. She leaned on the wall by my sink, quite separate from Manatree and the healer, and about as far away from me as it was possible to get without physically leaving the cell.

She was the tallest out of the three of them, a vaguely slouching figure in a puffy jacket and long black leggings that were starting to come apart a bit at the seams. She'd wrenched her hair into a short black ponytail at the nape of her neck. She'd be thirty-two now, a few months younger than me. I'd never seen her hair that short before. I hadn't seen her once in the past seven years, for that matter.

If you must know, her name was Wisteria Shien. People called her the Kraken, just like how they called me the Magebreaker. But I'd always called her Wist. She was the most powerful mage in the entire world, not just our fair country of Osmanthus. Only the second Kraken-class mage in all of recorded history. She was also the reason I'd been sentenced to life in prison.

Once we'd been pimpled schoolgirls together, studying magic (Wist) and mage healing (me). Once we'd been best friends. Once I'd been her dedicated healer. Now one of us was serving out a life sentence, and the other was an international celebrity with godlike powers. A lot can change in less than a decade.

CHAPTER TWO

30 Days Left

Again, you might know me as the Magebreaker, but my name is Asa Clematis. Family name: Asa. Given name: Clematis. The opposite of Wist, whose given name comes first. My name order is the standard version, by the way. Wist's got flipped to show that she was adopted by the Shien clan.

Once I'd dreamed of ruling the world. Okay, not the entire world, just Osmanthus. And I wasn't interested in ruling it per se. I mean, I did like the idea of holding power, but I wasn't planning to become a life-long dictator or anything. I would have been more than content simply to control things from behind the scenes.

And most importantly, it wasn't just a mere dream. At the time I'd been in my early twenties, with little job experience and only a partial education. I was a healer by birth, incapable of wielding magic myself. All I could do, in theory, was help fix up aching mages.

I was sick of mages looking down on us healers, and I was sick of seeing other skilled healers get courted for bonding, forced to become life partners with mages they didn't even particularly like. I was sick of living in the only country on the whole continent ruled solely by mages, with zero healers in any position of significance and absolutely no plans to change that.

Naturally, I wasn't the only one who had ever felt this way. But there was one colossal difference between me and every other failed rebel over the years. I had Wist—yes, the one and only Kraken-class mage in the world—on my side.

At least, I'd thought I had her on my side.

Seven years after my conviction, it was downright comical to reflect back on how much I'd trusted her. I'd believed wholeheartedly that the most powerful mage of all would stand by me no matter what, even if we ended up making the entire mageocracy our mortal enemy. Talk about naive.

I'm not a complete idiot. I'd learned not to expect anything from Wist anymore, of course. I certainly hadn't wanted or expected her to visit me in prison. She was the person who'd put me there. Why show up except to gloat? Anyway, she didn't show up, period. I hadn't so much as heard her voice since she testified against me at my trial. The least she could do for me was to stay out of my life—for the rest of my life.

So I'll confess that Wist's sudden appearance right here in my cell had me a tad shaken. I think I did a pretty commendable job of hiding it, mainly by keeping my eyes fixed on Manatree and her pet healer in the cardigan. At least focusing on those two let me pretend Wist wasn't lurking over there in the corner like some kind of lanky ghost.

And I didn't show anything on my face. I didn't let it twist the sound of my voice. Still, my heart pounded a sick beat in my chest. My familiar cell felt gray and hot. I'd never full-on fainted in my life. But knowing I was going to have to face Wist again gave me the sensation of blood pressure plummeting.

At least until I actually turned and made myself face her. Then, abruptly, I felt nothing except a resigned exhaustion. Why get all worked up? It was just Wist, my old nemesis. She'd already gotten me convicted for life. At this point, she could hardly do anything worse. The greatest risk right now was to my pride, and the best way to protect my pride would be to appear utterly unaffected.

I drew myself up and walked over to the sink. We stood there, squared off, as if we were about to have a tooth-brushing duel. I barely came up to Wist's shoulder, but that was nothing new.

"Clematis."

Her voice was lower than I remembered. Then again, Wist had never been much of a morning person.

"Your hair," she said next, apropos of nothing.

Instinctively I reached up to touch the back. I kept it quite short here in prison. Oh—she probably meant the white streaks. "I know," I said. "I look like a skunk. Cute, isn't it?"

"I didn't want to come here."

A white cold blanket of incredulity settled over me. It was remarkably calming. "That's funny," I said brightly. "Neither did I. Well, here we are anyway. Seems like I'm supposed to give you an examination. I'll make it quick."

She shot a look at Manatree. "I haven't agreed to this."

"With all due respect, Kraken," said Manatree, "you aren't in much of a position to refuse."

Now that was unexpected. Theoretically, Wist was very much in a position to refuse anything and everything. She had more magical power, after all, than the entire Osmanthus Board of Magi put together.

The best-trained duelists were nothing to her; nor were entire armies of combat mages. She had enough political sway to practically be considered a nation unto herself. She—

I put that thought on hold. Against my will, I'd grown intrigued. Wist edged away from me, but she'd trapped herself in the corner with nowhere else to go. Manatree watched with folded arms. The fresh-faced male healer peeked over at us from behind Manatree.

I focused on Wist, this time for real. Not on the black stub of her curiously short ponytail, or on the cap that shadowed her eyes. I focused on the magic that grew from the invisible core near the small of her back.

Nearly all mages have their magic core located in that same part of their torso. They get ranked according to the number of unique magic branches that sprout from it. For instance, Manatree—with nine separate branches—was a Class 9. That made her one of the highest. Everyone with double-digits on up got lumped together under Class S. Only a handful of Class S mages showed up in each generation, anyway. And only those with a genuinely countless number of magical branches would fall into the final class, the mythical class. The Kraken class.

Uncharacteristically, I was having trouble concentrating. I closed my eyes, pressed my forehead. With my physical eyes closed I could more cleanly perceive the skein of Manatree's magic sealing the room, the glow of Manatree's core, and the distinct divisions of the nine branches in her body, each devoted to mastery of a different magical skill. I perceived traces of past connections between Wist and the young healer. Despite looking like he'd barely made it out of high school, he must've healed her over and over. They might very well have been working together for years. No such history existed between him and Manatree.

Yet when I turned to Wist—

Her core sputtered deep inside her, dull and low, scarcely more than an ember. It was there, at least. But the infinitely branching threads of her magic, the myriad long tangled strands that had stymied healer after healer—they were gone. Only her core remained, like the sad stump of a world tree sawed down to nothing.

My eyes came open. Wist's gaze remained trained on the rim of the toothpaste-spotted mirror above my sink. There was no indication on her face that she'd known what I'd seen, or that she cared. My throat felt bitterly dry. I took a moment to swallow.

Manatree came up beside me. "You see?"

My brain started churning, damn the thing. "You've got a problem, all right. What the hell happened?"

"She claims not to remember," Manatree said.

"Convenient." I turned on Wist again. A sick thrill rose in me as I considered the implications. "You can't do any magic right now, can you? You can't so much as blow over a piece of tissue paper."

Something had rendered the almighty Kraken weaker than a Class 1 mage without training. Worse than that, even.

Yes, everyone in the world was technically either a mage or a healer. But the vast majority were classified as subliminal mages or subliminal healers, unable to actually use any sort of special ability. For most people, knowing whether you were a mage or a healer was like knowing your zodiac or blood type—a source of identity, perhaps, but with little practical value on a day-to-day basis.

Perhaps 1% of the population had enough magical power to require mage training for safety's sake, but well under 0.4% of people actually made their living as mages. Right now Wist the Kraken was a zero-branch mage with little left to her but the flickering remnants of a ravaged magical core. In other words, her magical capabilities had fallen to the level of your average neighborhood dentist, who might have been classified as a subliminal mage in childhood, but who had never actually worked a lick of magic in their life.

I couldn't help it. I started laughing.

I slapped my thighs. The laughter bent me in half. There were tears in my eyes. The joy tasted like bile. I certainly didn't expect anyone else to join in. It was all too ridiculous. I sounded like a monkey howling. But for quite a long time, I just couldn't stop laughing.

Once silence filled my cell again, Wist pushed off the wall. She passed me without quite brushing me, without looking down at me, and repositioned herself right by the steel door to freedom. "There's your second opinion," she said to Manatree and the healer.

Aftershocks of laughter jerked my chest like a coughing fit. "No one enters or leaves here"—I meant the whole prison island—"except by magic. You can't even make a scene of storming off."

"Clematis," said Wist.

She'd have to try harder than that to shut me up. I wasn't done yet. "You can't teleport. You can't walk away through the walls. You—you have to wait here like a prisoner till another mage lets you out."

Wist had always been difficult to read. That's how she managed to get away with stabbing me in the back, I guess. The last thing I wanted to do right now was indulge in flashbacks. Yet when I looked up at her, at the dark eyes and still face that revealed little other than hints of sleep deprivation, it reminded me of every other time she'd looked back at me like that over the years. Waiting for me to pick up the thread of the conversation. Revealing nothing.

It was the same this time. I saw no anxiety at the loss of her magic, no humiliation at her helplessness, no anger at whoever had decided it was a great idea to bring her here, to bring her to me of all people. Or maybe she felt all those things and more, but they stayed immersed somewhere untouchable inside her, sunk down miles below the ruins of her magic core. All that showed on the surface was an implacable watchfulness. It sure took all the fun out of taunting her.

"Clematis," she repeated. "We're on the same side in this. I don't want to trouble you."

The disbelief came on so strong, it almost made me dizzy. I looked to Manatree for confirmation that I wasn't losing my mind. "Are you hearing this shit?"

Manatree responded with a surprisingly unmilitary shrug.

I rounded on Wist. "Is this some kind of reverse psychology gambit? You don't want to *trouble* me? *You* don't want to trouble *me*?"

"I take full responsibility for recovering my magic." Now Wist seemed to be speaking as much to Manatree and the male healer as to me. A forced calm permeated her voice, as if she were performing final negotiations before a hostage exchange. "I know this puts Osmanthus in a difficult situation. But I can feel that my magic will grow back. All I need is time. There's nothing Clematis can do to facilitate—"

"Nothing?" I said. "How insulting."

Wist ignored the interruption. "You can't force Clematis to cooperate. And it isn't worth the risk. She won't find a way to bring my magic back faster. But she's the Magebreaker. She can definitely find a way to make the situation worse."

"You're worried I might seize this as my chance for revenge?" I asked, delighted. "Aw. You know me so well."

"See?" Wist said to Manatree.

Manatree, disregarding her, addressed me directly. "The Board of Magi sent us here to make you an offer."

"Is it good enough to stop me from plotting my vengeance?"

"If you can find a way to recover the Kraken's magic within a month from today, you'll get parole."

My pulse accelerated. "What if I cooperate, but she recovers naturally? Before the deadline."

"That still counts."

"I want that in writing," I said immediately.

"I'll have an agreement drafted."

"What happens if I fail? I just go back to enjoying prison hospitality for the rest of my life?"

"Correct," Manatree said. "Of course, if you fail, Osmanthus will have far more pressing issues to grapple with."

Yeah, I could see that. How many people in the world right now knew that the all-powerful Kraken had suddenly become useless? Those of us in my cell, plus the Board of Magi and perhaps a few of their bonded healers? What about foreign spies, international syndicates, enemy governments?

If this news ever leaked to the public, the geopolitical balance of the continent—no, the entire world—would turn upside down and inside out. The first reaction might be sheer panic. An increasing number of magical natural disasters had started occurring over the past few decades—massive vorpal holes, otherworldly beasts run amok—catastrophes of such a scale that only the Kraken herself could begin to address them. If anything similar happened while Wist was still in this state....

Although, frankly, that was none of my business. The world had gotten along fine before Wist was born. It would eventually figure out how to muddle through even if she dropped out of society or, say, never recovered her magic. Parole, on the other hand, was very much my business.

"I'm in," I told Manatree. "Get me that contract."

"Clematis," Wist said. "You don't want to do this."

"Oh? Why not? Enlighten me."

"For one thing, you hate me."

I stared at her. "Wist," I said, feeling something almost akin to pity, "It doesn't matter who you are. I'd kiss a serial killer to get parole."

"I put you behind bars. I want you to stay here."

A brittle edge had crept into her voice. This was starting to get fun. I stepped closer. Here we were in my cell, my tiny kingdom, home sweet home, the home Wist's betrayal had made for me.

"That's right," I said, sugary as tree sap. "You hate me, too. I disgust you? You can't stand the thought of the Magebreaker poking around in your magic again? Makes you sick to your stomach, does it? Poor Wist. Well, isn't that a real shame. Here I am, ready to work my absolute hardest just to help you." I nodded at Manatree. "Trust me, I'm extremely motivated."

"Excellent," Manatree said dryly. "You'll be coming with us, then. Welcome to the team."

"Where are we going?"

"The Kraken's tower. We'll spend the next month there."

"Talk about a dream vacation."

She didn't take the bait. "The goal is to get the Kraken's magic back in some kind of working shape before any foreign operatives gain concrete evidence of her ... current situation. Do you require any special equipment?"

"Just one request," I said. "I want a bodyguard."

For the first time today, Wist regarded me with a faint yet legible facial expression—one of unadulterated confusion. "I can't use magic right now."

"That's the whole problem, isn't it?"

"You're afraid I might try to hurt you? Physically, if not with magic?"

The thought hadn't crossed my mind, to be honest. But no need to mention that. "Hey, can you blame me?" I said smoothly. "Sounds like you really don't want me in that tower with you. Anyway, the more time passes, the more spies are bound to get a clue. If any of them penetrate the tower, I want a mage there whose job is to keep me alive. Me specifically."

I turned to Manatree. "It's not like we can rely on the Kraken for protection. And you have other work, don't you? I guess you'll be our main liaison with the Board of Magi—what if something happens while you're off giving a progress report?"

I saw Manatree start to open her mouth. I plowed ahead, cutting her off. "I promise you this isn't some kind of elaborate escape attempt. I haven't tried to escape in years. Anyhow, I couldn't have planned this, no? I'm just looking out for myself here."

"...You sound like you have someone in mind," Manatree said, visibly reluctant. "You understand I'll need to run this by the Board of Magi."

"Should be fine," I assured her. "He's got relatives in high places."

I gave Manatree my prospective bodyguard's details. Wist's face had closed up again, eyes mostly hidden by her cap. She appeared to be gazing over at the ice-thick glass of my cell's one sad airhole-size window. I suppose she knew she'd lost this battle.

Manatree—and by extension, the Board of Magi—was in quite a hurry. She wanted to whisk me off to the Kraken's tower right away. I asked her to bring everything movable from my cell: the bedding on the floor, the wall clock, my desk and ragged chair and notes, the child-safe kettle, the cup with my toothbrush. Porting magic would make it doable, and anyway, it wasn't much, all things considered. I wanted to remember what I'd come from, and what I'd be going back to if I failed.

Not that I would fail, of course. I'd long ago given up hope of any kind of freedom—if I'd clung to it, against all reason, it would've consumed me from the inside. I'd wanted nothing to do with it anymore. Mental survival depended on being at least minimally content with my lot. Past memories were a parasite; dreams of the future were a corrosive poison.

But now they'd thrust the slimmest of hopes back into my hands. So here I was, thirty-three-year-old Asa Clematis, gripping that stupid warped hope like a murderer with a shiv. Now that I had a real chance, however dubious, I'd fight like a rabid dog rather than be forced to surrender it.

CHAPTER THREE

30 Days Left

The Kraken's tower gave off the impression of a giant lance flung down from the heavens by a vengeful god. Wist was a mage, of course, not an architect—only through magic could such a strange-looking tower remain standing.

As for me, I was more enraptured by the sea of blue-green grass around the base of the tower, and the hugeness of the cloud-streaked sky above. The last time I'd seen a sky like that, it would have been nothing special to me, nothing worth carving in my memory.

Back then, it wouldn't have occurred to me that the wide open sky was a thing you could lose.

Perhaps even for the rest of your life.

Though technically it stood on Osmanthian land, the tower had a status more akin to that of a foreign embassy. Wist was king here—at least, she would be if she had any usable magic left inside her. Having been reduced to a powerless shell of her former self, she slunk off in defeat soon after letting us in.

Manatree pursed her lips as she looked around the entrance hall: a vaulted wooden space hung with gardening tools. It rather resembled a barn. "Where's the Kraken?"

"Snuck off somewhere," I said. "It's fine. Let the wounded animal limp away to brood in the shadows."

"This is going to make your job more difficult," Manatree pointed out.

"Don't worry about it," I said. "She's got no magic right now. She can't get very far. Anyway, I already got a good look at her core. I need a little time to think up a plan of attack."

Poking around the entrance hall rubble, I found an empty rack to stash my shoes, as well as a nice clean selection of guest slippers to choose from. I picked a dove-gray pair and slipped them on before shuffling back over to Manatree and the healer.

I was still in a prison jumpsuit—I didn't have much of a wardrobe to choose from. I'd gained a new accessory, however, courtesy of Manatree: a bright red string wound around my right wrist. The magic on it itched like ants marching across my skin. If needed, the string would let me step outside the tower and wander part of the meadow and woods around it. Only an authorized mage could adjust the permitted range or cut me free. Good practice for probation, I guess.

"I need to supervise a security sweep of the tower grounds," Manatree announced, back by the front door. Against the wood-plank wall nearby leaned a pitchfork, and a hoe, and a treacherous-looking garden ladder, and several rakes, and a baker's dozen of old-fashioned bamboo brooms.

"Have fun," I told her.

"Your things from prison are in an empty bedroom a few floors up."

"Thanks," I said. "I'll keep an eye out."

Still she lingered. I glanced from Manatree to the male healer. He was still in his own pair of house slippers—apparently he wouldn't be joining her on the security sweep.

"I know I'm the one who asked for a bodyguard and all," I said to Manatree, "but I think I'll be able to survive without your presence for a little while. No fear."

"The bodyguard's being vetted," she said. "He'll be here tonight at the earliest."

She remained unmoving, one hand on the door. Suddenly I understood. And once I understood, I couldn't keep my mouth shut. "You're worried about leaving us two healers alone," I exclaimed, utterly tickled. I pointed at the male healer. "Is it him you don't trust? Or is it me? I suppose it's me. You don't even want me here, do you?"

Manatree neither confirmed nor denied. I took that as a form of agreement. "Wist wants me here even less. And in the end, you're right there with her—you don't think I'm worth the risk. I can't imagine the Board of Magi would decide to turn to me all on their own, either. So who suggested it to them? Whose brilliant idea was it to rope me into this?"

A little cough. The young healer in the cardigan raised his hand. "Er, me," he said, a tad sheepishly. "That would be me."

I couldn't help but gape. It was the first sentence I'd heard him utter all day.

Manatree sighed with the air of one resigned to her fate. "I'll be finished around noon," she said. "Stay in the tower, and stay on task. Time is of the essence."

The door echoed ominously as it creaked shut behind her. The slight breath of wind it heaved in from outside sent dust motes dancing in curlicues through somber shafts of sunlight.

I turned to the healer. "Do I know you?"

He closed the distance between us in one long-legged step, seized my hand, and pumped it vigorously. I squawked.

Mages usually strove not to come in direct contact with me (if they could avoid it), and I rarely had the chance to meet another healer in prison. I briefly touched captive mages when I hobbled them, but that was simply part of the business of being the Magebreaker. I couldn't even begin to recall the last time I'd touched another human being outside of work.

Perhaps startled by my lack of dignity, the healer dropped my hand. But he still stood too close for comfort. He was a pretty kid, with annoyingly clear skin and soft hair to his shoulders—a warm fair color, difficult to describe. Almost pinkish.

"I'm Mori," he said, beaming. "Kuga Mori. I'm a doctoral candidate."

"And Wist's dedicated healer?"

He clapped his hands together in delight. "You could tell just from that quick examination? Of course you could. Ms. Asa, I'm your biggest fan. I've wanted to meet you for years."

Hoo boy. Maybe Manatree had been right to fret about leaving us alone together. I backed away.

"Listen," I said carefully, "I'm not sure what you expect from me, but I really am here just to earn probation. My political phase is a thing of the past. If it's a rebel leader you're looking for, best look elsewhere."

Mori tilted his head. Doctoral candidate or not, I'd put money on him being hardly a hair over twenty-two. Which probably didn't mean much coming from me, seeing how as I had no actual money to back up my bets. Anyway, the puzzled-dog look made me nervous. What was I missing here?

"Oh!" he said. "Ohhhhhhhhh. No, what I mean is I've read all your papers."

"I have papers?" I said, bewildered.

"Your prison writings. They've been shared with the National Healing Research Institute. Well—with a select few of us. You're a genius. You're practically the Kraken of healers! I've always wanted to talk to you. I have so much I want to ask you."

"How about this," I cut in hastily. "I seem to remember Manatree telling us something about staying on task. Show me around the tower, would you? I haven't been here in ages. And if you're Wist's main healer, there's a lot I'd like to check with you, too."

In retrospect, I was impressed by Mori's ability to keep a lid on it in front of Manatree. Trailing after her into my cell, looking for all the world like a complete afterthought, he'd had all the charisma of a garage sale table lamp. Now he chattered at triple-speed, as if to make up for lost time.

He showed me the plain room where they'd stashed my prison-cell possessions. He showed me the first of many sunrooms; a few hidden magic elevators; balconies and decks that stretched irrationally far into the sky yet remained stable. He warned me against straying into the living maze at the back of the main kitchen pantry. He taught me how to find floor maps in empty picture frames if I ever got lost.

The tower was much larger on the inside than it looked on the outside, and none of it made much spatial sense. Magic squished multiple rooms together where only one should have been able to fit, and linked doors thirty or fifty or hundreds of floors apart.

Truth be told, I didn't listen that closely. I really only needed to know the basics of how to get around and find the nearest bathroom. I recognized almost nothing of the tower from the last time I'd come here—which would have been before my arrest, obviously. Back then it had been much more sensible in scope. In the years since, Wist must've used magic to pile the tower up ever higher and higher, wider and wider. It was impressive on a technical level, but about as meaningful as a child playing with blocks. Seems like the all-powerful Kraken had a lot of free time on her hands.

I started paying attention again when Mori led me through a library filled with binders of research on magic and mage healing. None of it was Wist's own work—she wasn't exactly the scholarly type. Nor did I expect it to be particularly useful for my purposes. I just found it curious that Wist had bothered collecting these in the first place. Perhaps it was merely one of many rooms Wist had abandoned after creating. There must be entire wings of the tower whose existence she'd long since forgotten.

I stopped by a bay window covered in cushions. "Mori," I said. "How long ago did Wist lose her magic, exactly?"

It took him longer to answer than I'd expected. He joined me at the window, looked down at the bright blue-green field and the dark forest far below.

"The Kraken was missing for months, actually," he said.

"Missing?" I repeated, uncomprehending. "*Months*?"

"She didn't meet with delegations from any country since midsummer." And now it was autumn verging on winter, with cool sleepy mornings and sunset well before five in the afternoon.

"The Board of Magi never publicly announced that she was missing. They told us to keep covering for her. We searched everywhere, of course. Especially inside the tower. Then all of a sudden she just—reappeared in here. But she couldn't use any magic anymore. She couldn't say where she'd been all those months. That was three days ago."

No wonder everyone was in such a rush to fix Wist. She'd already been functionally absent for a full season. By now the rest of the continent must already be quite skeptical of the Osmanthian government's attempts to pretend nothing had gone amiss. I pressed the side of my fist to my mouth as I thought.

The more a mage uses magic, and the more powerful and many-branching their magic is, the more twisted up and painful it gets over time. It's not something you can see from the outside, but it's there. Like a plant getting choked up and root-bound after too much time in a too-small pot.

Healers like me and Mori were, essentially, supposed to act as chiropractors for mages. Personally I'd always resented being forced into that role (and just look what my resistance ultimately got me: a life sentence). To your average Osmanthian mage, though, we healers served as a vital form of pain relief. Some people considered us a type of doctor—but just as often they compared us to piano tuners or plumbers.

None of the analogies rang true to me. Ever since I was a kid, ever since I first started obligatory training as a healer, I would ask myself the same thing over and over.

Why do they call us healers?

I couldn't understand it. My teachers spoke as if the only possible course of action for a healer was to untangle twisted-up magic, to bring mages relief. As if we were little more than glorified massage therapists.

But if you know the human body well enough to cure it, surely you would also know of ways to precisely and effectively damage it. Similarly, if you're capable of smoothing the painful kinks out of someone's magic, why couldn't you simply choose to do the opposite? A doctor could stab you all over with a scalpel if they felt like it—and could surely do so with far greater accuracy than your average amateur serial killer, to boot.

Why are we labeled healers, I wondered, when we could just as easily break mages rather than fix them?

Long story short: there's a reason they call me, and only me, the Magebreaker. I can perform normal mage healing as well as anyone. Far better than most, actually. I also excel at reverse healing—a process that exists in none of our textbooks, and that most other healers could hardly conceive of, much less execute. Unfortunately, neither standard healing nor my patented magebreaking seemed applicable to whatever was going on with Wist right now.

"You've already tried all the usual healing procedures?" I asked Mori. Just in case.

He nodded. "Me and a few of the stronger Board-bonded healers. Nothing seems to affect her, positively or negatively."

"Have you ever seen any similar patients? No, wait." I rethought my phrasing—precision might prove key here. "It looked to me like something pruned all her magic branches. But pruning itself is nothing unusual. Mages do it all the time. The strange part is that she seems to have lost all her branches at once, and they aren't growing back." Even the slowest-growing mages could typically re-sprout a lost magic branch overnight.

"I've never seen anything like it, either." Mori stared into the still shaded aisles of the library, tugging at the ends of his hair. "Healing can help magic branches grow back faster, but only if there's some initial growth to work with. We tried with the Kraken, but we couldn't find even the tiniest signs of regrowth."

"Hm." I'd been kneading one of the window cushions in my palms. I tossed it back into its pile of fallen comrades. "Well, the next step is obvious, at least."

"Is it?"

"What's the one guaranteed way to accelerate mage healing?"

Those bright eyes blinked back at me, then fell to the carpet. "You think the Kraken should—bond with someone. With a healer," he said slowly.

"Yeah, and you didn't need me to tell you that. Why haven't you tried it already?"

For the first time in our tour of the tower, Mori seemed lost for words. He buried his hands in his cardigan pockets. When he did start to speak, he lowered his voice almost to a whisper, but somehow that only made it seem louder in the lonely air of the book-filled room.

"I did think of it," he said. "But I didn't feel right suggesting it."

Clearly there was more to this story. I leaned back on the windowsill and motioned for him to get on with it.

"I met the Kraken—three or four years ago, probably? I was in undergrad. Not nineteen yet. Almost done with my final year, though. I started college earlier than most people. After I graduated, I wanted to work for the National Healing Research Institute. But I was already scoring too high."

"A lot of top-class mages must have wanted you."

A shadow of remembered misery crossed his face. He was remarkably easy to read—the opposite of Wist. "My advisors all told me to just pick someone to bond with. They all refused to recommend me for a job. I got desperate and started writing to NHRI directors for help. No one responded."

"I guess your healer classmates weren't very sympathetic, either."

A dry laugh. "I wouldn't have dared complain to them. Some of my suitors were Board support staff."

"Any S-class mages?"

"Two."

"Any actual Board members?"

"One."

"A dream come true for the average healer," I said. "But a nightmare for you, huh? Suppose I can relate. So then Wist popped up and rescued you?"

Mori gave me a startled look. "You already knew?"

"An educated guess based on the info at hand," I said. "That's all."

"She was visiting campus for some kind of function with the top mage students of the year. But she came all the way over the to the healer labs to find me. She asked me to try healing her. Afterward, she said she'd heard there was a talented student healer who was having trouble finding work. She said if I became known as her dedicated healer, no one would ever dare ask to bond me again. And she wouldn't stop me from taking other work. She'd encourage it, even. Go to grad school if you're serious about research, she told me."

"Generous, for a mage," I said. "Of course, if anyone can afford to be generous, it's the Kraken. Must've been a huge relief for you."

He nodded vigorously. "But she said she wanted to be very clear on one thing. She was offering to hire me as a healer. She wasn't offering—and never would offer—to bond me. She'd decided long ago that she would never bond with any healer, she said. It didn't seem like I wanted that in the first place, which was part of why she approached me. Even so, she was extra careful not to get my hopes up."

You could heal a mage without being bonded to them. Bonding had enormous benefits for both sides, though. Since a mage-healer bond would last until one of them died, for healers it could sometimes serve as a guarantee of lifelong protection and employment. The mage could no longer be healed by anyone else, but in return, bonding would greatly facilitate and accelerate the healing process. More importantly, it usually led to a power boost equivalent to going up by at least 1 mage class, and sometimes several. The Kraken had no need for that, naturally. But I could certainly imagine healers flocking to her in hopes of one day being bonded—of achieving the highest possible status and security any healer could ever hope for—even if she claimed she'd never do it.

"Well, that's a touching story," I said. "And I'm glad you found each other. Very sweet. But right now Wist needs to get back her magic. She's in no position to be choosy. You'll be happy as long as you still get to do your research or whatever it is you care about, right? You've seen that Wist won't make you give that up. You'd be up for bonding her now, wouldn't you?"

Mori still had something of the air of a guilty golden retriever. "If she actually agreed to it, yes," he said. "I just don't think she'll be interested."

"Whatever her personal feelings are, she'll have to try it if she wants a better chance of growing her magic back." I rose from the windowsill again. "Don't worry. I'll persuade her."

Mori stopped me with a tug on the sleeve of my jumpsuit. "What about you?"

"What about me?"

"Um..." He let go of my sleeve, looked about awkwardly. "There was a lot of talk about you and the Kraken, wasn't there? Back in the day."

"Before she put me in prison, you mean? Clearly it'd be out of the question now." Taking pity on Mori, I patted him on the shoulder. He seemed like a good kid, and a smart one. After all, he'd called me a genius. "Where do you think she went to hide? No, I'll guess—one of the roofs?"

CHAPTER FOUR
30 Days Left

PREDICTABLE, REALLY. Back at the academy, Wist had always gone to hide on the roof when she skipped class. And here she was again, a woman in her thirties, sitting on one of the many roofs of her extravagant tower. They all managed to exist in the same space simultaneously. Don't ask me how. Whichever roof you currently were on became the true roof of the moment, I suppose. And right now we were on a roof largely covered in sheets of overgrown ivy, its leaves the size of bathtubs. It looked suspiciously similar to the roof of my shabby high school healer dorm.

Wist was cross-legged in a patch of sunlight, eating tuna straight from the can.

"Incredible," I said as I walked over, winding a path among the heavy green-black leaves. "Behold the mighty Kraken."

She looked up slowly. No indication of surprise at my having found her. After a moment she lifted her open tuna can as though proposing a toast. "Did you want some?"

"I'm not a cat," I said.

"I have crackers."

"Oh, how sophisticated. That's practically a charcuterie board."

Wist returned to concentrating on her tuna. I stood there with my hands in my pockets, my shadow falling just short of her, and studied the phantom light of her magic core.

"How's it feel?" I asked after a minute or so.

She stood up briefly and set the empty can on the flagstones a few paces away, then went right back to her original spot in a patch of sun. "How does what feel?" she said without looking at me.

I crouched beside her. "Having all your magic ripped out by the roots," I said softly. "Having nothing of it left to get all tangled and torment you. Feels good, does it? Feels amazing? Is this the first time you've been pain-free since you got rid of me?"

As usual, Wist's expression showed nothing. But perhaps it was just a bit more guarded than before. I relished that tinge of wariness. It brought back the old heady feeling of knowing exactly what to say to make her crack—even if the feeling itself was no more than an illusion. Seven years of prison had changed me plenty. I wasn't so foolish as to think that seven years on the outside would've done nothing to change her.

"I haven't been suffering," Wist said. "Mori's healing works just as well as yours."

"Liar."

She looked askance at me. "Where does that confidence come from?"

"No one else ever had the ability to heal you as deeply as I did. But now you've got no magic branches left to bother you. Congratulations! How's it feel to be free of all the knots and pinching?"

Wist eyed the empty tin can like an archer. "No different, actually."

"It still hurts? Even without any magic branches to get tangled?"

"I can still feel them there."

"Like phantom pain from a missing limb," I said. "Interesting. Unfortunately for you, treating imaginary pain falls outside the scope of my mission. Sad, isn't it? You'll just have to suffer."

She sat there motionless on the cold roof, her body pointed toward the tin can now set well outside her reach. Her magic core tensed in its direction, too, but a core is just a core. It can't extend like a magic branch; it can't actually do anything. A feverish-looking sweat shone at her temple.

The can rattled in place. So softly that it might have been an accident, or a quick touch of wind.

"Try that again," I said.

Wist's breathing was beginning to sound strained. After a few very long seconds, the can rattled again, this time more weakly. It didn't actually move anywhere. Wist tipped over on her side and lay there panting, as if she'd fallen off a bicycle. I prodded her in the back with my foot. Her eyes slid to look up at me.

A magic core really can't go anywhere. It's just a lump located in the magical—not physical—space inside you. Trying to move it would make about as much sense as trying to fling your kidney outside your body.

Even so, Wist had fought to move hers with the fury of a prisoner flailing inside a straitjacket. And she'd only shifted her core a tiny bit before it snapped back into place—such an imperceptible movement that I daresay most healers wouldn't have been able to detect it. Yet she'd strained her core just enough to create a kind of tiny magical wake, a pulse of seismic power so weak it couldn't even push an old lady over, couldn't even scoot an empty tin can two millimeters out of place.

"Neat party trick," I said. "Trying to brute-force it, are you?"

Wist gestured at herself with one limp hand. "Maybe ... my core is like the remnants of a fire. Not enough heat or tinder to start again."

"So you're doing whatever you can on your own to send sparks flying." I pushed her with my foot until she sat up again. "Not a bad idea. Get bonded and then try it again."

Because I was more or less kicking her as I spoke, I felt the tension shoot through her. I didn't wait for her to start mumbling in objection. "Listen, we're in agreement on at least one thing," I said. "Your magic is bound to grow back on its own eventually. The problem is the time frame. What if you're damaged so badly that natural regrowth would take centuries?"

"The Board of Magi won't approve of me bonding." She sounded raspy. "It would leave me too reliant on a single healer."

"Yeah, I'm sure that's what you've been telling them all these years. Well, good news: once you get your magic back, you won't have to worry too much about what the Board thinks anymore. Give them one mean look, and they'll go belly-up and beg for a chance to get on your good side. Besides, I already talked to your Mori about it. He's ready if you are."

Wist got up and retrieved the tin can. For a moment I feared she might be about to stick it right in her sweatshirt pocket. Instead she trudged over to rinse it off under a metal faucet that sprouted straight from the flat stones of the roof floor.

A lazy wind waded through the jungle of ivy all around us. The leaves were too ponderous to stir much in response. Ugly-sounding birds screamed at each other from somewhere deep in the shadows. I had to wonder how on earth they found their way up here.

"What do you usually do with your trash?" I asked.

Wist contemplated the can in her hand as if she wasn't quite sure.

"Add it to the tower," she said after a moment.

Great. Look at the two of us, standing atop a castle that I now knew was at least partly made from transmuted garbage. "Well, you'll have to wait on that. Stick it in a bag or something. Stash it in the kitchen. And stop holding it like that, for god's sake. You'll cut yourself."

"I won't bond Mori," Wist said in the tones of a final answer.

"What's wrong with him?"

"It's too dangerous."

"I think you being bereft of your magic is much more dangerous for everyone."

"I'm thinking of after I get my magic back. There are a lot of people who want to take down the Kraken."

"And from the looks of things, they've done pretty well for themselves."

She shook her head. "Clematis. You know what I mean."

"Behold the all-powerful Kraken, the glory of Osmanthus. How do we get rid of her? Nothing can hurt her. Worst of all, she's completely antisocial. Estranged from her adoptive family. No real friends. But oh, look, she bonded a healer. She must really care about them. We can't touch the Kraken, but we can murder her bondmate. We can shatter her bond." I paused. "Something like that?"

Wist said nothing. I rolled my eyes. "Nice of you to worry about Mori's safety, but he's already known as your dedicated healer. He's got a permanent place on your payroll, no? That's only a few steps down from bonding. If he were going to be in danger, he'd be in danger already. Either way, get your magic back, and you'll be in a much better position to protect him."

"You don't understand," she said flatly. Wist was always like this. Coldly immovable. Patient. Infuriating. "Bonding is completely different. Both for those bonded, and those looking in from the outside. You've never bonded anyone."

"Neither have you," I snapped. "So we're both clueless."

She opened her mouth, then closed it. She actually looked away, off the side of the roof. For a wild second I wondered if being stuck in prison had made me miss the celebrity gossip news of the century. But Wist said nothing further, and my original conviction only grew. For some reason Wist was irrationally afraid of bonding, despite having no actual experience with it. What a coward.

Wist turned the dripping tin can around in her hand. Then she did, in fact—very slowly and deliberately—tuck it away in her sweatshirt pocket. I bit back the urge to scream. "I hope cockroaches feed on your laundry," I hissed.

"You're forgetting how bonding works in the first place," Wist said. "The mage needs to extend a magic branch to the healer. I have no magic branches to reach out with."

"We could reverse it," I countered. "Start bonding from the healer's end. Reach into your core rather than accept an extended branch. I'm good at reversing things."

"You could. But could Mori?"

"He could try," I said. "He fails, so what? Cross that off our list and move on to something else. I'll go next."

"You'll what?"

"If Mori can't bond you," I said—beat by beat, for the benefit of her slow-rolling brain—"all that really leaves is me. I'll be the back-up option. If nothing else, I can guarantee you I won't fail."

Wist started to back away. She paused. Abruptly she turned and strode for the exit. Undeterred, I trotted after.

"No," she said. "I'm surprised I need to say this out loud. I'm not bonding you, Clematis. And I'm not bonding Mori. Besides, it's all hypothetical. There's not enough magic left in me to bond anyone."

A set of airy outdoor stairs wound down to a door leading back inside the tower proper. Our feet clattered a noisy beat as Wist tried to ditch me, and I scrambled to keep up.

"You said something about taking responsibility for recovering your magic," I called after her. "That was just lip service, huh? You'll look real hard at tin cans, and you'll work up a good sweat, and you'll strain your core like no one's ever strained theirs before, but you won't truly do anything and everything to get your magic back, will you? Not even the most sensible, obvious things.

"So what if a giant vorpal hole opens smack in the middle of Osmanthus City tomorrow, huh? What then? If that'd be enough to get you to try bonding, then why wait till the last minute? Why wait till you're desperate? Why not just do the adult thing and get a head start on recovering? Hm?"

Wist stopped in her tracks. I crashed headfirst into her back. Thankfully, her puffy jacket served as decent padding. I retreated a few steps, rubbing my nose. Our little chase scene had taken us to a corridor most likely located somewhere far separated from the physical roof. Succulents and cacti lined the walls like art pieces in a hoity-toity museum.

"You're trying to appeal to the common good," Wist said. "But you're only here for the promise of parole."

"So what?" I said. "Who cares about me? Do you have a conscience or not?"

She looked up at the nearest ceiling light as if she wanted it to blind her. "It might not make sense to you, or to anyone else," she said. "But it's because I have ... it's because I have a conscience that I really shouldn't—that I *can't* bond any healer. Not unless there's truly no other choice."

My irritation melted away into an icy calm.

Fine. I can accept facts.

The facts, in this case, were that Wist clearly had some deeper reason to resist bonding—one she didn't want to (or simply couldn't) coherently explain to me.

Wist being stubborn to a fault was nothing new, anyhow, and it was far from the only secret she was currently hiding. She had yet to explain how she'd lost her magic in the first place, for instance. The whole amnesia cover-up was downright laughable.

But I'm not one to lose sight of my overarching goal. I still thought bonding would be the best way to kick-start Wist's magic regrowth. If she wanted to be put in a position where she morally had no other choice but to go there, so be it. I still had plenty of time to figure things out. And in the end, Wist was the one who would regret forcing my hand. Not I.

CHAPTER FIVE

30 Days Left

Around dusk Manatree gathered us in one of the tower's lower parlors. By "us" I mean Manatree herself, me, Mori, Wist—and one other. My bodyguard had passed inspection.

We exchanged glances from across the room. I grinned. The bodyguard grinned back. I loped over. We slapped each other's hands multiple times, always perfectly synchronized and with a satisfying resounding smack.

"So this is Fanren," I said to the others. "Class 8-5 mage. He's a duelist. You might've seen him before if you're into magesports."

Fanren took a bow. "Nice to meet you all," he said. "I hear I'm a bodyguard now."

Since Manatree was the one who had brought him here, I figured she needed no introduction.

I skipped over her and pointed at Wist instead. "The Kraken," I said.

"In case you somehow didn't know. And that's her main healer, Mori. He's going for a doctorate."

Mori peered at Fanren. He peered at Wist. He peered at Fanren again. Wist. Fanren. Wist. Fanren.

"Are you related?" he blurted.

Fanren laughed. "I get that sometimes. Nah. We've never met before."

Personally I didn't see the resemblance. Superficially they were both tall, more on the thin side, dark-haired. Fanren could be a bit deadpan, but overall he was about a million times more socially adept than Wist. Fanren wore glasses more often, and he was still in his mid-twenties—over half a decade younger than me and Wist—and he was covered in piercings. You'd certainly never mistake them for each other close up. From far away? If you had bad eyesight, maybe. Then again, most people did watch magesports from far away. Perhaps that explained the confusion.

"How do you and Ms. Asa know each other?" Mori asked. When he started bursting out with questions like this, it was easy to picture him in the classroom—a well-meaning and enthusiastic student, perhaps to the point of making enemies of all his classmates.

"Prison," Fanren said lightly. "I'm an ex-con."

"To be quite honest," Manatree said, "I was astonished that the Board approved your presence here. And in a matter of hours."

She was doing her utmost to sound sour, but I could tell that—against her best judgment—she already kind of liked him. Fanren tended to have that effect on people. Especially older people.

"Nepotism and NDAs can work miracles," Fanren said piously. "I'll be sure to pull my weight."

He turned to Wist, who stood next to an inexplicable grand piano, staring blankly into the mysterious purple flames of the parlor fireplace. "Kraken," he uttered, with an experimental air. "Ms. Shien? Ms. Wisteria?"

Only then did Wist seem to realize he was talking to her.

"*Kraken* is fine," she said. "I'm used to it."

"Do you have any rules here?"

"Rules," she repeated, uncomprehending. "Rules?"

"It's your tower," Fanren said. "Your territory. I'm just a guest here. Wouldn't want to step on any toes. Especially not the Kraken's." He paused. Wist still wasn't getting it. "Rules for magic use," he clarified. "Or just rules in general. Rooms we should never enter. Types of magic we should never use. Taboo topics. That sort of thing."

"There's a maze at the back of the kitchen pantry," I said. "That's the only place I've been told to stay out of. Too easy to get lost, and it's unmappable to boot. The front part of the pantry is fine, though. Nothing else to worry about. You've been reading too many fairy tales."

"Hey, just trying to be a good guest." He tilted his head, as if attempting to get a better look at Wist's expression. Good luck parsing that, buddy. "Anything goes?" he asked. "Really?"

At last Wist looked him up and down. I found myself forced to admit that the resemblance—coincidental though it may have been—became a lot stronger when they faced each other across the fireplace mantel like that. They even had similar hair now, since Fanren had grown his out a few inches since the last time I'd seen him, and Wist had started chopping hers off drastically at some point in the last seven years.

"I don't have any rules for you," Wist said tonelessly. "I doubt you could do any serious damage."

For a flash of a second, the air in the room tasted like ice. I honestly had no idea if Wist mean it as an insult. You know what, though—she probably didn't. She probably wasn't paying the least bit of attention to how she sounded. Wist was just being Wist. The Kraken could always get away with saying exactly what she thought. But somehow that just made it worse.

Thankfully, Fanren was the furthest thing from a hothead. He looked at Wist almost curiously, as if waiting to hear what she'd come up with next. When nothing further emerged, he rubbed the back of his neck.

"All right," he said. "Agent Manatree took me around the tower a bit when we first got here. I wasn't sure if I should say anything, but..."

My ears perked up. "Yeah?" I said. "Go on, spit it out."

"Nothing too urgent," he said. "I just noticed that someone else was here. Quite a while ago. Like months ago. Not someone from Osmanthus, if I had to guess."

The lines on Manatree's forehead deepened. "We know there have been foreign operatives trying to case the tower. You think they left some kind of artifact? Are parts of the tower compromised?"

"No—no, nothing that serious. Not right now, anyhow. I just thought you might want to do some clean-up. It'll make more sense if I can just show you all, maybe." He ducked his head apologetically at Wist. "Sorry. I wasn't sure if you already knew or not."

Wist demurred. "If it was a few months ago, they came while I was away."

"And since you've been back, you've lacked the magic perception to notice any kind of intrusion in the first place," I finished for her.

"See?" I told Manatree. "It's a big tower. You're a busy woman. You can't be everywhere. We've all got our strengths and weaknesses. Aren't you glad I thought of bringing in a bodyguard?"

Manatree hadn't stopped frowning. "I find it hard to believe I would overlook a living intruder."

"Yeah, that's the thing," Fanren said. "Follow me."

The first place he took us was the kitchen (one of them, at any rate). Trust Fanren to be perfectly oriented within minutes of his initial visit to the most convoluted building on the continent. He scrounged up a few dish towels and soaked them in rice vinegar, offering airy excuses when Mori tried to ask why. "Love the smell," Fanren said. "Can't get enough of it. Vinegar's also great for cleaning. Ever used it on your laundry? No? Let me show you another day, then. You too, Clem," he added, with a meaningful glance back at me in my prison jumpsuit.

"Oi," I said. "You calling me stinky?"

"Wouldn't dream of it."

Jokes aside, I could see where this was going, and I didn't particularly care for it. But I kept my mouth shut and let Fanren lead the way. We marched up a few flights of stairs, passing a series of chandeliers—or art installations, perhaps—crafted from driftwood. I began to wonder in earnest if Wist was a hoarder.

Fanren stopped in front of a short sky-blue door. The paint was cheap, peeling around the edges and in long vertical strips like claw marks. All and all, it looked eerily similar to the door of my fourth-year academy dorm room. I suppose Wist was no natural-born interior designer. She had to get her inspiration from somewhere.

If I stilled my senses, I could detect magic skimming the door frame. Wist's magic, of course. An old branch, long ago broken off by Wist herself and grafted to this door to serve its purpose. All the magic in the tower worked that way—it was the reason the tower itself remained functional, despite its master no longer having any intact branches left in her body.

Most magic cuttings can keep functioning independently for as long as their creator remains alive. Thus Wist, even in her current state, could open a door on the bottom floor of the tower and magically step out onto the roof. And that was how I, though not a mage myself, could do the exact same thing. The old branch of magic she'd snapped off to establish the portal, however many years ago, did all the work for us.

I could still remember the first time I saw Wist prune herself, back when we were in school together. The instant she cut one branch, two—no, far more than two—unfurled in its place. It was honestly a bit disgusting, like the swarming legs or antennae of an entire hive of insects.

That was how Wist had always worked. She'd never needed to plan her pruning or to budget her magic with the care of lesser mages. She could rip through her branches with the speed of a lawn mower and still come out on the other side, seconds later, looking like she'd somehow ended up in possession of even more magic branches than she'd started with. That was part of what made the current bare desolation of her core so hard to swallow.

"It's in here," Fanren said.

The five of us studied the blue door. It was taller than my head but shorter than everyone else's.

"Better have Wist open it," I warned. "She's left some kind of trap on the room. Should be safe as long as Wist herself lets you in."

Wist stepped forward to reach for the knob. I grabbed Mori and pulled him back a good long distance from the door, all the way down to the next staircase landing. Fanren, watching, tossed us two of the vinegar dish-cloths. They made a nasty wet sound when I caught them.

"We're not going in with them?" Mori asked.

"Leave it to the mages," I said.

"But why?"

"How's your tolerance for gore?" He looked puzzled. I tried again. "Ever seen a dead body?"

"No?" he said, still not getting it.

"Then no need to start today," I concluded. I pressed one of the squishy cloths into Mori's hands. "Should be better back here, but breathe through this if it starts to get smelly."

There had been no hint of an odor in the area just outside the sky-blue door. No doubt the magic trap kept everything sealed in the room beyond.

Well, if we were extra lucky, the magic trap might very well prevent foul air from emerging even after the three mages stepped inside.

From down on the landing, we could just barely glimpse the partway-open door. We couldn't see anything of what lay beyond it. Voices filtered through the air, their words unclear. Mori gazed up with round eyes, craning his neck to look past the driftwood chandeliers dangling above the stairs.

Fanren jogged out first, his mouth pressed in a straight line. Unfortunately for us, some of the stench came punching out with him. I retreated a few more steps and resigned myself to getting my nose and mouth covered in vinegar.

"How many?" I asked, muffled by my dish towel.

"Three bodies."

"How old?"

"Well, I'm no expert," Fanren said, "But they're at that stage where everything kind of melts together. Agent Manatree says she'll bring in a forensics team tonight. We've got to keep out of the way in the meantime. Should be fine as long as we stay off this floor."

Mori listened to us with his eyebrows halfway up his forehead. He seemed to be trying to whisper through his towel, but it didn't work very well. He coughed pitifully. "Did—did someone kill them?"

"The Kraken," Fanren said. "In a manner of speaking. But this isn't a standard murder investigation, if that's what you're asking. It's more like the house itself killed them."

"But how can you tell?" Mori asked.

Fanren gestured back up the stairs. "The magic trap on that room seems to be made so that if anyone other than the Kraken opens the door, it seals them inside the room and binds them in place."

"For how long?"

"Until the Kraken shows up in person to release them. Look—it's a gentle trap, as far as these things go. Not deadly at all. But at the time, no one was there to check on them. And when the Kraken came back from wherever she went traveling, she didn't have enough magic perception left to realize the trap had been sprung. Very large tower on the inside, isn't it? Must be hundreds—thousands?—of rooms she doesn't visit regularly."

"Yeah, better hope most other rooms don't have this same kind of trap on them," I said. "How do you think they died? Thirst?"

Fanren spread his hands. "If they're spies, maybe they had poison pills. Who knows—might not have been such a bad way to go. All things considered."

Mori was taking the news of death much better than I'd thought. Or perhaps he was simply not one to let any discomfort or squeamishness interfere with a fresh surge of academic interest.

"How come you knew they were there?" he said to Fanren. "All this time, and we didn't have any idea."

"Agent Manatree's team had been scanning for living creatures."

"And you scanned for dead bodies?"

"Mm—not exactly." Fanren rotated his wrist as he spoke. "I don't have very good natural magic perception. Can barely see anything, actually. To make up for that, one of my branch skills is a type of magic scan. It shows me all the magic nearby. Broken branches, attached branches, passive and active. When I first got here, I ran a check of the whole tower. Just out of habit."

Mori's eyes widened. "But the tower is huge. And it's packed with the Kraken's magic cuttings. Wouldn't that just give you information overload?"

"It's full of magic, sure, but a lot of it is passive—only activates when someone needs it. Like in the elevators. The constantly active bits of magic in the tower are mostly there for safety. To keep the building hanging together and such. It's extremely efficient, actually. Very impressive."

"Wist did always have a thing for trying to get maximum results with minimum effort," I commented. "Lazy to the bone."

Mori still looked unpersuaded. Fanren continued: "The binding magic in the room back there was pretty much the only bit of active magic in the whole tower that didn't have an obvious, necessary purpose. You know? Didn't seem like it would make any difference to the tower if you just turned it off. Yet for some reason it had been left activated for weeks or even months on end. I didn't know for sure that there were dead people in there till we actually opened the door, though. It was just a strong hunch."

"The instincts of a duelist," I said. "Well, I'll feel much safer with you around here, that's for sure."

We had to wait a little longer for Wist and Manatree to emerge. They came out slowly, stopping along the way to prop the death-room door wide open with a heavy chair. Manatree had pulled her long locs back into a ponytail. Wist was ashen. Halfway down the stairs, she sat with a thump, head in her knees.

"Didn't know you had such a weak stomach," I said.

It took a moment for Wist to respond. "Big words for someone who didn't even enter the room," she said without looking up.

"Well, it's not *my* tower," I said sensibly. "Why aren't you using your towel?"

"Hate the smell of vinegar."

"If you'd prefer to breathe in dead bodies, all the more power to you."

Wist's shoulders flinched, but she said nothing more. Once she seemed able to stand again, we paraded in silence to the nearest sink to rinse off our vinegar cloths and wipe our faces.

Soon afterward, Manatree had to rush away to organize her forensics team. Those of us left behind congregated in the comically vast kitchen. The air clinging to us still smelled stickily of sweet vinegar and dissolving flesh gases.

I asked Fanren to see if he could make a pot of hot coffee. Mori popped on over to help him hunt for beans. Wist sank into a chair and stared into space. I watched her reflection in the dark wall-length kitchen windows. The twilight sky outside was smeared deep navy blue, with only the faintest scabs of red left near the horizon, a dimming glow as weak as Wist's battered magic core.

"Going to have any?" I asked Wist once the smell of fresh-brewed coffee wafted over. She didn't react.

"She'll have some," I told Fanren. "Put a good splash of brandy in it. Or rum."

"You got it, chief." Fanren came over with two steaming mugs in each hand. He placed them carefully around the wooden table by the window, one for each for us. I pushed Wist's close in front of her, eventually forcing her to look at it. She reached out, took the mug in her hands. She lifted it to her nose and breathed the scent quietly, without drinking. I took small sips of mine to keep from scorching my tongue.

I was perched on a stool rather than a chair—which meant I got to be taller than everyone else, for once. I could look right down at the top of Wist's dark head. That's where I fixed my gaze as I said, "So. Wist. What was in that room up there?"

She didn't move a millimeter. Neither did her reflection.

"What was so special," I said, "that you needed to guard it with a death trap?"

"Nothing," Fanren said. I shot him a glare. I hadn't asked him to come to Wist's rescue. Whatever the answer, I wanted to make her squirm for it. But Fanren just set his mug down with a gentle clink, unrepentant.

"Absolutely nothing," he went on. "It was almost bare. Like a room

up for rent. Except for the people decomposing on the floor, I mean."
A brief silence. He eyed the tall windows as if he were attempting to
reconstruct the blue-door room in his memory.

"Oh, just one thing," he said suddenly. "There was a flower pot on a
desk. A kind of classroom desk. Literally nothing else, though. Just that
single flower pot. It was growing real well, too, somehow—even though
no one could've been coming by to take care of it. One of those pretty
weeds, with a lot of tiny florets in bunches. All different colors. Red
and pink and orange and purple and blue and white ... don't think I
know its name. I'm not too good with flowers, sorry."

"A lantana?" I said.

"Is that what it's called? Pretty sure I've seen them around the city
before. Growing in corners of empty lots and such."

"Definitely a lantana, then."

Lantana, I repeated to myself. Lantana. A lantana plant. When was
the last time I'd seen one? What did I know about them? They were
toxic. The little flower clusters changed colors as they grew. They were
strong and unkempt, bushy, attractive enough to be cultivated for
ornamental purposes but stubborn enough to also be considered a type
of weed. They were—

I took a larger gulp of my coffee. It didn't sit well in my stomach.

"Huh," I said to the top of Wist's head. "So you let three people die
miserably for the sake of an empty room and a worthless shrub. Well
done."

Mori shrank in his seat. Wist stirred as if she were about to say
something, but in the end, she didn't bother. How unsatisfying. I
studied the side of her face reflected in the window. Her jaw was set.
Strangely, she didn't look sick at all anymore. One month to go, I
thought. What a rollicking start.

CHAPTER SIX

29 Days Left

I HAD NO IDEA where I was when I first woke. I lay there breathing like I'd just swum a river to hell and back. My floor bed felt the same as in prison, but the walls were a ghostly white, not dark grey.

Stupid quantities of moonlight flooded the rectangular room—apparently no one, myself included, had thought I might need a set of curtains. I sat up slowly; my legs were clammy with sweat. I hadn't found any hooks on the wall to mount my familiar black clock, so it lay tipped morosely against the back of the desk, pointing at somewhere between one and two in the morning.

The gray house slippers were startlingly cold on my feet. When Wist got her magic back, she'd better crank up the heat all over this godforsaken tower.

Last night Manatree had ordered us to stay off the floor with the mystery corpses. The main kitchen should still be fine, though. Right?

Down in the kitchen, I stood by the wide black sink to drink half a glass of water. I didn't turn any lights on. Afterward, I held my empty right hand in the air over the sink and watched critically as it shook. I tried flexing my fingers, making a fist. Still didn't help.

"Same dream again?" asked Fanren.

I didn't jump—I'd heard him coming up behind me. "Same dream," I said shortly.

Every single night I slept, I dreamed of dying. The dreams followed me everywhere: at home with my parents, in the school dorms, in my old city apartment, in prison, and now here. Fanren had heard it all before.

"Going to stay up?"

"I'll go back to bed in a little," I told him. "What's that look for?"

Moonlight from the window above the sink glinted off Fanren's piercings. "Something I've been wanting to ask." He lowered his voice. "Why don't you try to escape now?"

"Who says I'm not?"

"Doesn't look like you're going anywhere at the moment."

I shrugged.

Fanren persisted. Noble of him. "Getting off the prison island would've been the hardest part, right? Just by leaving it, you're already halfway to freedom. And more than that—I thought your biggest reason for not running was that you knew they'd just end up sending the Kraken after you. No way not to get caught by her. But now she's in no shape to chase you. All you need to do is make it somewhere without an extradition treaty. You'll be set for life."

I raised my right wrist to show him the red string on it. "Only an authorized mage can cut this," I said. "I'm guessing you're not authorized."

Fanren shook his head. "Sorry."

"It'll have to be Manatree, then," I said, resigned.

"Can you force her to cut it?"

"Sure. I can figure something out. But I'm not doing it till the last minute."

"Why wait?"

My hand wasn't shaking nearly as much anymore. Talking to Fanren must have helped.

"Look," I said. "If I make a run for it now, and I get caught, they won't let me come waltzing home to this tower for another happy-go-lucky round of trying to cure Wist. They'll just send me straight back to the island. But if there's only a few days left in the month, and Wist isn't looking any better yet, I'll be about to miss out on my shot at parole anyway. Might as well bolt. Plus, the later it gets, the more likely it gets that outsiders will show up to run interference."

"Like those dead guys upstairs."

"Exactly. With any luck, things could get nice and chaotic. That's when I'll take my chances. In the meantime, I'm counting on you."

Fanren scratched his head. He must've at least taken a nap earlier—his hair stuck out like horns sprouting in three different directions.

"You're the boss, Clem," he said. "I owe you my life and all. You know I'll do whatever you say. But for the record, I'd rather not hurt anyone."

"Didn't think you were such an idealist." I poured the rest of my water glass down the sink. "Well, I won't make any promises. But if we do anything overtly criminal, and it doesn't immediately bring Wist's magic back, they'll probably yank that promise of parole right out from under me. I won't go overboard. What's your magic skill set nowadays?"

Fanren counted his magic branches on his fingers. "Scan. Barrier. Body Double. First Aid. Reflect. Zero Gravity. Piercer—"

"Oh, that's more than enough," I said. "Lovely. Which ones are branch-breakers?"

"Just Body Double."

"Can you do it without breaking your branch off? By controlling the doppleganger directly, for instance. Like a puppet. Instead of making it go off and do its own independent thing."

"I'd have to stay close," he said. "Maybe six, twelve feet away at most. I wouldn't attempt that in the arena—too much work to puppet it. Should be possible, though. Why?"

"Just an idea," I said. "Give me a couple of days to pull it together." Ready to head out of the kitchen, I turned away from the sink. "Nice talk, friend. I think I'll—"

"Clem."

I looked back over my shoulder. Fanren didn't seem particularly cold, even in a raggedy nighttime T-shirt and sweatpants. "What was it about that plant?" he asked. "The la—ladybug? Laurel?"

"Lantana," I said. "What about it?"

"You seemed kind of disturbed."

"It's nothing," I said. "It can't be anything."

Then I reconsidered. Fanren was the closest thing I'd had to a best friend—or any friend, period—since my conviction. No harm in telling him.

I pointed at myself. "You know what a clematis is?"

"A little orange fruit?"

"No, you doofus. It's a type of flower. A climbing vine. Mostly purple or blue."

"Like morning glories?"

"Not really, but sure. Anyway, the point is, my parents like flowers. Originally they were going to name me Lantana. They changed their minds because a lot of people think lantanas are a weed."

Fanren tapped his lip ring. "Think it's a coincidence?"

"That there was a potted lantana in the sealed-up room with those corpses? It has to be. I've never told anyone it was supposed to be my name."

"Not even the Kraken?"

"Not even her. I'd completely forgotten about it myself. I don't think I've thought about it since my parents first told me. When I was a tiny little kid. Maybe not even officially diagnosed as a healer yet. I just remembered randomly when you started describing the lantana flowers. So—it can't mean anything. It's impossible."

So much for going back to bed. I hugged myself for warmth. Prison jumpsuits didn't have great insulation. "I do wonder what she was really hiding in there, though."

Much of the tower was rife with vegetation, from thick-stalked shrubs in vat-like pots as tall as Wist, to greenhouse vegetable gardens gone halfway feral, to outdoor decks with wildflower meadows and even tree-lined streams of water winding through them. That single lantana plant might very well be a capricious form of decor, like all the rest. Or else a simple distraction.

"My scan only picks up on magic," Fanren said slowly. "I told you I didn't see anything special in the room, but if there was something like a hidden trapdoor, or a secret compartment—anything concealed physically, without using magic—I could've overlooked it."

We decided to go back there—just the two of us—and search the blue-door room once more. First we needed to wait for the forensics and cleanup teams to clear out.

It was a full-blown sunny morning by the time we stepped through the safely propped-open door, scarcely half a day after Fanren first led us there. The three bodies were gone, with hardly a stain left on the light hardwood floor. The cleanup crew must have made liberal use of magic to leave the room in such a pristine state. Even the air smelled fresh and scrubbed, with a tinge of lingering bleach.

The potted lantana was gone, too, with no sign it had ever been there—perhaps whisked away as evidence, or destined for disposal as a potential biohazard.

Fanren and I got down on our hands and knees. We poked the floorboards and rapped at the walls, pretending we knew what we were doing. Nothing gave off a telling rattle. Nothing sounded different from the rest. I stuck my arm in the front compartment of the single desk in the room—its solitary piece of furniture—and found it to be indisputably empty. Eventually Manatree came to chase us away. I left the stark room in a cloud of annoyance, wondering what in the world we still weren't seeing.

CHAPTER SEVEN

24 Days Left

Rest assured, I hadn't given up on getting Wist to bond with Mori. In the meantime, however, I chose to step back and explore other angles of attack. First, I tasked Mori with pulling together research on the very first Kraken-class mage. The original. There had only ever been one other before Wist.

The previous Kraken was said to have lived on a faraway continent, well over two thousand years ago. What we knew of her life now seemed like a complicated mix of fogged-up facts and myth, with much of it lost in translation. But I figured even tall tales might contain some kind of helpful hint. And if not, then on to the next thing.

Mori looked a bit worried. "History isn't my area of specialty."

I jerked a thumb at Fanren, who was busy washing breakfast dishes. "Well, you're definitely more of an expert than he is."

"Don't drag me into this," Fanren called over his shoulder.

I ignored him. "Anyway," I told Mori, "you obviously have access to more scholarly resources than the rest of us. Just do what you can."

As for Fanren, I put him to work as Wist's nutritionist and overall coach. Each morning, I marched over to rouse her at a nice healthy hour. My body still ran on a precise prison schedule—I, for one, needed no alarm to wake up. I dragged Wist down to the main kitchen and watched Fanren fix her a beautiful tray of food: nutty grains, grilled fish, hot soup, fragrant tea, colorful pickles, neatly rolled eggs, perky salad....

Wist, for her part, would gaze upon this lavish spread and inform us, pathetic as a wet cat, that all she wanted was a simple can of tuna.

"Canned fish is great," I said. "But you can't live on it!"

"Actually—"

I cut her off. "No. Wouldn't you feel stupid if it turned out that your magic isn't growing back because you're lacking in some dumb little mineral or vitamin? Or because you're not getting enough sleep? Or because your overall physical health is a bit crap?"

Wist looked plaintively at the fresh bowl of salad to her left. It was the most emotion I'd seen her show in a while. "I can't eat leaves this early in the morning."

I plopped down in the chair across from her. "I know you think your physical condition has nothing to do with your magic. Granted, I can't whip out scientific proof that it absolutely, definitely has some kind of effect. But duelists and most other high-class mages are athletes of a sort, if you think about it. They have to take real good care of themselves if they want to excel.

"As the great Kraken, you've always had so much power to spare—but that just makes you a special exception. You were the best from the start, with no need to optimize. Up till now, you never even had to bother to try to get into peak condition."

Fanren came by to refill everyone's tea. "Top chess players say it takes enormous amounts of physical stamina simply to get through a match. Even though it looks like they're just sitting there. It's kind of like that."

"Right," I said. "Anyway, being well-fed and well-rested and well-exercised won't *hurt* your magic regrowth, that's for sure. If it ends up helping, all the better."

A few meals later, Wist admitted that Fanren was, in fact, a brilliant chef. And she obediently made for her bedroom when we told her it was time for sleep, hours before midnight. So far, so good.

Manatree seemed a tad perplexed by all the fussing over Wist's lifestyle, but after a few days of this, I could see her start to relax. Perhaps I'd managed to convince her that I wasn't about to plunge my new housemates into a dastardly life of crime.

She softened still further when Fanren presented her with a tin of fresh-baked ginger cookies to take home to her family. Her absences from the tower, though still occasional, began to grow longer than before. This was quite important for my purposes, since some of the experiments I had in mind could only be run while Manatree was out of the picture. Not that I planned on mentioning any of these to her, of course.

As for me, I'm quite capable of focusing on more than one thing at a time. I hadn't forgotten about the mystery room with the mystery corpses, not for one second. The door was pushed permanently open now to prevent any new accidents, since the trap would still fire if the door closed once more, and anyone other than Wist subsequently attempted to open it.

Unfortunately, Fanren and I never did manage to uncover any hidden cabinets or loose floorboards. Wist could be difficult to understand, sure, but she wouldn't lay a magical trap in one of her tower rooms for no reason. No matter how bare it looked. She'd been determined to protect—to hide—something inside there. To my mind, there remained only one possibility.

Wist's bedroom was laughably tasteful, with one huge glass wall, and the rest of it all clean lines and cream paint, straw-colored cedar wood, colorless bedding. I was fairly sure she'd copied it straight from one of the old magazines sitting piled in a downstairs bathroom. There was no way she had the interior design sense to come up with this on her own.

After close to a week of wandering the tower, I could tell that there were some rooms she'd constructed deliberately—copying from film and theater, from famous buildings and paintings—and some rooms she'd left to develop on their own, bubbling up from her subconscious to take form in the tower like growing springtime buds. The latter tended to resemble places I'd been before: the academy cafeteria and lecture halls, for instance. A few of the opulent higher floors called to mind parts of Wist's adoptive childhood home, which I'd only seen once, though it left quite an impression. Like many mages who showed great promise at a young age, she'd been adopted into money.

Yet the place she'd made to lay her head to sleep resembled nothing from her past.

I crossed the muted carpet and looked down at Wist curled on her side. She had four different pillows and somehow managed to use all of them at the same time. She slept with the curtains wide open, apparently unbothered by sunlight. We were high enough up in the tower that—from this vantage point in the middle of Wist's bedroom— nothing showed through the window-wall but a bleak expanse of blue morning sky.

I leaned closer and asked softly, "Where'd you hide the lantana?"

Wist opened one dark eye at me.

I sat on the edge of the bed beside her.

"The flower pot," I said. "From the room with your murder victims. You took it, didn't you? Not Manatree's clean-up crew."

Wist rubbed her face. After a moment she tried to roll over and bury her head in the crevice between two pillows. I gave the blankets a hard yank to make her look at me.

"This is just a warning," I said. "If it's anywhere in this tower, I'll find it eventually. But if you explain to me why you want to keep it hidden so badly, maybe I'll understand. Maybe I'll agree with you. So why not tell me?"

"Mm. Maybe I have nothing to worry about," Wist said. Her natural voice was already quite low, but sleepiness plunged it deeper, a raw sound that seemed to scrape along the very bottom of her throat. "Maybe it's no longer in the tower. Maybe it no longer exists."

"If it was important enough for you to protect with a trap like that, I doubt you'd let it leave your territory. Much less destroy it."

Wist sat up on her elbows. Crow-black hair fell forward around her face, escaping the scrawny ponytail in back. "Even now that three people have died for it?"

"Not that I care," I said, "but if it's any consolation, they were probably up to no good."

That was the last time I brought up the lantana flower pot with her. I'd said what I came to say. If she refused to tell me about it, all that remained was to find it on my own time. In my own way.

There were twenty-four days left till my deadline when Manatree returned with the full report from her forensics team. She made us all come meet her down in the barn-like entrance hall—apparently she had to rush off soon. This time she didn't even take off her boots.

As Mori and I came over to greet her, a brown-black tortoiseshell cat slinked past one of the haphazardly-stocked wooden shelves lining the entrance walls.

"Wist has a cat?" I asked. It was my first time seeing it.

"It kind of decided to live here on its own," Mori said. "A year and a half ago, maybe?"

"What's her name?"

"Turtle."

"And whose brilliant idea was that?"

Mori gave an embarrassed laugh. "Mine. The Kraken didn't want to name her."

"Where is she?" Manatree demanded, unamused by our small talk.

"Turtle? Right over there." I pointed at the cat crouched on the shelf.

"The Kraken will be here any moment now," Mori said hastily.

"She's slow in the morning," I added.

Manatree would need to invest in a good mouthguard if she kept grinding her teeth like that. But I wisely—for once—elected to keep this thought to myself.

Fanren and Wist showed up shortly afterward. The cat leapt straight into Fanren's arms as soon as she saw him. Of course animals would love him. They must have already gotten well acquainted at some point in the last six days.

"The three bodies were all adult men," Manatree said, now that we were fully assembled. "Varied ages. Twenties, forties, fifties. One healer and two mages. We ID'd them as Extinguishers."

No one looked surprised.

"What's that?" I said, since no further explanation seemed to be incoming. "Some kind of firefighter?"

Mori and Manatree stared at me. Fanren made a small noise of understanding. The cat on his shoulder rubbed its face against him and purred as if trying to hold a conversation. Wist appeared lost in thought.

"Come on," I said. "They didn't exactly bring me the daily newspaper in prison. And now I'm stuck in this tower in the middle of nowhere.

You can't expect me to be all caught up on current events. Who are the Extinguishers?"

Three answers came simultaneously.

Mori: "Cultists."

Manatree: "Terrorists."

Fanren: "A crime syndicate."

They looked at each other. "All true." Manatree sounded resigned.

"Give me the simple version of it, then."

"The organization has been around for a very long time, but they only became publicly active some time after your conviction," Manatree said. "Their stated goal is to eliminate the Kraken."

"To snuff her out like a candle?" I said. "How poetic."

"They blame the Kraken for—well, for almost everything bad happening in the world today," Mori added. "But especially vorpal holes. They talk a lot about how ever since the Kraken was born, vorpal holes started manifesting faster and faster—from once every few decades to once every few weeks."

I myself hadn't seen a vorpal hole in person in years. But some news of them reached me even in jail.

Vorpal holes were great gaping wounds in the fabric of reality: the magical equivalent of a sudden tornado or earthquake. No one knew why they formed, and only the Kraken possessed enough power to fully seal them.

Some were borderline harmless. They just sat there, a bizarre gap in reality, posing no particular danger unless you were stupid or unlucky enough to walk straight into one. Those who passed through to the other side would never return.

Yet sometimes vorpal holes formed right in the middle of a road or a stadium or a block of apartments or a school, with little or no warning— instantly erasing from existence any people or buildings in the way.

Sometimes, even if everyone was careful not to approach the hole, vicious magical beasts would come streaming out from the other side.

The worst type of vorpal holes were the ones that slowly yet inexorably expanded, unstoppable. If no one could contain them, they would one day become a threat to perhaps the entire continent, or even the entire world.

From Osmanthus to Jace, there were people in every nation who had lost loved ones to vorpal holes or the beasts that occasionally emerged from them. I could see how the sheer random unfairness of it might drive you to the edge. And yet—

"So the increase in vorpal holes correlates with Wist's existence," I said. "Right. But you could say that about literally anyone from our generation, no? Hell, maybe I'm the one causing them."

"Agreed," Manatree said. "Still, regardless of whether or not their philosophy makes any sense to us, the Extinguishers exist. And killing the Kraken is their calling."

"Not that they had any chance of succeeding before," I pointed out. "Now, on the other hand—all I can say is you'd better have the tower perimeter guarded real well right now."

"As best as we can manage. Without drawing undue attention."

"There are a lot of mages working guard shifts," Mori piped up. "Can't see them from here, but they're out there."

I gave Fanren a hearty smack on the back. The cat in his arms bristled. "Hope your First Aid's up to snuff, too."

"The best case scenario would be not having to use it," he said. Such a paragon of common sense.

"Really, though, how good is it? I'd like to know in case we get attacked. Can you use it on yourself?"

"As long as I'm conscious," Fanren said. "It works to buy time, but only in cases where buying time is helpful."

"Meaning?"

"My variant of First Aid makes your condition degrade slower. If you're losing a lot of blood, it can make you lose much less. If you're going into shock, it can help you stay stable. But I don't think I could stop someone from dying if they got staked right through the heart. And definitely not if they got their head cut off."

"Hm. Can you apply it to multiple people?"

"One at a time. Unless I sever the branch. Takes me twenty or thirty minutes to regrow it."

"That'd be a bit of a problem if all of us got injured."

Fanren scratched behind the cat's ears. "Now you see the downside of hiring a solo duelist."

"Well, I knew what you were when I requested you. You'll just have to do an extra good job of protecting us. And by *us* I mean me."

"I'll start by hoping such a situation never arises."

"Ha, ha, ha. I'm counting on you, buddy."

A few minutes later, I caught at Manatree as she tried to take off again. "Question for you," I said.

"What?"

"How have you been explaining my absence?"

"Your absence from what?"

"From prison duties," I said patiently. "They've had me working startup hours for years on end. I can only assume my services are in extremely high demand. How're they going to get by without me hobbling all those sentenced mages?"

Manatree regarded me the way a germaphobe might look down at a kitchen drain trap in need of cleaning. "You're terribly ill," she said. "A persistent stomach flu. That's the story. The justice system can cope without you, the same way as it did prior to your sentencing."

The next words she spoke were much quieter, pitched for me alone to hear. "You're a convenient tool, Magebreaker. But only as a prisoner, secure in the Board's control. You're convenient, not indispensable. Surely you haven't forgotten that you were originally supposed to be sentenced to death. The Board's mercy spared you. Even if atonement is impossible, you should be grateful you've had the chance to make yourself useful. In prison, and now here. Don't make them regret letting you out."

I reached out as if to seize Manatree's hand. She leapt back to the door, immediately beyond my reach, displaying astonishing reflexes for a stiff-backed bureaucrat not many years away from retirement.

I grinned. "Just trying to show how very grateful I am. Why, I could hug you. Where's the harm in that?"

Manatree stalked away. She'd let me stand closer to her than before. Sometimes she appeared to be relaxing her guard. But clearly she hadn't forgotten who she was dealing with.

CHAPTER EIGHT
24 Days Left

I HAD PLANS OF MY OWN for today, of course. Once Manatree left, I recruited Fanren and Mori to help me put Wist through a series of magic evaluation tests. Most were the type normally used for very young mages, as part of the process to eventually bestow them with an official classification.

I'd been hoping to stumble across some kind of interesting irregularity, but the results merely told us what we already knew all too well. The Kraken was now a zero-branch subliminal mage.

We'd been working in one of the larger dining chambers, which I selected mainly because it had a banquet-size table, with plenty of room to spread out all the tools Mori had gathered for me. Fanren and Wist helped prepare by pushing the table runners and candelabras off to the far end; it lent the space the air of a ransacked castle.

We took lunch right there in the same room—it was, after all, originally a dining room. Accustomed to brief prison meal breaks, I polished my sandwich off faster than anyone else.

Mori wasn't finished eating yet, but he sidled over as soon as I'd swallowed my last mouthful. "Ms. Asa," he began in hopeful tones.

"I've told you, you can just call me Clematis."

"There's something I've been wanting to ask," he said. "It has nothing to do with helping the Kraken. But if you've got time..."

"If I can wrap it up fifteen minutes or less, sure."

"I heard you talking to Manatree earlier, and it made me curious." He paused. "Well, I've always been curious," he admitted. "You know how most of my personal research has to do with mage healing? I'd really love a chance to watch you hobble a mage."

"Oh, so you want to see the Magebreaker in action." I'd almost forgotten Mori was my self-appointed biggest fan. "I don't mind, but there's only one usable mage here right now."

I stuck my foot out to nudge Fanren on the ankle. "You in?" I asked him.

Fanren nodded. Well, I'd have been shocked if he refused. Fanren was usually game for anything.

"I'd like to see it too," said another voice.

I'd tuned Wist out so completely, it took me a moment to realize she'd spoken. And the instant I understood, it made me want to flat-out refuse. But Mori was already watching me with those bright puppy-dog eyes of his.

Right. I'd give a demonstration because Mori was the first to request it. Not because of Wist.

"Got a watch?" I asked Mori. He raised his wrist to show me. "Great. You can be the timer. Your magic perception is pretty strong, right?"

"I think I'll be able to tell when the hobble wears off," he said.

"Perfect. I'll do one for five minutes, then."

Fanren, who knew what was coming next, got up out of his chair. We moved over to the light by the large arch-shaped windows. Mori followed right behind us. He'd whipped out a notepad and laid his watch across the top of it; he looked poised to start scribbling. Wist drifted a little closer, too, hands deep in the pockets of her thigh-length sweatshirt.

The captive mages they usually brought to me wore custom clothing, cut quite differently from my plain prison jumpsuit. Their tops were waist-length in front but cropped much higher in back, with a thick band of fabric wrapped around the lower half of their torso instead—a corset-like belt. Usually I would slip a finger or two inside the belt to touch the naked small of their back, the closest place to the root of their magic.

Years ago, when I first met Fanren, he too had been wearing the specialized uniform of a mage convict. Happily for him, he could pick his own clothes nowadays. He turned his back to me, as obedient as ever, and hiked the hem of his shirt up to give me easier access.

"Do you always have to touch bare skin to make it work?" Mori asked.

The answer was no. With effort, I could do it through clothes. But I prefer not to lay all my cards on the table at once. I nodded as if to say that, yes, the Magebreaker was like any other healer, and that both healing and its reverse required skin-to-skin contact. If I'd learned anything after getting a life sentence, it was to never reveal more of my abilities than I absolutely had to. The element of surprise was priceless, and once you surrendered it, you could never get it back.

Normally, a healer would touch a mage's back to untangle their magic branches, to straighten out the painful kinks. But I could perceive how one might instead knot their magic up further, like tying a knot in a hose. I could knot their magic up to the point that not a single branch would be usable. And I could do it with the thoroughness of a tourniquet, so their magic could be completely tied up without causing them any undue pain. Most crucially, I'd figured out how to knot their magic in such a precise manner that it would naturally unwind itself over a set period of time.

The end result was that a mage I broke would be rendered completely incapable of using magic for the stipulated length of the hobble—be it a few months, a few years, or decades. Yet when the hobble finished unwinding, they would be perfectly capable of using magic again, and as pain-free as if they'd just been treated by a highly skilled healer.

In short, my job in prison was to hobble convicted mages for the exact length of their sentence. Whether they served their time behind bars or went right back to society, it was an absolute guarantee that they couldn't commit assault or go on a crime spree—at least not by using magic, that is.

Of course, not everyone I hobbled was a violent criminal, or even an intentional one. I saw political prisoners (would I count as one of these?). I saw detained foreigners (mostly Jacians). I saw guilt-wracked mages who'd lost control of their magic and gravely wounded or killed someone they loved.

Healing mages isn't crucial just for relieving the agony of tangled magic, I should add. Mages who get their magic too twisted eventually go berserk. Most of the time periodic healing is more than enough to prevent it, but some people are simply more prone to drastic tangling. And with bad enough luck, any unbonded mage could snap without warning, without any real provocation, the way a perfectly healthy-seeming person might suddenly suffer an aneurysm.

Many mages who'd snapped were desperate to hurry up and get hobbled. They begged for a chance to see me. They actually thanked me for it. It was a strange feeling, to say the least.

I laid my palm against the small of Fanren's back.

"Give me a countdown," I said to Mori.

"3…"

I closed my hand into a fist, still touching Fanren, as though gripping an invisible handle.

"2…"

I took note of each of his eight magic branches. I called them to gather together.

"1…"

I pressed the side of my fist harder against that spot on Fanren's back and *twisted* without physically moving a muscle. The thing I twisted was the bundle of his eight magic branches. The ripple of motion I'd initiated flared from end to end of each branch, fast as pressure flying out from an explosion. The branches curled into a single intricate knot.

Without magic perception, it would look as if we were both standing there meditating in the light from the window—doing absolutely nothing on the outside. But anyone with semi-decent perception would notice Fanren's strands of magic all twisted up like a nest of snakes inside him.

"Don't forget to watch the time," I told Mori. "Five minutes."

I took my hand off Fanren and backed away. He made a show of trying to use magic, gesturing at the pile of candelabras at the other end of the table. His magic core wriggled a bit, but nothing happened.

Exactly five minutes later, Fanren's knotted magic branches came slithering apart again, smooth and separate and perfectly usable. He demonstrated by generating a quick barrier in the air. Mori rapped his knuckles on the hard shimmer of the nigh-invisible wall. Then he rounded on me with shining eyes. Oh, no.

"How do you do it?" he demanded. "Right down to the minute—no, down to the second. How can you tell it'll take the right amount of time? How do you decide what kind of knot to tie? How can you figure it all out on the spot like that? How—"

"Remember," I said. "You called me a genius. That's how."

"But—"

"I showed you what you wanted to see. Let me have my trade secrets."

I looked at Wist. She had her gaze fixed on Fanren's torso. "Could you actually perceive any of it?" I asked. She shook her head. I'd figured as much. Well, this made for a good segue into our final test of the day. I warned Wist to stay out of the way while the rest of us got everything set up.

"You know," I told Mori as we worked, "for the record, I only became known as the Magebreaker during my trial."

"Really? But I thought—"

"I never did anything but properly heal mages right up until Wist turned on me. Nowadays loads of people seem to think I got arrested for being the Magebreaker. But that name came way later. I didn't harm a single mage until there was already a warrant out for my head. At that point I figured I had nothing more to lose, right? So maybe I went a little wild. The original charges against me were much more boring."

"What were they?"

"The original charges? A few counts of espionage," I said. "That sort of thing."

"Not sure if most people would call that boring," Fanren said mildly.

I called Wist over to get her started on the magic perception test. Mori had laid a few sheets of blank paper across one side of the table. Arranged atop them, standing neatly upright, were a series of mana stamps—the decorative sort, with round doll-like bodies and hand-painted faces.

I'd suspected there would be at least one set of them squirreled away somewhere in the colossal tower, and I'd been right. Mori managed to discover an entire abandoned storage room packed with miscellaneous magic tools, including several extravagant sets of mana stamps. Some were patterned after zoo animals; others could be used as fancy chess pieces. The flat-faced dolls I'd selected were among the simplest of the lot.

"Here's a pen," I told Wist. "Take a good look at each stamp. Fanren touched some of them with magic just now. Draw a circle on the paper by each stamp if you see traces of magic on the doll body. Draw an X if you're sure you don't see any magic. Draw a triangle if you just have no idea what you're looking at."

Wist began quietly working her way down the line of stamps. We left her to it.

"I was wondering," Mori said to me, sotto voce, "Would you have been able to hobble the Kraken? When she had access to her full power, I mean."

I shrugged. "Who knows? Would've been interesting to try."

Before testing Wist, we'd taken turns testing each other for practice. I had by far the sharpest magic perception out of the three of us. No surprises there. Mori was on the higher end, too. Fanren was pretty dismal. That was why he wore glasses most of the time: they were designed to aid his magic perception, not his vision of the physical world. I'd heard such glasses were extremely expensive, but I guess it wasn't too much for a top-class duelist.

Magic perception was simply another sense, in some ways no different from your sense of smell or hearing. It didn't necessarily track closely with your abilities as either a healer or a mage. Sometimes even subliminal mages and healers turned out to have extremely good magic perception. Sometimes even S-class mages needed special glasses.

So I was quite lucky to be both a genius healer (Mori's words, not mine) and to have naturally excellent magic perception. Wist had always possessed top-class magic perception, too, but I reckon that was just part of the whole package of being the Kraken—an exception among exceptions.

Now, though? She'd tried to watch me hobble Fanren, and she'd claimed to see nothing. Her magic perception seemed to have shattered right along with her magic itself, even though those two things really weren't supposed to work in tandem.

Then again, I'd never seen a mage with damage all the way down to her core, with lost magic branches that refused to show any sign of regrowth. Something abnormal—likely something unprecedented—had wounded Wist's magic and her magic senses alike. That much was obvious, even if she refused to say what had happened to her. Even if she pretended not to remember.

Wist appeared to be about halfway through the test. Sure was taking her time.

"I haven't used mana stamps like this since I was a little kid," Mori commented.

" It's similar to the perception tests we took in school," I said.

"Wow—really?"

"It was a very old academy. They liked old-fashioned tests."

Wist and I had been around fourteen when we first met at the old academy, a government-sponsored vocational school for healers and mages over a certain rank. Back then, no one knew her as the Kraken. Years passed before she officially became reclassified. At fourteen she was still considered an S-class mage. Even that in itself was something extraordinary—it'd been at least five or six years since the last time an S-class student graduated from the academy. And at the time, I'd never met another S-class mage in my life.

"What was it like?" Mori asked. "Going to school with the Kraken."

"Fishing for old gossip?"

He colored a bit. "I just—my school was for healers only."

"Ah. You want to hear about the co-ed experience." I tipped my head back to study the vaulted ceiling. "Not very exciting, actually. We had some combined classes, but other than that, we were strongly encouraged not to mingle. They didn't want any healers and mages getting especially close. Don't tell me you're about to ask why not."

Mori's look of embarrassment deepened. Poor kid. "Uh...."

"You've got a bunch of teenagers," I said. "Let's say an S-class mage falls in love with an absolutely piddling healer. Or vice versa. Let them start thinking they're soulmates, and they might miss out on a more logical bond pairing later on. Look, I didn't say it was a beautiful or romantic reason. But that's the reason they mostly kept us apart."

Mage-healer bonding wasn't inherently romantic in nature. Yet it wasn't inherently *un*romantic, either. Especially considering that it never worked between close blood relatives, and almost never worked between otherwise unrelated people who had been raised together like siblings since birth.

Among those ranked highly enough to make a career out of magic, healer-healer and mage-mage marriages were actually much more common than mixed relationships. And many of those people were bonded to mages or healers outside their marriage, purely as work partners. They wore a wedding ring for one person on their finger, and a bond thread for someone else around their neck. Take Wist's adoptive parents, for instance: both working mages.

But whatever the reason, when healers and mages became romantically involved, they nearly always ended up either bonding or breaking up. It was almost unheard of for a mage to be married to one healer but bonded with another.

Of course, Osmanthian society as a whole was a completely different matter—perhaps because subliminals didn't need to worry about bonding. Take my parents, for instance: one a subliminal healer, the other a subliminal mage.

Once Wist finished her magic perception test, I asked Mori to preside over the scoring. We shuffled closer around the long dark dining table.

I won't pretend to know exactly how it works, but mana stamps contain a substance that liquefies when touched by magic. Stand them up on a piece of paper, and they won't leave a single mark. Stand them there and brush them with a bit of magic, and their innards melt like ink.

Mori lifted the first stamp. Wist had drawn a triangle to say she didn't know the answer. The paper was snow white—no magic.

Mori lifted the second stamp. Wist had drawn an X to say she thought no magic had touched it. But this time the paper below the stamp was marked with a wet vermilion square. Wrong answer.

And so on. If anything, the results were all downhill from there. By about halfway through, I felt assured that Wist wasn't faking it. She genuinely couldn't tell the difference. In terms of magic perception, right now she was all but blind.

As Mori bent down to take a note of the final score, Fanren and I exchanged looks over his fair head.

"Wist," I said. "You got any glasses for that? Ones like his." I pointed at the thin-framed pair on Fanren's face.

She said no. Of course not. She had normal glasses for normal eyestrain, but nothing to help with seeing magic. She would never have needed them before. And they were a far rarer artifact than mana stamps. I'd looked through the whole storeroom and hadn't spotted a single magic perception aid.

As far as I was concerned, this was excellent news. My only worry was that Manatree might try to scrounge up a pair of magic glasses for Wist, especially if Mori mentioned today's test results. Given their rarity, though, finding a spare pair Wist could use would take at least a few days, if not weeks. I had some other things I wanted to get done before then.

CHAPTER NINE
23 Days Left

IF YOU ASKED ME whether I had any fond memories of Wist from before she put me in prison—anything at all—my first answer would be: absolutely none.

But if I thought about it a little, one small thing came to mind. Just one.

From the first time I spotted her in school, right up until I got sentenced, Wist had always had the longest hair of anyone I'd ever met. That's why I was so surprised to see how she now kept it cut nearly to her nape.

She used to wear it in a single thick floor-length black braid, sometimes with a few coils looped casually around her neck like a pet snake. The long tail end of it would swish back and forth by her legs with a mind of its own, a kind of magical tic. She wove a strand of magic all down the length of her braid to control it.

Now, I wasn't a friendless pariah in those days. But neither was I famed for diplomacy, not even in situations where—in retrospect, anyway—it might have been smarter to keep my big mouth shut. Yes, it might have been a good idea to avoid antagonizing the low-class mage grandchildren of Board members, and accidentally humiliating healer classmates who couldn't keep up with me. But I did it anyway. Simply put, there were a lot of students who had some kind of motivation to hassle me.

Whenever my enemies got me cornered in one hallway or another, Wist would come drifting over, usually in her dingy gym tracksuit instead of a proper classroom uniform. She'd walk on by without looking at me, like she didn't even know me. But as she stepped past, her black braid would lash out behind her like a whip, knocking the hooligans away before they even realized what was happening.

Only then would Wist halt and glance over her shoulder, waiting to see if I would join her. Sometimes I ignored her and made a brisk exist in the other direction. Sometimes I trotted over, and we'd walk away together without looking back, her braid swinging up around my shoulders like the weight of a protective arm.

Sure, I'd call that a fond memory. But not because of Wist, really. Because of the dumbfounded looks she put on their faces. Because of the brutal sound of her braid thwacking flesh. Believe me, that thing hit hard.

And yes, plenty of people like to bray and moan about how revenge will just leave you feeling more empty inside, and retribution will only lead to more suffering. You know what? Screw 'em. Sometimes nothing tastes better than a nice meaty serving of petty vengeance.

On that note, today was unseasonably cold. I wore pajama shorts anyway, and tried to compensate for it by bundling up on top. I had my reasons. I was also irritated that it had taken nearly a week to realize

I could get away with wearing whatever I wanted in the Kraken's tower. No need to stick with my increasingly fragrant prison jumpsuits.

Can you blame me, though? I hadn't expected there to be spare wardrobes lying around—entire rooms outfitted like walk-in closets, a surprising amount of it in my size. Wist told me to take whatever I wanted. It felt like looting a mall. Meanwhile, Wist herself seemed to rotate between a handful of the same baggy tops and a few different pairs of decrepit old leggings. Or, for all I knew, maybe it was the same pair all along.

In the morning, Mori shared what he'd gleaned about the previous Kraken. She'd lived over two thousand years ago, mostly on a faraway continent. Vorpal holes and deadly vorpal beasts were far more common in those times. Must've been a cruel and wild world to grow up in.

Courtesy of the Kraken's power, the kingdom of her birth rose up to become the Blessed Empire—now fallen, but historically the largest and longest-lasting superpower in all the world. The old country that existed here before Osmanthus was easily defeated and absorbed by the Empire.

Certain scholars said this explained why Osmanthus, in the process of fighting for independence, became such a strict mageocracy. Subjugated by forces associated with the greatest mage of all, Osmanthians resisted by reorganizing themselves around magical power. Osmanthians developed the modern classification system for ranking mages; Osmanthians flipped ancient continental culture on its head.

In the truly olden days, healers were revered as oracles and priests. Honored, respected, protected at all costs. Osmanthus ripped away the veil of mystique and repositioned healers as a scarce natural resource meant to be governed and utilized by powerful mages, carefully divvied up for maximum efficiency.

Some records claimed that the previous Kraken walked the earth for hundreds of years or more. Some claimed she herself brought down the Blessed Empire that she had once led to such glory.

Bloody conquests aside, though, the Kraken was also known for declaiming the great taboos of magic use. Never attempt to revive the dead. Never attempt to change the flow of time. Never attempt to create new life. And so on.

I'd always thought it was a bit of a moot point. Other mages might try as much as they like, but of all the mages in the world, only a Kraken-class would have even the faintest hope of succeeding. If failure was all but guaranteed, where was the harm in merely trying? It was like telling a subliminal mage child to wash their hands and brush their teeth and, oh, be sure not to accidentally transform into a butterfly overnight. They wouldn't wake up as a winged insect even if they wanted to, regardless of whether you went to the trouble of warning them against it.

Nevertheless—and here we were definitely getting into the territory of myth—rumor had it that if you made the slightest effort to break one of the great taboos, the previous Kraken would show up and vanish you away like a vorpal hole, never to be seen again.

I'd heard a few of these first-Kraken stories before, of course, but others were new to me. History hadn't been a particularly crucial subject for healer students. Besides, all we got fed were government-approved textbooks, written to give you a nice warm glow of patriotic pride.

None of the information Mori now brought to me sparked any brilliant ideas for fixing Wist, but it did make me wonder. Sources disagreed over whether the previous Kraken had ever bonded with a healer—and, if so, who that healer had been.

Other named figures showed up alongside her in tales of the Blessed Empire's rise, but what about later on? If the first Kraken really did live for centuries on end, did she bond with healer after healer, one by one, moving on to the next after each died? Or was she alone the entire time? If it were me, which route would I have chosen? Wist, for one, seemed bent on going it alone.

Later in the afternoon of the same day, Mori left with Manatree. They needed to visit the guards posted on the distant perimeter of the uninhabited land around the tower.

"How long will you be out?" I asked.

Mori tilted his head, thinking. "They all need healing ... it's a pretty good number of people, actually ... couple of hours, maybe? We'll try to be back in time for dinner."

"Looks cloudy," I told him. "Don't forget your umbrella."

After seeing Mori and Manatree out, I turned back to the empty entrance hall. The bare wood walls and ceiling made the room feel half-finished. The tower suddenly felt very quiet and tense, the silence of a held breath.

What a relief, though. I'd been starting to fear that Mori and Manatree might never step out at the same time. I almost suspected them of staggering their departures from the tower on purpose.

I've always had a slightly paranoid mindset, but if anything, age has only taught me that I was right all along. Just look at how trusting Wist saddled me with a life sentence.

I dusted off my shorts and went to fetch some implements from Fanren's room. Next, I headed over to join Wist and Fanren in a sunroom located very high in the tower. It perched on the roof area of a architectural offshoot that stuck out from the main tower body rather in the manner of a sawed-off branch.

The sunroom was set up like a greenhouse, with tall glass walls, a domed glass ceiling, and a decidedly amateur assortment of decorative potted houseplants and unenthusiastic-looking trimmings in vases. The sky above was stuffed full of cottony clouds the color of wastewater.

Light filled the room, but it was a wan, diluted light without any sharp edges or shadows.

Wist sat cross-legged on a white wicker couch, struggling to use magic to stir the droopy leaves of the plant across from her. I forget what the plant was called, but its leaves hung down like something you'd see on the head of a lop-eared rabbit. Rather endearing.

After a week of performing the same exercise over and over, Wist had become adept at producing a little wind, just enough to swish unresistant leaves back and forth. It was still little more meaningful than a party trick, though. She did it the same way she'd poked at that tuna can— furiously working her magic core, just enough to send out faint ripples of pressure. No signs of magic regrowth ensued. And she was aching from the strain of it: her fingers clenched the edge of the wicker seat like claws.

I told her to keep going anyway. Wist wouldn't get any mercy from me. You've been through seven days of this without any progress, I said. Work harder. Break your limits.

Fanren and I watched her for around an hour before I sent him out of the room. He returned with Mori trailing in his wake. Wist glanced over, her efforts faltering.

"We finished up with the guards early," Mori said.

"You sure know how to pick efficient healers," I told Wist. "Well done. But don't get distracted."

Wist returned her focus to the lop-eared plant. I threw an arm around Mori's back. Fanren and I walked Mori a little closer. The three of us looked down at white-knuckled Wist.

All that struggling, and nothing to show for it. The clouds crowding in above the glass ceiling had at last given way to a soft drizzle, almost too quiet to hear. It seemed, in fact, that the clouds were starting to descend around us—melting down into a fog that enveloped the entire outside of the room. I could see nothing but a dim, suffocating whiteness in all directions.

"You know," I said to Wist, soft and conversational, "You were right to worry about allowing me in your tower. Manatree was just as worried as you, too. She only pushed you to let me come here because she was following orders from the Board. Good soldier mindset."

Wist said nothing. She probably thought I was testing her focus.

"If I learned one lesson in prison," I continued, "it was how to bide my time. How to hold out for the optimal moment.

"Truth is, I had some initial worries when I came here. The magnificent Kraken can't really afford to concern herself with individual lives, now can she? The Kraken has to prioritize the common good. The Kraken has to watch over all of society.

"Getting back in this tower was the chance of a lifetime for me. I'll admit, at first I got quite anxious. Even when you had all your magic, maybe you usually just stayed cooped up inside. Maybe you only ventured out into the world if they really needed you. Maybe you were careful not to get to close to anyone. Like I said, the Kraken has to be fair and benevolent to all, right?

"But I shouldn't have worried. I waited and watched. Thanks for that, by the way. Prison taught me patience. I owe it all to you, Wist."

Now she was starting to pay attention. I was warm all over, just about vibrating with adrenaline. Or maybe shaking from cold, especially my bare legs. I couldn't tell which. Mori stood next to me, docile, cozy in one of his big woolly cardigans. I wore something similar, a chunky knit sweater with yarn so thick it looked as if someone had braided it out of rope. I had a thermal undershirt on beneath it; the two conspired to trap so much heat that my whole torso was already soaked through with rapidly chilling sweat. Ugh.

And that wasn't all. Between the sweater and the undershirt, I had one of Fanren's knives strapped to the small of my back. I reached behind me and closed a clammy hand around the hilt.

Fanren's Body Double skill far exceeded my expectations: Mori looked and sounded exactly like the real thing. He smiled quizzically down at Wist. The hair brushing his shoulders was almost as pale as the fog crushing up against the sunroom windows, except his hair had that signature blushing tint to it, just a hint of pink, the gentle hue of blood stirred into bathwater.

Wist, who had been sitting cross-legged all this time, slowly unfolded herself, putting her feet flat on the floor. She turned her body to face us. She looked a bit—no, considerably—haggard from her nonstop yet utterly fruitless attempts to distend her magic core, or otherwise somehow trick it into sprouting new magic branches.

I wondered if she were capable of thinking straight right now. Hopefully not.

"Clematis," she said hoarsely, "what are you talking about?"

"Not to be a whiner," I said, "but you know you took my whole life away from me. My ideals. My ambition. No matter. That was a different Clematis."

Wist stiffened. She cast a look at Fanren as if asking him to intervene. When no help seemed forthcoming, she turned her gaze back on me. Her dark hair and eyes were even duller than usual in the dimming light of this fog-staunched sky.

"What?" I asked. Rhetorical question. "I'm not lying. Even if you told me you could put me right back where I was before they arrested me—no, even if you told me I could get the Board of Magi to pass all the laws I wanted without any violence, without any scheming—I'd say no. I'd walk away. I don't want any of that anymore. Osmanthus can burn, for all I care. So rest easy. I won't ask you to give back what you took from me. At this point it's impossible, anyway."

"But you want something," Wist said cautiously.

I laughed without humor. "I want a lot of things, Wist. Most of all, I just want to balance things out a little. I mean, what could you possibly do to make up for a life sentence?"

At this point I spoke so rapidly, I wasn't sure if she could even understand me. If I stopped to breathe, I was afraid I might stumble and falter. Momentum was everything. "Now, it won't be nearly enough to even the scales. But this time it's my turn to take something precious."

As Wist watched, I put an arm around the perfect copy of Mori, holding him in place. With my other arm I drew the knife from its sheath at my back.

Don't worry about where you hit, I reminded myself. Don't worry about the exact positioning of the muscles and cartilage, the trachea and the arteries. It doesn't have to be right. It doesn't have to be perfect. This Mori won't struggle as hard as a real person. Fanren has full control of the body double and what becomes of it. All you need to do is get things started. Fanren can take care of the rest.

Mori gave me a slightly confused look. My heart stuttered out of rhythm. The reaction was almost too real. What if—but no, he wasn't turning his head all the way. He left the side of his neck conveniently exposed.

Maybe a second—no, much less than a second—had passed since I'd drawn the knife. A million thoughts roared down through me like the pounding of a waterfall, turning into sheer white noise, turning into nothing. I felt briefly helpless, fragile as a ninety-year-old, the way you sometimes do in dreams. Almost too weak to hold into the knife.

The illusion passed. I stabbed Mori hilt-deep in the side of the throat, then yanked it out again for good measure.

Fanren's knife was extremely sharp, but that didn't mean it was easy. A grunt sounded in my chest, surprised and ugly. So much blood came out of Mori. He sagged in my arms as if the floor had given way beneath him. His neck made a hissing sound, a whistling, a gurgling.

Wist didn't move a muscle. Fanren gave me a sharp look, a *What next, boss?* sort of look. I couldn't believe how much blood my sweater was capable of soaking up. It was absolutely sodden—red-black and sagging with the weight of all that liquid—by the time I came to my senses and shoved Mori off me and scrambled to my feet, knife still in my hands. My hands were wet. Mori hit the tiled sunroom floor with a horrible splat.

Stray flicks of blood painted the white wicker couch where Wist sat up very straight, a far cry from her usual posture.

"I never told you this," she said to me. Distant. Implacable. "There was a time when I swore to myself that I would never again react on my first impulse."

Out of all the things I could be feeling right now, my primary emotion seemed to be sheer indignation on Mori's behalf. "Incredible," I said as the body double's blood pooled to fill up my socks. "Absolutely incredible. So you'd sit there and watch your healer bleed out because, what, you just don't want to try to save his life *on reflex*?"

"That isn't Mori," she said.

"You're magic-blind right now," I snapped. "You can't know that for sure."

Wist dipped her head at me, almost apologetic. "I know you wouldn't take such a huge risk with no guaranteed pay-off."

"The pay-off is hurting you."

"You want parole more than you want to hurt me," Wist said.

As if she had any idea what I was thinking.

I turned. I walked with squishy blood-soaked socks over to the nearest glass-topped side table, leaving dark footprints that someone was going to have to clean up eventually. I, for one, wouldn't lift a finger to help.

I contemplated the table's cluster of yellowing cuttings in cloudy-water vases. The algae seemed to be growing faster than the plants. I took a deep breath and, instead of screaming, swept the vases to the floor. They all shattered in one quick flash of sound. Dirty water spread in puddles.

I looked over at Wist with all the composure and dignity of a holy saint. "Yes," I said. "I really, really, really, really want parole."

I backed up between rows of pots, all the way up to the end of the room. The glass was very cold. Fog still pressed in on all sides. I braced myself against the wall. I raised Fanren's knife and waved it in the air.

"Can you see my leg?" I asked. "It's not blocked by the plants?" Wist didn't answer, but I watched her eyes go to my bare thighs. Good.

"It's a very sharp knife," I said. "But I'm not very strong. And I like to be prepared. Wasn't sure if I'd really be able to stab through fabric, you know? Maybe it's not as easy as they make it look. That's why I wore shorts."

I adjusted my grip on the knife; I held it with both hands now. I already felt faint. The bloody sweater had grown so heavy, it was like someone had filled it with training weights. I focused all my attention on the sullen glow of Wist's magic core, over on the other side of the room. I put my mind in that place where it has to go when I heal or hobble mages, a place walled off from the physical world.

I plunged the knife into my thigh. Wist was on her feet. I couldn't quite see the look on her face, or on Fanren's. I'd made an awful noise. Blood dribbled down warmly, almost comforting. It felt a lot like peeing on myself, to be honest. But I wasn't bleeding nearly as much as Mori.

"It's—a kind of roulette," I croaked. "How long will it take me to hit the artery? I hear the one in the leg is pretty big. Hard to miss, actually. Hey, I'll probably get it next time."

For a moment I feared I might not have the strength to pry the knife free. Yet somehow I made it work. It was as if time skipped forward, just by half a second. There I was pulling at the knife, that dream-weakness running like numbing ice through my fingertips, some rational part of me understanding that if I took too long with this, it would start hurting for real, and the pain would be far too much for me to force myself to keep going.

Then a brief blankness, a white-out of the mind. Then the knife was free and in my hands again.

"Here I go," I said. "Three, two, o—"

Something smashed me clean off my feet. I didn't understand what had happened. I understood only that I was now lying with my cheek to the stone-textured tile floor, and that I'd lost hold of the knife. As I fell, I'd heard it clatter somewhere out of sight.

At the same time, both close and far away, I heard a hideous sound I'd never heard before. A sound like a saw rasping on my skull. A sound like a mosquito licking my eardrum. It wasn't a real noise—I could tell that much, at least. It was a magical noise, a noise experienced with magic perception, and it ripped across the sky overhead like a comet, and it made me want to reach in and rip my own brain out.

And then it was gone.

I wasn't lying in such a way as to have the wind knocked out of me, but it felt like I'd lost it all anyway, like gallons of air had gone gushing out me instead of spurts of heart-blood. I didn't know how to restart my lungs. I gasped shallowly. Everything burned.

Footsteps. Fanren crouched over me, eyes half-hidden behind his glasses, muttering something. Then his First Aid magic covered me like a hot bath.

I could breathe again. I sat up, holding onto Fanren for help, delirious with relief.

"You hear that?" I demanded.

"I heard something in the distance," he said. "No idea what. Worry about yourself first, Clem."

Thanks to Fanren, the rivulet of blood from my right leg had almost completely stopped. I looked down at my self-inflicted stab wounds: the first very deep, the second barely a nick.

"Would've gotten the artery with that second one," Fanren said grimly. "You're very lucky your gamble worked."

"Did it?" I asked, brain finally starting to catch up with me.

He jerked a thumb at Wist. She remained rooted in place in the shadows at the center of the room, Mori's body double now a limp corpse toppled beside her. So little sun made it in through the fog—or low-down clouds?—that I could no longer tell where she was looking.

Magic, however, needed no light to illuminate it. I perceived her magic with perfect clarity. The embers of her core. And one single bright new magic branch. The fresh-grown branch thrashed behind her like a long angry tail.

My leg pounded with a nauseating heat. I had absolutely no desire to try walking on it. But triumph surged at the back of my throat.

Fanren heaved a sigh. As he pushed himself back up to his feet, he reeled in his own magic branch, the one still connecting him to Mori's body double. The dead body double dissolved in a puff of air and flaky particles—like ash drifting from a bonfire. Or dandruff.

Unfortunately, nothing changed about the state of my soggy sweater, or the long irrigation canals of blood running down the grout between the floor tiles.

"I'll go find Agent Manatree, see if she can get us some medical backup," said Fanren. "You two stay here. Don't kill each other."

The door banged shut behind him.

"Come here," I said to Wist. "Show me up close."

She didn't budge.

"Fine. I'll go to you."

I shifted onto my uninjured leg, trying to maneuver it beneath me. My right leg pulsed and pulsed, but Fanren's magic had patched it well enough. A little movement shouldn't do any serious damage. I sucked in careful breaths and clung to the wall to draw myself up. Just needed to take it slow. Just needed to make sure I didn't pass out along the way.

As I started to take my first tentative wobble away from the glass wall, Wist's lone regrown magic branch lashed out like a whip, lengthening freely, coiling around me like ropes trussing up a kidnapping victim.

My stomach clenched. "Um—"

Wist's magic tail heaved me off the floor, hurtled me across the room like a human cannonball, and dumped me on my back on the lightly-cushioned wicker couch.

This time, I most definitely had the wind slammed out of me. I choked like a fish, eyes smarting.

"Don't be like that," I said once I could speak again. "It worked, didn't it?"

I'd never seen her with a look like that before. Wouldn't even know how to describe it. Horror. Revulsion. Strangulating rage. Suddenly I felt tremendously glad that I'd shocked her into recovering merely the tiniest portion of her magic, a single derpy branch that only seemed good for use as a blunt weapon, or perhaps a kind of makeshift third arm.

"You shouldn't have done that," Wist said at last. Her voice was tight, but far more controlled than her expression. "You had no way to know I would save you. You had no way to know I'd even be capable of saving you."

"It's like those hoary old stories of mothers lifting boulders off their children," I said. "There's a grain of truth in there. Adrenaline can make you do astonishing things."

With that, all trace of emotion vanished from her face. "Then you miscalculated."

"You grew back one branch in an instant. How many did you have before? Zero. It's a start."

"Don't expect a mother's love from the Kraken, Clematis."

That got a good laugh out of me. "Oh, c'mon. It was just one example. Anyway, I don't know why you're throwing a tantrum over this, but you can go ahead and relax. It was a one-time trick. Trust me, I've got zero desire to play the same card twice." I patted my right leg for emphasis, then immediately regretted it. Wist made a sardonic noise in the back of her throat.

We waited in silence for a little while. It was a truce of sorts, I suppose. I contented myself with lying painfully on the couch. Wist paced down her sad aisles of half-grown houseplants. I gazed at the ceiling, head empty, as I listened to her footsteps stalk the room.

Then the footsteps drew closer, marching right up to me.

"Why?" Wist said through her teeth. "Why is it always you?"

She might have been referring to anything. But on a gut level, I kind of understood what she meant. "Hey," I retorted. "I could ask you the same thing."

Wist flung herself down on the far end of the couch. A few inches in the other direction, and she'd have smashed my ankle. She dropped her head in her hands like she wanted to crush it.

Her newborn magic branch had retracted quietly inside her, but it was still very much there. The way she'd wielded it reminded me of how she used to wield that long braid of hers—hands in her pockets, cool as you please, while her hair casually pounded bullies out of the way. There had always been a sick kind of pleasure in standing side by side with such a powerful mage.

CHAPTER TEN

22 Days Left

WIST, THANKFULLY, refrained from mentioning the body double Fanren had made of Mori. It'd have been a bit awkward to explain. We'd created it for the express purpose of slaughtering it in front of Wist, and we hadn't bothered asking Mori's permission to use his likeness.

Manatree was understandably skeptical when I insisted that all the blood on the sunroom floor and furniture had come from me. Then again, no one else appeared to have been injured. I got all up in her face and babbled this and that about how the goal had been to put on a big show and shock Wist as much as possible. I didn't offer much in the way of coherent details, but Manatree probably ended up assuming that most of the blood came from squibs.

There was no way to disguise the fact that I'd stabbed myself in the leg, though. That night I collapsed into bed with Manatree's acerbic lecture ringing in my ears. You seem to have forgotten that the government covers your health care, she said. Well, I recovered one of the Kraken's magic branches! I shot back. It's the only attempt that's worked so far. That's practically priceless.

One of Manatree's medically-skilled subordinates helped patch my thigh up with magic. It still throbbed, but I could limp around more or less normally. I expect Manatree thought a perfect, instant cure was far more than the likes of me deserved. She'd probably ordered them to make sure it still hurt.

Neither the remnants of pain lancing deep in my leg nor the echoes of Manatree's scolding were enough to stave off the usual dreams. I dreamt of being strangled, of having my head held underwater, of six-foot-long magical lances flying swift as arrows through the air to impale me.

Dark figures watched me die, or sometimes murdered me with their own hands. I could never quite see who it was, but it felt like I knew them. Then again, they'd been killing me in my dreams every time I slept for at least the past three decades. At this point, why wouldn't they feel familiar?

The following day, I planned on putting Wist's solitary new magic branch through its paces. She'd gone from a subliminal mage to a Class 1—that had to be worth celebrating.

Unfortunately, my plans fell apart before Wist and Fanren and I finished cleaning up after breakfast. Mori and Manatree, whose visit to the guards in the forest had been rudely interrupted by my medical emergency yesterday, had gone traipsing back over to the outpost first thing in the morning. Fanren gave them a basket of peanut brittle and toffee to take in apology.

Yet scarcely half an hour later, Mori burst back into the kitchen, alone.

"They found"—he was gasping for air as he spoke, possibly more from overexcitement than exertion—"They found a vorpal hole in the woods. A new one."

I stopped drying dishes. "How close by?"

"Within range of your..." He pointed at the red thread on my wrist. "How new is it?"

"The analysts said it formed less than a day ago."

Wist took the remaining plates away from me to dry them in my place, but she appeared to be listening. She did have her one newborn magic branch. It was hardly enough to seal up a vorpal hole on its own, though.

"Is the hole expanding?" I asked. Mori shook his head.

Good news, then. The tower was located in the middle of government land, a vast national nature preserve permanently closed to the public. It was just about the best possible place for a vorpal hole to form, in fact: barely any roads nearby, no residences at risk, no hiking traffic.

Put up strong enough magical barriers, and even birds and deer and bears and little critters in the underbrush could be safely deterred from falling through. If vorpal beasts started wandering out from the other side, that was another matter—but Manatree already had plenty of combat-ready mages posted in the tower vicinity. Surely they could handle whatever came up.

"Could be a lot worse, huh," I said.

And yet there was an uncharacteristically sickly cast to Mori's face. I thrust a glass of water at him and forced him to take a stool at the counter. "So how precise is the analysis?" I asked. "Can they tell exactly when it formed? Yesterday, was it?"

He swallowed. "A little before ... a little before four-thirty in the afternoon."

I did a bit of mental math. Then I did it again.

That awful grating sound came back to me. That sound like sawing at your teeth with a pizza cutter. That sound that had actually felt worse than stabbing my own flesh with Fanren's knife. That indescribable sound had keened through the air—drilled through my head—right after Wist's regrown magic slapped me down to the sunroom floor.

Right after a brand new branch burst to life from her seemingly dormant magic core, in other words.

Right around the time when this new vorpal hole had simultaneously birthed itself in the woods close by.

"Ah," I said. "You're worried that the Extinguishers might be onto something."

Wist silently put away the rest of the dishes and shut the cabinets. Fanren dried his hands on a dish towel. Mori sat with hunched shoulders, looking utterly miserable.

I patted him on the head. It felt like trying to comfort a guilty dog again.

"Look at it this way," I said. "The Extinguishers claim that Wist is the one making vorpal holes form, right? But vorpal holes have always been a thing. Even before the first Kraken's time. And they were a thing in the decades and centuries before Wist was ever alive. So there's absolutely no way every single vorpal hole is her fault.

"Anyway, if you think about it, the Extinguishers have had years and years to make their case. They wouldn't be considered extremists if there were obvious links between the Kraken's activities and vorpal hole formation."

Mori took a big gulp of water. At last he glanced up at me. "But—"

"Now, this vorpal hole might be something different. Wist was never bereft of magic before. The timing does line up perfectly with her getting a bit of her magic back. Maybe it's a coincidence, maybe not."

I spread my hands. "I'm just saying it doesn't make sense to draw any big conclusions yet. Stick to what you know. Think like a scientist."

Slowly he nodded. "Right … you're right. Guess I—I got a little shaken." He gave Wist a stricken look. "I'm so sorry," he said. "I just—I don't know why—I just assumed the vorpal hole was because of you."

Something unreadable crossed Wist's face. A repressed spasm like a dinner guest fighting to disguise the fact that they'd gotten a fish bone stuck in their cheek. "Nothing to apologize for," she said, oddly gentle. "Perhaps you're right."

"Are we allowed to go take a look at it?" I asked Mori.

"I think it'd be okay if Manatree comes with us."

"All right, then," I said. "Time for a field trip."

After getting in contact with Manatree, we needed to wait a little while for her to find a free moment. She was far busier than the rest of us slackers.

Once all five of us had assembled, we trekked across the prairie-like meadow surrounding the tower. Bluish grass swished wetly against our legs. No more fog lingered down here on the ground, and bracing scraps of blue showed through in parts of the sky, but the top of the tower was lost to low-hanging clouds.

Our destination wasn't far enough for Manatree to bother with porting magic. That didn't mean it would be an easy walk, though. The forest beyond the prairie was centuries old and bore few trails fit for human use. Supposedly it had grown back over the remains of a massive battlefield; from time to time parties of archaeologists would be permitted to come do a dig. Few other people ever passed through, except perhaps for the occasional poacher.

In an unexpected display of common sense, Wist had opted to wear actual pants. She and Fanren kept getting smacked by cobwebs and low-hanging vines that posed little threat to the rest of us—the drawback of being a head taller, I suppose.

Speaking for myself, I hadn't set foot in anything resembling the natural world since—well, since I was a scrappy kid still chasing bugs. I'd probably never seen an old-growth forest before in my life. Between whining vociferously about my leg and striving not to inhale mouthfuls of bugs or twist my ankles on slippery moss, I didn't have much time to look around and think poetic thoughts. But the biggest of the trees made us humans seem about as significant to the world as a pack of squirrels.

We trudged over heaps of leaf-buried rocks and twisted our bodies to avoid vast fungi growths that looked like coral reefs. Along the way, I asked Mori and Manatree if that horrible sound yesterday had been the sound of the vorpal hole ripping open. Apparently the answer was yes. But even over at the outpost, only Mori and a few of the local guards—those with the sharpest magic perception—had been able to hear it.

And yet Fanren had heard it loud and clear, I thought. Fanren, who had such mediocre magic perception that he'd invested in pricey custom glasses to correct it. The glasses would do nothing to help him pick up on magical sounds, of course. Had he been able to detect the noise yesterday because he was right there in the same room with me and Wist? If Wist really had somehow unintentionally spawned the vorpal hole, it might make sense.

I stuck close to Wist once Manatree said we were almost there. I told Wist that my leg was killing me. I told her that if I tripped and fell, I'd make sure she went down with me. A couple of times, her magic branch shot out to catch me as I slipped. It felt eerily cold to the touch, like being grabbed by a rope made from clear mountain water.

Eventually I just wrapped it around my wrist and clutched it like a leash. It wasn't physically visible to the naked eye, but I could make out its outlines with my magic perception, a glassy distortion like a long tail snaking away from Wist's lower back.

"There," Manatree said.

She pointed across what was evidentially a man-made clearing: the earth scraped mostly bare and trodden with footprints, huge piles of old leaves and hacked-up shrubbery heaped around the sides. A scattering of uniformed guards saluted us smartly. All mages, though a few were subliminal. No healers.

Someone had built a makeshift fence around the center of the clearing. Rough-hewn wooden stakes and straw-colored rope acted as scaffolding for a spiderweb of caution tape.

In the space at the heart of the circular barricade, maybe six feet off the ground, the air became malformed. It was barely the size of a serving platter. It was difficult to look at directly—it felt wrong, dangerous, like having a staring match with the sun.

I could see that it was, as the name suggested, a hole. But I couldn't begin to tell you what lay on the other side. It wasn't darkness. It wasn't light. It wasn't blankness. Some kind of information existed there, but neither my eyes nor my magic perception had any idea how to process it.

The meat in my right leg pounded, even when I strove not to put weight on it. I looked away from the vorpal hole. "But that's tiny," I said to Manatree. "That's nothing." There was something strange about my voice, as if I'd forgotten how to talk.

Manatree didn't answer, but she looked profoundly unamused. Yeah, yeah. I didn't need her to tell me. Vorpal holes can be dangerous regardless of their size. Still, at least none of us were at risk of accidentally falling all the way through it.

I glanced at Wist to see her reaction. My breath caught in my throat. The entire walk here, her magic core had shown no reaction. Now I could see its surface dimpling. A subtle roughness forming. It was only the tiniest of changes—nothing anyone else in the clearing would notice.

I only picked up on it because I'd been glaring at her core throughout the hike, and yesterday, and every day before that. To me, it looked like her core was preparing to sprout hundreds—no, thousands—no, a countless number of new branches.

CHAPTER ELEVEN

22 Days Left

I took Wist by the arm. She flinched the instant I touched her. I chose not to be offended. There were more important matters at hand. "Let's get a little closer," I said, indicating the taped-off vorpal hole up ahead. I wanted to put my hunch to the test.

But Wist took a heavy step back, dragging me with her. She shook her head wordlessly.

Mori and Manatree were discussing something with the guards. Only Fanren had an eye on me and Wist, but he wouldn't intervene unless I called for him.

I tugged at Wist to slow her retreat from the clearing—from the vorpal hole. "What?" I asked, just loud enough for Wist alone to hear. "This isn't your first vorpal hole. Running around sealing them up is practically the Kraken's main gig."

She wouldn't look me in the eye. "It was a bad idea to come here."

She peeled my fingers off her arm, one by one. When I reached for her again, her one full-grown magic branch batted my hand away, quick as a cobra. "I'll go back first," she told me. "You can stay."

I shifted to block Wist's exit from the clearing. Gnats danced giddily in the air between us. "All right," I said. "Give me one good reason why I shouldn't yell to Manatree about what I see happening in your core right now."

Wist's magic clapped over my mouth like a kidnapper's cold hand trying to squash down a scream. Muted, I raised my eyebrows at her. Her mouth started to form a word that looked like it might be *Please*, but she never actually said it. Her eyes dropped as if she were trying to get a better look at her own magic core.

Then, with zero forewarning and her magic still clamping down on my mouth, Wist leaned forward and picked me clean off the ground. If I'd been able to make noise, I'd have screeched my head off. Instead I was reduced to ingloriously grabbing at her neck for balance.

"I need to get away from here," she said in my ear. "Whatever you saw, keep it to yourself. I'll make it worth your while."

Rest assured, I may not have been capable of screaming, but I was perfectly capable of struggling like a caught fish, or at least of beating Wist black and blue with my hands and feet. That ought to have been my first reaction, and yet instead I went rigid in her arms, frozen in place like a small prey animal.

Finally Wist deigned to make eye contact. Whatever it was that she saw in my face, it prompted her to take the magic off my mouth. I sucked in a pitiful breath. Wist's eyes darkened.

"Clem?" Fanren said.

Wist swung around to face the clearing again, still holding me up, but didn't take a single step closer to the vorpal hole. "Clematis won't be able to make the walk back."

Now Manatree turned to look at us, too. "What?"

"Her leg."

"She did say it was hurting her a lot on the way here," Mori commented. He gave me an apologetic look. What a sweet kid. I doubt anyone else would've described my incessant whining so kindly.

Fanren caught my eye. I shook my head ever so slightly, just enough to let him know to stand down. I'd play along with Wist for now. I clung tighter to her neck, hopefully tight enough to give her some real nasty aches and pains tomorrow.

"I've seen enough," I said to Manatree, with all the dignity I could muster. "Could you port us to the tower? Unless you'd rather force Wist to princess-carry me the whole way back."

Manatree looked as if she were battling the urge to strangle me. "You were the one who originally insisted on hiking all the way out here."

"Yes," I said. "I got mud all over my ankles. I witnessed the vorpal hole. It was extremely edifying. Now it's time to go back. I've only got twenty-two days left to restore the Kraken's magic."

Based on my observations to date, Manatree's porting skill didn't appear open-ended—she could only send people or objects to specific predefined geographical points. I also suspected her of being limited to places she had already visited in person. On top of that, there was probably some kind of cap on the maximum number of endpoints she could maintain at one time.

I didn't care much about the finer details, though. Simply put, it probably wasn't worth it to her to make this vorpal hole clearing one of her set destinations. Wist's tower was a different matter; Manatree had to return there constantly. So while it might have been asking a bit much to make her port us to the vorpal hole—hence the thrilling, insect-ridden trek to get here—I had zero qualms about requesting the opposite.

I watched as one of Manatree's nine magic branches flowed like a thin stream of blood down her leg. It pooled in the toe of her left boot, which she then used to scrape a shallow line in the soft dark earth. Her magic poured out to fill the depression. It flared the golden-red color of lava.

Manatree motioned to Wist. "You first," she said tersely.

The moment Wist carried me over the glowing line in the ground, Manatree's magic wrenched us far from the harsh-sounding birds in the clearing, far from the vorpal hole seething behind its makeshift wooden fence.

It didn't feel anything like moving. Ever seen the trick where someone whips a tablecloth out from under a full set of dishes and glasses without disturbing them? It felt a bit like that—as if she'd whipped the ground out from under us, but not even long enough for us to miss its presence.

Now we were in the sea of grass again, facing the tower's streakily painted back door. It had nothing written on its nameplate—nothing but a subtle etching of wisteria blossoms. Very pretentious.

"You can put me down now," I said to Wist.

I felt the breath hitch in her chest as she let me slide to the ground. It had taken a lot of effort for her to keep holding me up. Maybe I should've made her do it longer.

Manatree had other business to attend to, but Mori and Fanren soon followed us through the temporary portal back to the tower. I told them Wist and I had something to work on in private. Mori perked up, the very picture of innocent curiosity. I distracted him by giving him homework: I wanted him to look up data on vorpal hole emergence, plus any detailed information he could find about the Extinguishers.

He wouldn't be able to perform much in the way of serious research until the next time Manatree took him into Osmanthus City, but he could at least start drafting a detailed to-do list.

Hopefully that would keep him busy for a bit.

Fanren needed no explicit instructions, of course—I could trust him to read the room and make himself scarce elsewhere in the tower. He wouldn't bother us.

Just to be safe, though, I told Wist to take me someplace the others were unlikely to follow. She led me up to her bedroom, which still looked as if it had been plagiarized straight from the pages of *Osmanthus Design Digest*, albeit not one of the very latest issues.

She tugged open the bi-fold closet door. She pulled down two midnight-blue bathrobes, shrugged one on over her clothes like a coat, and tossed me the other. Then—without a word of explanation, mind you—she walked straight through the back wall of her closet and vanished.

There was some kind of magic cutting grafted to the closet interior, but I couldn't tell what it did simply from looking. I tried shrugging on my bathrobe (I guess it was mine now) in the same way as Wist. Though the gray-painted wall still appeared perfectly solid, my hand passed straight through it as if through a curtain of water. I cinched the bathrobe shut and stepped through to the other side of the wall.

I emerged in a vast, dimly lit room that immediately made me lose my sense of what time it was outside the tower. The very concept of *outside* began to seem incredibly distant. My footsteps echoed as if in a cave, or some kind of after-hours cathedral.

Most of the room was filled with a wide indoor pool, one much too shallow to actually swim in. Some kind of enormous foot bath, then? Strings of firefly-sized lights hung down from the ceiling in tangled gobs like ragged stalactites. But the seamless black stone of the floor seemed to suck up almost every last bit of illumination, leaving little to see by.

Wist had curled up in a pool chair near the edge of the water. She'd taken her bathrobe off again. Now she held it bundled in her arms like a furry pet. As best I could tell, it would only be possible to enter or leave this chamber if you happened to be wearing one of these specially designated bathrobes. I wondered how many of them she kept in stock.

Wist hadn't invited me to sit, but I pulled over a second pool chair for myself all the same. It made a noise like squeaky chalk. She'd better not bill me for any damage done to the flooring.

"Pretty gloomy in here," I said.

"It's good for headaches."

"Your head hurt?" I asked.

"Not much," Wist said. After a moment, she seemed to reconsider. "Not yet."

"Heh. Bet I can help you with that." I hugged my knees to my chest.

Magic perception had nothing to do with light or the lack thereof—I could still see Wist's core quite clearly. By now it had reverted to its previous state of smooth dormancy, with no hint of the spiky agitation it had shown near the vorpal hole in the forest.

"So," I said. "Decided how you're going to convince me?"

Wist's arms tightened around her bathrobe.

"I'll give you a day," I said. "But right now I don't see why I shouldn't let Manatree know. I could just tell her that sticking you next to a vorpal hole looks like it might be a shortcut to regrowing your magic. And once I tell her, it doesn't matter how you feel about it. She'll summon an army to drag you over there if she has to. Won't be able to put up much of a fight with your one measly magic branch."

"I said I would make it worth your while."

The cavernous room lent Wist's voice an unfamiliar resonance. I wasn't sure if I liked it.

"Yeah? How?" I cut her off before she could answer. "Keep in mind that my chance at parole might be on the line."

She tipped her head to look over at me. At some point her hair had come loose; it hung in listless black hanks just long enough to tuck behind her ears. I wondered if her hair tie lay trampled somewhere among the moss and ferns of the national forest.

"I can't ask you to keep any secrets, can I," she said. It sounded like a rhetorical question.

"I mean, no one's stopping you from *asking*," I said. "Then again, you're the one who identified me as an enemy of the state. Shouldn't take a lot of emotional intelligence to realize that maybe I'm not super motivated to honor your wishes."

"I'll speak at my own risk." Wist kept twisting the end of her bathrobe belt as if trying to wring blood from it. "Would you like to know something I've never told anyone else?"

"That's what you're trying to trade me? Gossip? You think that'll be enough to make me keep my mouth shut?"

"The Extinguishers are right," Wist said.

She rose abruptly from the pool chair. She stooped and hiked up the legs of her pants, then stepped down into the shallow water. The black surface rippled uneasily, and so did the myriad rice-grain specks of golden light scattered across it like fistfuls of glitter.

"Right about what?" She really needed to use more words, I thought. "About you making vorpal holes happen?"

"All vorpal holes—no. Most of them, yes. The recent increase in vorpal holes is because of me."

"What do you mean, because of you? Because you exist? Because you happened to be born as a Kraken-class mage? It's not like you chose to—"

"No."

Wist turned around. She'd cleared her face of all expression. She hadn't rolled her pants high enough to avoid the water; I could see it seeping up into the fabric bunched around her knees. "I chose it. I broke one of the taboos."

"One of the first Kraken's taboos," I heard myself say dazedly. My surging curiosity—and the sheer intrigue of it—were so powerful they left me light-headed. It was a pain much like physical hunger.

"That's why more and more vorpal holes have emerged throughout our lives," Wist said. "So many more than before we were born. I've been trying to fix what I started. Trying to fix it is how I lost my magic. But vorpal holes keep spawning anyway, and not just yesterday—all this time, all over the continent, at the same rate as before."

Her mouth tugged sideways in a ghost of a smile (or half a grimace), soon gone. "I might have sacrificed my magic for nothing."

I planted my feet on the ground, leaned forward to the edge of my chair. "You can get it back, though. Just stroll on up to that little vorpal hole in the woods. Your core will wake right up, grow new branches right and left. From what I saw today, I'd bet my whole career as the Magebreaker on it. I'd bet anything."

Wist shook her head. "I want my magic back. But not that way."

This flat refusal again. "Why not?" No response. So I went straight for the heart of it. "Which taboo did you break?"

In the ensuing pause, I could hear nothing but the faint lapping of the pool water. Wist may as well have been a decorative statue.

At last she said: "I can't answer either of those."

I feigned surprise. "Amnesia? Again?"

At least that got something out of her—a whuff of air like a deflated laugh. "Might as well be. I can't talk about it."

"Can't talk about it, or won't?"

"Won't."

"Not even to little old me?" I batted wounded eyes at her. "Thought we came here to have a heart-to-heart."

"Not to anyone. Especially not you." An ironic edge had entered her tone.

"Hah." I plucked the bathrobe off Wist's abandoned chair and chucked it in the water beside her. Together we watched it sink like a corpse.

"Well," I said. "This makes you an enemy of the state, too, doesn't it? You broke one of the first Kraken's taboos. Can't say I understand the exact mechanism, but if that really does accelerate vorpal hole formation—well, then you're a greater threat to the people of Osmanthus than any foreign conspirators. How does it feel to read news of vorpal holes in the middle of towns and cities? How does it feel to browse the obituaries?"

"You're not wrong," Wist said evenly.

Something that I had no words for whirled inside me. I'd risen to my feet without quite realizing it. I stood with my toes right at the edge of the black pool, for once much taller than Wist.

"Look at you," I snarled. "Making it seem like you've confessed some deep dark secret. Awfully crafty, aren't you? You haven't handed me nearly enough rope to hang you by.

"How about offering up some real proof of exactly where you went wrong? Write it down on parchment and sign it in blood, for instance. The way things stand, not a single government official would believe if I walked out of this room and tried to inform on you. Like how you informed on me."

Wist observed me with an air of very faint trepidation. As if concerned that I might stamp in rage and slip on the edge of the pool and crack my head open like a melon on the merciless stone-slab floor. The only reason I didn't scream was that I doubted it would change anything about her reaction. I took a furious breath.

"Listen," I said. "None of this adequately explains why you refuse to just go stand next to a vorpal hole. It would be the easiest thing in the world. But for your own private, top-secret, inexplicable reasons, you're dead set against it. All right then."

I stepped noisily down into the pool. From above it had looked ice-cold, but instead it turned out to be unsettlingly warm. If Wist had thought I wouldn't follow her in, she'd thought wrong. A little water wasn't nearly enough to keep her safe from me. I didn't bother hitching up my pants first, either—they weren't really my own clothes, anyway.

Abandoned at the bottom of the pool where I'd thrown it, her bathrobe lurked like a clump of dead seaweed. I kicked it out of the way and sloshed right up to her.

"If you refuse to experiment with going near vorpal holes, you'll have to boost your magic regrowth some other way. At this point there's only one other choice, really."

I reached behind Wist and tapped the small of her back, pinging her one full-grown magic branch. It curled awake. I grabbed it in my fist, as if clutching a transparent snake under the chin, and yanked it up in front of her face. "You've got a functional magical branch now. It's not the greatest, but it's there. In this case, one working branch is all you need. There's nothing to stop you from bonding a healer.

"Yeah, you already said no to that. You can't say no to everything. So which will it be? The vorpal hole or bonding?" I shook the end of her magic branch like a baby rattle for emphasis. "I know you don't want either, but at this point you're in no position to be picky."

Wist's magic branch went long and narrow, shooting out of my grasp as fast as a shard of soap on the run. After escaping back behind her, it slashed restlessly from side to side through the dark water. She had her head bent. She didn't show it, but she must've been thinking furiously. At least I hoped she was. I preferred not to be the only one wracking my brain here.

My pants stuck unpleasantly to my legs. The damp had crept almost all the way up to my crotch. There was something eerie about how I could see the long strings of lights leaking down from the ceiling, but couldn't glimpse anything of the ceiling itself—it was too high up and too shadowed. It felt like there might be miles of lethal rock up there, or absolutely nothing at all, nothing but the suffocation of a permanent night sky.

Wist took my hands. I startled, floundering. I'd forgotten how close I'd gotten to glare up at her. Pool water slopped about our legs. Wist's fingers were strangely chilly at the edges. Her grip tightened. I couldn't remember what I'd stomped over to demand of her. Something about bonding. Right. I'd given her an ultimatum.

"It's not that I don't want to bond," Wist said.

She spoke with painstaking care, as if uttering the wrong word might set off a bomb. I found myself staring like a dimwit at her fingers curled around mine. Her nails were a fraction longer than mine, but somehow managed to stay much cleaner. She wore no rings.

I heard her say my name and then trail off, lost for words.

I didn't want to see what kind of look Wist had on now. Probably nothing. Probably the usual inscrutable face.

I wrenched my hands free and climbed hastily out of the pool. Or bath. Or whatever it was. Wist could bend down and save her bathrobe from drowning all by herself. And if she ever wanted to leave the room, she'd have to put it back on, still soaking wet from wallowing at the bottom of this stupidly massive bathtub.

The thought cheered me a bit. I dug my nails into my palms to center myself. A mere five seconds later, and already I had no idea what her hands had felt like on mine.

See? That was how very little it mattered.

I was my usual composed self when I glanced back at her. Left behind in the pool, Wist had indeed reached down to rescue her bathrobe.

"Why'd you get in the water, anyway?" I said by way of accusation. "Now we're both wet."

She stepped out onto the dark stones, sodden bathrobe over one arm. "I'm used to being able to dry off instantly."

With one of her infinite magic branches, of course. Such was the life of the Kraken. "You'd better not go jumping off the tower roof just because you're used to being able to fly."

"I did almost make that mistake a few times."

Sometimes it could be difficult to tell if Wist was joking. I cleared my throat. "Bonding, then," I said briskly. "You'd better at least dry off first. You'll have to use a towel like the rest of us peons. Want me to go tell Mori to get ready?"

"No," Wist said. "You."

"Me?"

"I'll bond with you. If you're willing."

We were both dripping profusely. Yet my throat remained painfully dry. "You always did have a weird sense of humor."

Wist stopped in her tracks and scrutinized me like she had no idea what I was talking about. Drip, drip, drip. It was way too quiet in here. "When you first came to the tower, you said if Mori couldn't bond me, then you would."

"Don't tell me you took that seriously," I said.

"Was it a joke, then?"

"Not a joke," I snapped. "A threat. I said it to motivate you. And you sure sounded dead set against it at the time! Which was all of, what, a week ago?"

Wist raked her hands through her hair, attempting to pull it back again. She appeared to realize midway through that she was all out of spare ties. Her arms descended belatedly. Her solitary magic branch rose to grip her hair in place instead, prehensile.

"The only progress I've made this past week was when you stabbed yourself in front of me." Her hand touched her right thigh, the same place where I'd wounded myself. "That's not a sustainable method. The only other hint of a change came when I went near the vorpal hole today. But I don't want to use that."

"So basically," I said, drawing myself up, "You've decided I was right all along, and the most logical next step is to try bonding a healer. Great. You can bond with Mori."

Wist put the heavy wet bathrobe down gently on one of the pool chairs. Empty-handed now, she turned to me.

"Clematis," she said, "If I absolutely have to bond a healer, I want to bond with you. But it's up to you. You can tell me no."

I couldn't help myself. I looked up at Wist looming there next to me. Like she had all the time in the world. Like she would be content to stand here patiently bickering with me in the darkness until we both withered away into skeletons. Was she doing this on purpose? I wondered wildly. She couldn't possibly have engineered a better way to grind my pride to dust. But I could still save myself. She'd said it herself. All I had to do was tell her no.

"How"—oh, listen to that, my voice cracked—"How could you ever expect me to say yes?"

Wist watched as if waiting for me to elaborate. As if elaboration were even necessary. When I turned toward her, she was so close that I didn't have to look at her face anymore. I could just stare at the round neckline of her dark red scab-colored sweatshirt as if talking straight into the wall of an empty room.

She still smelled the same, even after all these years—despite the fact that during my time in prison, I couldn't have recalled or properly described the first thing about her scent. I just instantly knew that it was the same as before, and it was hers. Wist was still Wist. I'd gladly stab another knife into my leg if only it would let me turn around and walk away and forget her.

"Wist," I said to her neckline. "Remember when they arrested me? You were there in the room. Nostalgic, right? Remember how I called out to you? You didn't even turn your head.

"I kept saying your name. I was so confused. They started to haul me away. I started to struggle. I reached for you. I begged for help. Do you even remember that? Were you even listening?"

I heard her breath catch. Or perhaps it was mine. I felt a hand—tentative, barely there—on my head.

"Don't—touch—me." By now I could barely get the words out.

Wist immediately let go.

I had to clench everything to keep it together—my eyes squeezed shut, my fingers gripping the edges of the long bathrobe sleeves, my lungs burning in my chest. At least I managed to force a semblance of calm back into my voice. "Well, I know why you're trying to choose me." I opened my eyes again.

Wist actually took a step back. "You do?"

"You're worried the healer you bond will become a target. Of the Extinguishers or whoever else hates the Kraken. If someone's got to be in danger, better me than Mori, right? I can understand that." I raised my chin. "But how could you possibly think I'd just roll over and say yes? You never explained why you decided to turn me in. You never even tried."

She crossed her arms as if she were cold. This was really such a bizarre room to be having it out in—the water lapping slowly to utter stillness behind her, the overgrown masses of fairy lights suspended ominously from the unseen ceiling above.

"A Board member died." Her tone was devoid of emotion, simply stating the facts. "I know you only meant for him to be delayed, to miss the vote. I doubt the Jacians were plotting a full assassination, either. It could even be described as an accident. But in the end, he died."

"So I deserve my punishment."

Wist began pacing. "I informed on you because I could see how it would all play out," she said, low and clear. The water in the knee-deep pool had gone completely motionless. "If I tried to shelter you, the entire Board of Magi—all the surviving members and their factions— would have turned on us. It would have meant war."

"You're the Kraken," I said caustically. "You didn't think you could win?"

"Of course I would have won," Wist said, as if it wasn't ever even in question. "The two of us, against every mage and healer in Osmanthus? We would have crushed them. There would be incredible bloodshed. And what next, after civil war? How would you transition to peace? Rule forever as a dictator, with me as your enforcer? Turn around and leave the country in ruins?"

Full disclosure: I won't try to claim her answer was a total surprise. I could understand why Wist wouldn't want to go to war with all of Osmanthus for my measly sake.

"Yeah, it all sounds very reasonable when you put it like that." I reached out and jerked at her sleeve to stop her from moving, to make her face me again. "So why didn't you tell me you couldn't defend me anymore? Why didn't you tell me that you'd have to report me to PubSec?"

For the first time, Wist's face twisted. She stared down at me as if she wanted to shake me. "Would you have fled quietly into the night, never to be seen again?"

"Yes!"

"No," Wist shot back, with such certainty that it actually succeeded in shutting me up for a few seconds. "Maybe now you would. If the exact same situation happened right now, maybe you would look for a way to flee to Jace, or even further. But the Asa Clematis of seven years ago? You would have gone underground in Osmanthus. You would have joined the Jacian agitators, or a subliminal insurgent group. You would have found a way to fight back. You'd have nothing to lose anymore—you'd strike at more Board members. And then the government would hunt you down and destroy you. With or without my help."

"Wow. Listen to you, Wist. Never realized you had such an active imagination." Somehow, miraculously, my voice remained steady on the surface. "Okay. That explains why you didn't give me any advance notice. It doesn't explain why you had to let them drag me away like that. In the end I screamed for you. I've never screamed like that before, and never again. You didn't look at me once."

I was clutching her sleeves with both my hands now. When had I started doing that? The slightest hint of her scent still made my throat close up. "You think—you think it would be a simple matter for me to let your magic in?"

For another long moment, Wist was as still as the water. I started to pull away. I couldn't breathe right. Then her voice sounded near my ear, soft and raw, breaking over the line between empty whisper and audible speech. "Can I...?"

Her arms were around me. At first barely holding me, leaving room for me to shove her away. I suppressed a noise in my chest. I didn't have the words to answer. I nodded jerkily into her shoulder. Her arms tightened, pressed the air out of me.

Then I was gripping her too, fingers clawing the back of her sweatshirt. She smelled like our twenties. Like our teens. Like the academy. Like the sky soaring above the school rooftops when she first talked about building a tower with magic, a secret place far away from her family, far away from the seat of the mageocracy in Osmanthus City, a sovereign tower meant just for the two of us.

And as she held me, I remembered the side of her face when PubSec came to take me. All I'd been able to make out was a pale reflection in the dark window behind her. She'd been in a chair by the window, utterly immobile, as if sitting to have her portrait painted.

At first I'd thought it was some kind of prank. I waited for her to crack. But they weren't letting me go. They had an arrest warrant. None of them addressed Wist after a cursory salute in her direction, a few brief words to thank her for her service.

I began to panic. I cried out for her. It was an ugly and undignified struggle. I was in hysterics. I'd never cared so little for how I looked or sounded. I just wanted Wist.

Seven years later, I had Wist in my arms, and all it did was bring the memory back to jagged life. I'd never wanted to feel like that again. I hadn't thought it was possible to ever feel like that again.

Yet here we were anyway. Wist's magic branch coiled around my back like a rope tying me to her. Her hand cradled the back of my head. It shook minutely, as if from a bone-deep cold. Her face was in my hair.

I swear to you, I hadn't missed this. I hadn't missed her. I'm no innocent victim, but Wist threw me to the mercy of the mageocracy and never looked back. I would be a sucker to long for scraps of the unreachable past.

"Wist," I mumbled into her shoulder. "You know I hate you."

"As you should," she said, barely audible.

"Why would I ever agree to bond with you?"

She pulled back a little to look me in the eye. "Is that a no?"

"Bonding is for *life*."

"I realize that."

Exasperated, I blew out a big breath. "Oh, come on. I should parrot back all the objections you raised seven days ago."

Finally I found it in me to wriggle away. Wist's arms released me at once, but her magic branch tried to cling to me longer. It trailed forlornly off my shoulder as I shrugged myself free.

"You'll bond with Mori if I say no?" I asked. "If he's still up for it?"

She gave a very small nod.

"Good. Let me—let me think about it," I said. "Just a little. Just tonight."

I had no idea what kind of face I was making right now, but it definitely wasn't one suitable for viewing in broad daylight. Thank goodness for the shadows welling up in this cavernous room, and for the comparative faintness of the fairy lights.

"I was too weak," Wist said. It sounded as if she were speaking half to herself, half to me.

"Too weak for what?"

"When Public Security came for you. If I looked at you, if I answered you, I wouldn't ... I wouldn't have been able to let them take you. I was afraid of what I might do. That's why I ignored you." She held her wrist to her chest, clenching it as if delivering a punishment. "Originally they offered to come while I was out. I insisted on being there. In the end, it hurt you more."

"I'll punch you if you start apologizing," I said, although I was strongly tempted to punch her regardless.

"I wasn't going to. But—"

"I mean it," I warned.

"I never forgot the sound of you calling for me," Wist said. "I never forgot how you sounded. Not for a second."

I don't remember what else we talked about afterward. Maybe nothing. Certainly nothing important.

I still wanted to punch her. I wanted to push her backwards into the water and watch her smash her head on the bottom of the pool. I wanted her to look at me one more time and say it again, say she'd never forgotten me, say it in that low strained voice like the words were being strangled out of her.

Not that she deserved to complain of any serious grief. But it thrilled me to think that even a sliver of what I'd felt at the time had ricocheted like shrapnel to pierce Wist, tiny splinters staying buried in her all these years, working their way inexorably up toward the fragile meat of her heart.

Anyway, that's what filled my head as we departed the pool room. Wist peeled her wet bathrobe off the pool chair where she'd left it and pulled it on little by little, wincing as she went. I drifted after her, following her back through the wall into her bedroom closet, and then into her bedroom itself, painted corner to corner with sunlight. The brightness made my eyes water.

When I finished blinking, Wist was in her loose gray undershirt, digging around for drier clothes to wear. The sun pierced the old thin fabric hanging off her as if it were made out of mist. Something caught at the back of my throat. I trained my gaze firmly on the wide windows, which framed the torn-up aftermath of a battle between vivid blue sky and blustery clouds.

Someone would bond for life with Wist soon. And with any luck, bonding would jump-start the rest of her magic regrowth. But it didn't have to happen this this very instant—surely it could wait a little longer. No matter. Someone would be bonded with Wist by this time tomorrow.

CHAPTER TWELVE

16 Years Ago

WIST ONLY TOOK ME to her childhood home once. Once was more than enough.

We were around seventeen or eighteen, I think, getting close to graduation. It would have been shortly after Wist became officially recognized as a Kraken-class mage.

For most of our time in the academy, she'd been identified as S-class—though any fool could see that there were distinct differences between her abilities and those of every other S-class mage on record. Then again, there had only ever been one other Kraken, and the previous one had lived thousands of years ago, long before the modern Osmanthian ranking system came into existence. I could understand why Osmanthian officials might hesitate before anointing a second Kraken.

Of course, even a mere S-class mage would have been considered a precious gift. Wist retained little memory of her biological parents—the

Shien clan had adopted her when she was only five or six, almost immediately after she started showing signs of being a once-in-a-generation talent. No doubt her birth parents had little choice in the matter; hopefully they at least got paid well. Since magical strength didn't run reliably in families, the most influential mage clans made strategic use of adoption to preserve their power.

The Shien clan was one of the wealthiest in Osmanthus, with high-placed mages in every branch of government. Yet their adoptees still had to follow the usual naming laws, which was why Wist's official name order got inverted when they added her to the family registry. Legally she belonged to the Shiens, but no one would ever forget that they'd adopted her. It was carved into the very sound of her new full name: Wisteria Shien.

This is all to say that Wist's family home was both as luxurious as an ancient palace and deeply uncomfortable. Her parents' biological children—and there were quite a few of them—all heartily resented her. At the same time, they didn't dare offend the newly reclassified Kraken, the king of all mages, the second coming of a legend, the pride of Osmanthus.

Face-to-face, everyone was extremely sweet and caring. Surrounded by glittering chandeliers and enchanted mirrors, breathtaking muraled ceilings and servants better-dressed than me, I chose to pretend I was staying at a hoity-toity four-star hotel.

I didn't mention to Wist how her siblings looked at her when she glanced away, or the muffled things I heard them saying as I prowled corridors where I wasn't supposed to wander alone. Wist didn't need me to come tattling. She'd grown up with them, after all. She wasn't oblivious.

We were on our two-week summer break from school. Wist had spent most previous breaks in the academy dorms, same as me. She rarely went home, and rarely stayed there more than a day when she did. But now that she'd been declared a Kraken-class, her parents insisted that she come for a visit. And they insisted on meeting me for the first time, too. I guess word had gotten out that Wist never let anyone else heal her.

Soon it became clear that I was Not Worthy of being this close to a mage of Wist's caliber. My parents? No-name subliminals. My grades? A mixed bag. Now, I could run circles around any of my healer classmates, and they knew it, but taking the top rank in every subject would just have made me a bigger target. Why bother?

Landing a high-class mage wasn't part of my life plan to begin with. I didn't want to be the meek little supportive healer hovering politely behind my big-name bonded mage, forever at their beck and call. Some healers dreamed all their lives of bonding the perfect mage, and some were like me. The whole idea of it kind of creeped me out.

Then Wist's parents looked down their elegant noses at me and inquired ever so delicately about my background. Her siblings scanned me up and down and made backhanded remarks about how generous Wist was to look past appearances and manners. Yeah, sorry for being short and butch and for not knowing exactly which utensil pairs with each course, or which soups are meant to be slurped and which aren't.

Nothing they said set Wist off. I could see now where she'd acquired her poker face and her stony patience. But she studied her food very carefully whenever we all sat down for formal dinners, cutting it into needlessly tiny pieces with the intense precision of a surgeon.

As for me, I didn't crack till the third or fourth or fifth time Wist's parents tried to press us about our future plans. They subtly hinted that we would both be much better off if we separated and went to different colleges, institutions suited for honing our respective abilities.

You're only young once, they said, albeit in fancier phrasing. You should experience life apart from each other. You should try working with other mages and healers. They offered to introduce me to mages who would be just *perfect* for me, given my test scores and upbringing. They hinted to Wist that the most eligible young healers in the nation were clamoring to meet her.

I took Wist's hand under the table. I smiled beatifically at each and every face around the table. "Oh, but we couldn't," I said brightly, the picture of happiness. "We're already bonded."

All hell broke loose. It was magnificent. Tears, rage, disbelief, incoherent accusations. Spit-laced threats to sue me, my parents, our teachers, the entire school. Wist's siblings nearly toppled out of their chairs in horror and glee. Wide-eyed servants peeked nervously around the corner to see what was happening. I'd just barely turned eighteen, and Wist was still seventeen—too young to consent, they cried. There must be a way to annul it. If no way existed, they'd make one.

"How?" I asked, increasingly cheerful. "Gonna kill me?"

An elite squad of lawyers arrived on the scene hardly half an hour later. And still Wist kept her fingers laced tight through mine, not saying a word. I think we waited till the last possible moment to enlighten her parents. That moment came several days later, when they were on the verge of hiring magic-perception experts to formally examine our alleged bond. Until then, I took to wearing a makeshift bond thread—just a bit of colorless kitchen string—purely as a way to rub it in.

In the meantime, Wist refused to let me out of her sight. I appreciated it, honestly. Assassination was starting to feel less like a paranoid fantasy and more like something the Shiens might consider a legitimate last resort to get rid of me.

At some point in those brief days when Wist's family feared we might be bonded, Wist turned to me and said she'd thought I didn't want to bond anyone.

"Well, I've always been sort of against it in principle," I said. Wist already knew that. "But I would totally do it to spite them."

Yet we never did bond, not even after coming of age at twenty. I guess it was our way to defy both the people who said we should and the people who said we shouldn't. We had nothing to prove—and more to the point, we could get by just fine without it. I could already heal Wist better than anyone, and she was the last mage in the world who needed a power boost.

We talked about it sometimes, but we were never in any big rush. I liked just being a healer and a mage, without getting locked into the roles expected of a bonded pair. We were more than best friends and less than a couple. It didn't matter what others called us. From beginning to end, we were just Clematis and Wist.

At the time it had given me quite a superiority complex. Look at us—we didn't need bonding or labels or legal contracts to tie us together for life. We were freer than all the rest of those chumps out there. We were together because we chose to be together, over and over.

I was the real chump, of course. My first night in prison, the truth dawned on me with frigid clarity. I was no different from any of the other healers who clung to their station in life by virtue of a mage's benevolence.

At least those who bonded a mage had the good sense to make it extremely difficult to get rid of them. In refusing to bond with Wist, all I'd done was make myself easier to dispose of. I'd thought I was so much more enlightened than the desperate-seeming healers who chased after high-status mages and clung to them with all their might. But one way or another, without even acknowledging it, I'd been just as dependent on Wist's aura of privilege, on her silent protection.

CHAPTER THIRTEEN

21 Days Left

I DIDN'T SLEEP WELL that night in the tower, the night after Wist said she'd bond me (if I would have her). The dreams of death were unusually detailed and gruesome. Each time I startled myself awake, my mind raced off in a different direction.

At one point not long before sunrise, a vision of having nails hammered into my skull started to leak sideways into reality; I woke with an ice-pick headache behind my right eye. I lay curled in the darkness begging it to subside.

The spiking headache felt like it took forever to fade. In reality, it was probably a matter of minutes. My room still didn't have proper curtains, but Mori had helped me tack some towels over the windows to mute the moonlight. As agony ceased stabbing the back side of my eye, I began to smell ozone, a powerful hint of incoming rain. The towel-curtains stirred.

Had I forgotten to shut a window? I couldn't even recall shoving them open.

I shambled over to find the windows tightly locked. Yet the towels kept puffing like sails. The wind touched me, too—chilling my nose, running fingers through my hair. It was an outdoor wind inside a sealed room, a wind from nowhere.

Goosebumps pricked my arms. I went to my stack of pilfered clothes in the corner—the clean stack, hopefully, although I kept getting them mixed up—and dug out a sweater and jeans.

When I opened the door, the ozone scent grew stronger. I found Fanren poised in the hall outside my room like a guard dog. Though not typically an early riser, he too was more or less fully dressed, glasses and all. I asked him how long he'd been there.

"Couple minutes," he said. "It's raining in the kitchen."

"The ceiling's leaking?"

Fanren shook his head. "Regular rain, normal in every way. Just indoors. Come take a look."

Mori stood waiting outside the kitchen with an armful of umbrellas. The cat named Turtle crouched miserably by Mori's feet. I borrowed a red umbrella and opened it up as I stepped inside, barefoot. The kitchen was more than raining—it was pouring like a tropical monsoon, so loud that I couldn't hear myself think. I beat a hasty retreat. The umbrella wasn't very effective protection.

"Mori came and woke me maybe twenty minutes ago," Fanren said.

"You heard the rain?" I asked Mori. "Isn't your room much higher up?"

"I woke up with a headache." He put his hand near his right eye. "A short, stabbing one. It went away fast. But it got me awake enough to notice something was wrong. My room smelled like a flower shop. And there were little green lizards all over the ceiling, looking down at me."

"Where's Wist?"

The two of them exchanged glances. "Not sure," Fanren said. "Not in her room." He tapped the earring he usually used for communication. "Agent Manatree isn't responding, either."

A sick sensation began to expand in my ribcage. The indoor wind and rain, the inexplicable scents—they bore a powerful tinge of magic. In fact, magic was the only logical explanation. But it didn't feel like magic crafted with any kind of deliberate purpose. This was the kind of wild magic phenomena that materialized when inadequately healed mages went berserk.

I caught at Fanren's shoulder. He had past experience with losing control of his magic. It was the reason he'd been convicted, the reason we ended up meeting in prison all those years ago.

"What do you think?" I asked under my breath.

He scooped the distressed cat up in his arms. "It's probably what it looks like," he said. "Let's check out the tower entrance."

The entrance hall was filled with pearly white snakes. The cat took one look and leaped about ten feet in the other direction, then bolted far out of sight. Fortunately, the snakes didn't seem particularly interested in us passing humans. Their slithering produced a constant shushing noise as they writhed across the wooden floor, twined up around garden tools and onto dusty shelves.

Fanren led us on a careful path among the busy snakes. The front door appeared unlocked. He pushed it open. We stepped through and proceeded to emerge from the back door, coming right back into the barn-like hall we'd just left.

Next we tried leaving through the back door—and, no surprise, found ourselves crossing over the threshold of the front door. We experimented with climbing out a few second-floor windows. Doing so deposited us without warning in random rooms throughout the tower. There was no sign of Wist, and no way to escape.

We reconvened in the piano parlor where Manatree and I had first introduced Fanren to Mori and Wist. The fireplace, though still burning, overflowed with a riot of morning glory vines. They seemed immune to the flames. The hand-sized purple flowers were constantly furling and unfurling. They began to look to me like baby birds holding their mouths wide open for food.

"None of my branch skills would work to break us out of a closed loop like this," Fanren said. "That leaves us with two choices. We can sit tight and wait for Agent Manatree and her friends to realize something's wrong. We've got plenty of water and food. It might take some time, but if she gathers enough mages, she'll be able to break in eventually."

"Or instead of sitting on our butts, we can go search the tower for Wist," I added. "What's your recommendation?"

Fanren poked at one of the morning glories. The petals whipped shut. It took him a few seconds to tug free. I was mildly relieved to observe that he hadn't lost any fingers in the process.

"Waiting and doing nothing is obviously the safest option," he said. "As your bodyguard, that's what I'd suggest. You're the boss, though."

Mori looked a bit stunned. "But—the Kraken might be hurt. She might be suffering. It might get worse if we do nothing."

"Are you one hundred percent sure she's the one behind this?" Fanren gestured at the morning glories by way of example, although this time he did so from a safe distance.

"It's Wist, all right," I said. "The signature is more degraded than in a regular magic branch or cutting. But I'm positive it's her."

Fanren still seemed skeptical. "She's Class 1-1 right now. There's wild magic all over the tower. Seems a bit unbalanced."

"Maybe she regrew more branches."

"In her sleep? And then immediately got over-twisted and snapped?"

"Stranger things have happened," I reasoned. "Mages aren't supposed to be able to lose all their magic in the first place."

"Well, if you want to hunt her down, we'd best stick together for safety." Fanren yawned, flexed his hands. "My Scan skill won't help much with all this wild magic floating around. Where do you want to start?"

If Wist and I were bonded, it wouldn't even be a question. I'd be able to nudge her mind-to-mind. I'd be able to locate her in an instant. I'd already know if she were hurt, if she were conscious, if the rest of her magic really had come back in a sudden fit like spontaneous combustion.

But we weren't bonded. And I knew nothing.

The main problem with locating Wist was that the tower didn't fit together in the same way as a regular, sensibly constructed building. Both Mori and I had a general sense of where the wild magic was coming from. But just like how the tower's front door now looped straight into the back door, getting over to somewhere on the right might require going left.

With each room we entered, the source of the wild magic emanated from a clear and specific direction. We were never in disagreement over where to go next. But the exact direction changed drastically every time we crossed a new threshold.

All the stairs to the various roofs were broken, smashed to smithereens as if by an angry giant. Fanren had to float us up there with Zero Gravity. We found no traces of Wist, not a single footprint or half-eaten tuna can. We ventured back to Wist's empty bedroom and donned navy blue bathrobes to sneak into the dark cavern concealed behind the closet. Nothing. We searched sunrooms with swarms of yellow fish swimming peacefully through the air, and banquet halls whose rugs had sprouted mushrooms as tall as Fanren.

The sick feeling clenched tighter in my chest. The tower floor maps were useless, blotted out with thick white-and-black globs like bird shit. None of us had access to thorough blueprints, and I doubted the tower layout would deign to remain static over time, anyway. Searching it from top to bottom could take months, and that was assuming we didn't get hopelessly lost in the process.

Since we weren't making any headway, I made the executive decision to stop trusting our senses. We'd tried tracing the wild magic to its source. Now we tried going the opposite way.

Doing so took us past massive dangling sculptures of driftwood that hung on invisible wires like something in a museum. These I remembered seeing before. I paused outside the blue door—still propped safely open—which led to the room where the three Extinguishers had died all those months ago.

At this point, it was one of the most ordinary-looking rooms in the whole tower. No army of snails moisturizing the walls with a nice thick coat of slime. No gilded frames with their painted canvases dripping horrifically down to the floor, like bodies slowly bleeding out. Just wan wooden floorboards and that one empty desk.

I stepped inside just to see if anything would happen.

"Ouch," said a voice.

I jerked back. There'd been something lumpy underfoot. Fanren and Mori, still out in the hallway, hadn't reacted. I motioned them over.

"What was that for?" said the same voice.

The three of us looked down at a human face buried in the floor. The face didn't resemble anyone I could remember meeting before. For an instant I mistook it for a fallen mask. But no—it emerged fleshily from the solid floorboards like a sea mammal just barely coming up for air. It didn't seem capable of rising any further.

Its eyes rolled toward me accusingly. "That hurt."

"Sorry," I muttered, after taking a moment to master my stupefaction. It seemed like the thing to say. "Didn't see you there. Who are you?"

The pale eyes widened so far that I feared they might pop clean out of their sockets and roll away. This creature needed a breath mint—its exhalations were starting to make the small room smell like sweaty feet. The thick lips stretched into a variety of soundless shapes before forming audible words again.

"Help," the trapped face whispered. "It hurts. Please help."

Mori twitched. Fanren held an arm out to stop him from getting any closer to the face in the floor. Good man.

"What's happening to you?" I asked.

"Becoming part of the tower," hissed the face. "Becoming one with the tower."

"You came here from outside?"

"Trash must be recycled." It spoke with a peculiar conviction. "Does it hurt? Something hurts. Something always hurts. Step on me again. Please. Crush me like a leaf. The floor must be stepped on. The floor must—"

I spoke over the voice. "Where's the rest of you?"

The eyeballs rolled up toward the upper lids, then down toward the puffy lower lids. Then, with startling fluidity, they slid away in opposite directions, becoming perfectly wall-eyed. Straining to see the floor on both sides.

"Down," said the face. "Down, down, down."

The nose and forehead and eyes and lips slipped down below the floor like a turtle diving out of sight below the waves. Nothing remained but clean, varnished hardwood.

I tried pushing at the empty floor with the toe of my house slipper. No reaction.

I pictured the mystery face sinking further down. From the floor of one room to the ceiling of the next. Down, down, down. A new thought crackled to life at the back of my brain.

"Hey, Mori," I said slowly. "Does the tower have a basement?"

CHAPTER FOURTEEN

21 Days Left

MORI BLINKED. He put a hand to his mouth. He looked at me with very big eyes. "Oh, no," he said, muffled. "I'm so sorry. I didn't even think of that."

"So there is a basement," I said.

"Technically, yes."

"Technically?"

"It's more of a storage space, I guess. The Kraken said it's where she puts her mistakes. Rooms she ended up not liking. Failed magic experiments and such."

"A trash bin for the tower," I concluded.

I sketched a mental image of the barn-like entrance hall. The rest of the first floor was mostly devoted to a vast aquarium, with relatively tame vorpal beasts (and a few brave fish) swimming about in monstrous tanks.

I couldn't recall spotting any trapdoors or stairs leading further down. None of the elevators had buttons for basement floors, either.

Color me stumped. "How do we get down there?"

"I've never been to the basement myself," Mori said. "There probably aren't any permanent access points, physical or magical. I don't think even the Kraken goes there—she just transfers a few rooms down there every so often. I've never heard her talk about visiting the basement in person."

"You don't have any kind of porting magic, do you," I said to Fanren.

"Afraid not."

"Then we'll just have to break in through the first floor. What's your weapon skill again? Piercer?"

Fanren extracted a little scrap of fabric from his pocket and started cleaning his glasses. He checked the lenses carefully in the light from the window. "I think that face in the floor changes the risk equation, Boss."

"I'd argue that it lowers the risk," I countered. "We understand a lot more now."

"Do we?" Mori said hopefully.

"Here's my hypothesis." I gestured up at the ceiling, in the rough direction of Wist's bedroom. "Another party of intruders accessed the tower late last night, or extremely early in the morning. Maybe Extinguishers, maybe not. They could've used magic to breach the upper floors. Or they could've simply dug a nice long tunnel through the prairie to reach the basement.

"Wist's room looked undisturbed. If they were mages, they could've moved her lower in the tower with little noise or fuss. Her one measly magic branch wouldn't be hard to subdue. Or maybe Wist noticed something wrong and left her room on her own. Maybe she walked in on them and surprised them."

Now I motioned down at the floorboards.

"An altercation took place. Either it happened in the basement, or it resulted in all of them moving down there. Along the way, something induced rapid regrowth of at least a few of Wist's other magic branches. And eventually she snapped, going into full berserker mode. Or maybe it was the opposite—maybe going berserk was what brought more of her magic back. Regardless, her wild magic is what's warping the rest of the tower. Seems like the attackers haven't fared too well, either."

"Still leaves a lot of unknown variables," said Fanren.

"Is her wild magic causing the tower lockdown?" asked Mori. "Or is it the—the intruders? Whoever they are."

"Could be either," I admitted. "Let's have another look."

Back in the entrance hall, Mori and I took turns glaring at every inch of the front door. It was difficult to decipher through the miasma of wild magic in the air, but when I got down on my hands and knees, I thought I saw traces of an unfamiliar mage's magic cutting grafted subtly to the threshold.

Don't blame us for missing it earlier. With so much uncontrolled magic wafting around, picking out the home invader's work was the equivalent of trying to distinguish a single unfamiliar thumbprint on a water glass already covered in all kinds of blurry finger-marks. Using only your naked eyes, of course.

The front door still looped into the back door—which meant the mage who'd locked down the tower was still alive. At least for now. Magic cuttings never outlived their creators.

I told Mori to wait by the door, and to try leaving every few minutes. "If you ever actually make it outside," I said, "Run to the nearest guard post."

At first he was reluctant. He very much wanted to come to the basement with us. I patted him on the back—a token show of sympathy—but refused to budge.

"Fanren can do a better job of looking out for one of us than both of us," I explained. "And don't take this the wrong way, but he's here as my bodyguard, not yours. If something threatens both of us, he'll save me first. Let's not put him in that position."

To his credit, Mori was simply worried about Wist. He thought it might be better to have more than one healer ready to help her as soon as possible. Treating a berserk mage was by far the trickiest and most tasking type of healing.

I overcame his objections by asking how many berserk mages he'd neutralized before in his life. He was a prototypical honor student (and it suited him!), and he'd gone much further in higher education than me, in spite of having just turned twenty-two. But his experience with bringing broken mages back from the brink was absolutely nothing compared to mine.

Once our roles had been decided, Fanren removed one of his communication earrings and offered it to Mori. This way we could talk to each other across floors, should the need arise. More importantly, whoever had less going on at the time could try to contact Manatree again as soon as the tower lockdown lifted. Mori, who had no piercings, cradled the black drop earring carefully in his hands.

"All right," I said to Fanren. "Break the floor."

Mori and I backed up to the wall to avoid getting in the way. The white snakes were much calmer now compared to before. They coiled up along the shelves in cozy little groups. Fanren shooed a few undulating stragglers out of the way in order to clear most of the broad-beamed hall floor. Then a long black lance materialized beside him with zero forewarning.

That was one characteristic of a particularly capable mage—they could execute branch skills on the spot, without giving you any hint of what was coming next.

Fanren remained immobile, studying the floor, as the slim lance rose up over his head. His Piercer skill manifested the lance, but his Zero Gravity skill controlled its movement. He didn't turn his head or move his eyes around. He didn't gesture in the slightest.

Again without warning, the lance plunged halfway through the dusty floor. It yanked itself free. Eight or nine new lances popped into the air around Fanren. They joined forces to brutalize the floor like a battering ram. Next to me, I felt Mori wince at the noise.

Fanren's relaxed stillness was another sign of what made him so effective as a duelist. Many mages used physical gestures as a crutch when moving objects around with magic, controlling the targets of their telekinesis like a conductor directing an orchestra. That wasn't strictly necessary, but it did greatly reduce the mental load. Fanren, on the other hand, could freely juggle his lances without so much as twitching a muscle. He made it look deceptively easy.

Said lances evaporated as soon as they'd stabbed a satisfactory hole in the floor. It appeared about as wide around as the mouth of an old-fashioned well.

Before approaching the hole to the basement, I caught at Mori's hanging sleeve. He was wearing another one of his soft pastel cardigans. It went all the way down to his knees.

"Be careful," I warned. "Staying up here doesn't mean you're out of danger. There's a good chance that the attackers did something to the guards on the perimeter, too. If you get out there before Manatree responds, stay quiet and don't announce yourself. Try to get a glimpse of the situation at the outpost before you let anyone see you."

Mori nodded earnestly. At least I knew I could trust him to take these types of instructions to heart.

"You be careful, too," he said, still cupping Fanren's earring like a living thing. "Please."

"No need to fret," I said. "We'll bring Wist back up here like nothing ever happened." Easier said than done, no doubt, but I didn't want to give the poor kid a hernia. I slapped him on the shoulder, radiating reassurance and competence.

The hole in the floor revealed a grandly decorated space, one rather too large to be called a mere room. I couldn't quite put my finger on why, but it felt unpleasantly familiar.

At the edge of the hole, Fanren took hold of my elbow. We both hovered off the ground, buoyed by his magic, light as dandelion seeds. He floated us neatly down into the area of the basement just below the entrance hall. Wouldn't ever need a parachute as long as you had Fanren around to slow your fall.

Our feet touched down not on the floor, but on a spacious oval dining table with an elaborate floral centerpiece. On our right were an array of oversize musical instruments waiting dormant on a stage, as if dinner here always came with live music. On our left were a variety of over-the-top amenities, such as a spacious bar that would put most top-tier city restaurants to shame, and impeccably lit display cases filled with tiny pastries laid out like the finest of jewelry.

I tilted my head back. Sure enough, a baroque mural spread across the entire ceiling. Except for the part where Fanren had punched a hole, of course. Finely painted debris littered the creamy tablecloth and most of the tastefully upholstered chairs.

All in all, it seemed like a flawless copy of the Shien family dining room—missing only the well-bred accents, bitter looks, whiffs of pricey cologne, and general air of sophisticated dissatisfaction. But no sign of any living occupants, Wist or otherwise. We moved on.

Most of Wist's childhood home seemed to exist down here in

replica—outdoor gardens and all, with a mystical facsimile of sunlight emanating from sky-like ceilings. On the far side of a sprawling display of sculpted rosebushes, distant walls blocked off the horizon like painted stage sets.

Fanren and I worked our way lower, sometimes finding a convenient ladder or staircase, sometimes using his magic to puncture another hole straight to the next floor. We passed rooms that looked like government offices and rooms that reminded me of the academy. We passed half-finished spaces devoid of sound and color and gravity.

When we reached a simulacrum of Wist's old dorm room, I motioned for Fanren to follow me inside. He had to duck to come through the door, reminding me of how often Wist had bashed her head on it. Everything about the interior was exactly the same as in my memory. Even the bedspread still bore stains from that one time I'd gotten a bloody nose.

I touched the carpeted floor, a mottled blue-green-brown material designed to survive nearly anything we students threw at it. The carpet was warm to the touch and seemed to beat like a heart. Yet the beat was very, very slow. I imagined a huge animal sleeping. A whale. A vorpal beast. A dragon.

Fanren crouched beside me. "Bingo, is it?"

"One last request," I told him. "Do what you need to do to keep me alive. But you can't hurt Wist."

"Can't hurt her, period? Or no fatal wounds?"

"No fatal wounds," I said.

I'm a realist. There was no way to predict how a berserking mage might react to us.

This time, Fanren was much more delicate with his levitating lance. Unlike most non-magical weapons of the same shape and size, it could be used for far more than just direct stabbing. It had no handle, since he never actually held it. The entire long surface was just as lethally sharp as the pointed tip. Kneeling down, hands in his pockets, he made it saw delicately though the carpeted floor. It was like watching a pastry chef make surgical incisions in an unmarked cake.

Fanren didn't let the lid he'd cut in the floor fall through itself. The end of his lance shimmied inside the slit and lifted away a perfect circle of liberated floor, depositing it on Wist's bed. I leaned forward to peek down through the manhole-sized opening.

What happened next came so quickly that I had zero time to react. I saw it clearly, but it was as if any connection between my vision and my physical reflexes had been completely severed.

Before I could glimpse anything of what lay in the room below, a mass of gray hands shot up through the hole in the carpeted floor. They were hand-shaped but made of something vague and shifting, a thick choking smoke or mist. They surged toward me like striking snakes.

A wall of magic—flat and transparent like glass—materialized a finger's width away from my nose. Fanren's Barrier. The hands slammed into the wall and stopped. They melted. They recovered, reshaping themselves, splitting off in different directions, slithering up and down and left and right in search of a way around the barricade. More walls snapped into place to block them, closing me and Fanren off in a perfect cube.

Some of the smoky hands reformed into smoky drill-bits. Some were open palms. Some were fists. Light flickered across the magic barriers as the drills ground away and the remaining hands pounded at every available surface, over and over. It was a light like something you might see flashing through the heart of a thunderhead. The swarm of hands now surrounded our protective cube so thoroughly that we could hardly see anything else.

"This might've been a bad idea, chief." Fanren already sounded strained.

The hands had Wist's magic in them, but from here I couldn't tell if it was another wild phenomenon, or something that berserk-mode Wist had unleashed on purpose.

"They'll chase us if we try to flee," I said. "Might as well stick to the original plan. Let's go in."

"And how do you propose we do that?"

"Distract them with Body Double? Hide ourselves with Reflect? You've got all kinds of useful skills," I said. Fanren looked skeptical. "Hey, I'm just spitballing."

Was it me, or had it started to get kind of misty here inside Fanren's cube? I waved my hand in the air to see if the mist would clear. Fanren's face still looked foggy. A nasty premonition started to creep up the back of my neck.

"Fanren?" I said, praying for a response. "Fanren, you didn't put a barrier below us, did you? Maybe try—"

The thing I'd thought was Fanren collapsed into a pile of empty clothing and glasses and piercings and teeth and ashes. The clothing and other detritus transmuted into dry brown leaves. The leaves and ashes scattered in a mini-whirlwind that went screaming into the walls around me with a sound like peals of far-off laughter. Yet the barriers remained. For now, at least.

Which meant that Fanren was still alive. Somewhere out there.

If I sound strangely calm, it's because I had no choice but to keep my wits about me. It's one of the first things they teach us healers (and subliminals too, for that matter). We have absolutely no defense against magic. We can't use it ourselves, after all.

If a mage turns on you, all you can do is keep an eye out for opportunities to escape, unlikely though it may seem. And if you can't escape, you can at least be trained to hold onto your reason against all odds, to wall off your fears, to become capable of bearing meticulous witness.

Hey, it might come in handy if you survived to see your assailant in court.

I'd internalized those lessons as well as anyone. But my mind went blank a moment later, when the once-solid barriers dissolved into a vapor like dry ice.

The next coherent thought I had was: Fanren?

No. This didn't have to mean Fanren was dead. He might just be having trouble concentrating. He was one of the top-ranked duelists in Osmanthus City. Surely—

The gray hands looked as intangible as a miasma, but they felt just like human hands when they grabbed me. They were warm and alive, moist like the hot breath of a giant.

All those hands—it was the closest thing I'd felt in ages to the first time I got arrested. The PubSec agents hauling me away from Wist. The heat and cold racing through me. My feet scraping the floor in a futile effort to hit the brakes. Cascading irritation, confusion, humiliation, terror. A wordless cry tore out of me as the torrent of hands dragged me down through the hole in the floor.

CHAPTER FIFTEEN
21 Days Left

SOMETHING AKIN to an enormous spiderweb broke my fall. But I didn't stick to it; I bounced awkwardly off the rope-thick threads. Now the misty hands seemed to ease me to the ground, letting go of me as I landed.

The patch of floor where they put me down was the first thing that riveted my attention. It was a pliant material, white as new snow.

You might wonder: what kind of fool would choose to install pure white carpet?

Answer: one with the money and power to procure magic cuttings that would keep the carpet looking clean no matter how many people trampled it.

In this case, the fool was the Osmanthian government. I knew this room—or its original version, anyway, which existed in an Osmanthus City courthouse far from the Kraken's tower. I'd spent hours during my trial squinting down at the blinding wall-to-wall carpet, struggling to spot flaws.

The next thing I noticed after the stark white carpet was the stench. I'll spare you the details. Suffice it to say that the room smelled like people cut wide open. There are a lot of things cased up inside the human body that it's best not to think about too closely, and best not spilled free in polite company. I smothered my mouth and nose with the sweat-dampened end of my sleeve. It didn't help much, but felt somewhat preferable giving up and drinking the air straight, no chaser.

My pulse was still skidding out of control, spiked with adrenaline from how the flock of disembodied hands had yanked me through the hole in the ceiling overhead. Apparently getting me down here had been their only goal, though. They soon retreated, dissipating into formless skeins of smoke.

I looked around and promptly wished I hadn't. I'd expected bodies, but there were too many to count at a glance. Most in some kind of combat gear. No sign of Fanren. The enchanted carpet strove to avoid getting soiled; blood formed gelatinous puddles atop it rather than soaking in. On the whole, though, there was far less blood than there should have been.

Some bodies were stuck half-in, half-out of the walls. The colossal wall panels bore the same paintings as the ones I'd memorized over the course of my trial: empty landscapes depicting each vivid season in the Osmanthus countryside. I suppose the implication was supposed to be that justice had no season, or that justice would come for you regardless of the season.

Of course, in the real courtroom there were no staring human faces buried in the panels showing clouds of soft pink cherry trees. The faces protruded and retreated, wet their lips, ground their teeth. In the real courtroom there were no shadowy shapes shifting like ghosts—or submerged corpses, more likely—just beneath the surface of the picturesque painted scenery.

In the real courtroom there were no naked abandoned arms sprouting seamlessly from the seats of empty chairs, monochrome tattoos swirling from their wrists to their inner elbows. It was the mark chosen by the Extinguishers, or so Mori had told me. Candle stubs with just-snuffed wicks tattooed at the wrist. Streaks of dying smoke curling across the inner forearm.

Whether partial or complete, twitching or motionless, all the Extinguishers and their body parts had one thing in common. Fleshy umbilical cords drank from them, stretching through the air or criss-crossing along the walls or ceiling or floor. This haphazard net was what I'd crashed into as the wild-magic hands pulled me down through the vast replica courtroom, down to the very bottom.

It was like looking at a mass of pipes or wire, but alive—each cord sheathed in a transparent whitish material, twisted and bumpy on the surface, shining wetly. Some cords were plugged directly into visible human flesh. Others were plugged into the furniture, or seemed to plunge toward those dark figures bulging out from behind the painted walls. Regardless, all the cords led to the same destination. From every corner of the grand courtroom, high and low, they reached for the judge's throne.

The throne was not whole. Some fierce force had shattered its pedestal. The seat was mostly dismantled, its pieces just more elegant debris atop a heap of rubble. The flood of umbilical cords came together at the top of the heap. They connected to a broken figure with long dark hair that clung like a stain to the remnants of the judge's throne and its pulverized foundation.

Wist. It could only be Wist. I saw her magic pulsing through the cords of corrugated flesh connecting her to all the scattered Extinguishers. I saw her magic glistening like water in her suddenly-long hair, loose and black as tar, a mass that reached all the way down to the inconceivably white floor. But—

I stood up to see better, trying not to make any noise. Dizziness hit me. I gripped the edge of a bolted-down courtroom chair.

Very little remained of Wist's torso. Umbilical cords filled the space on the left where her heart and half her lungs and ribs belonged. They plugged up the gaping space where usually there would be a liver and kidneys and pancreas and stomach and intestines and ovaries and all those other organs whose names I've forgotten.

At first glance it appeared that the cords were filling a terrible hole. At second glance it appeared that they were jostling to feed on her, hungry pale fish wriggling and clustering in the way fish do. Her eyes were closed. She didn't seem to be breathing. But then, how could she breathe in such a state?

My own thoughts in my head felt like the voice of someone distant, someone with no real connection to this stinking room. Wist's magic was alive and moving. Therefore Wist was alive. No matter what had happened to her. No matter how she looked. The Extinguishers were alive too, weren't they? Most of them, anyway. Their trapped faces blinked at me. Their teeth chattered. Unlike the talkative specimen from earlier, they seemed to lack a voice down here.

Study the magic, I told myself. A different magic branch coursed through each of the pulsing cords. Wist's magic had grown out nearly as impressively as her hair. Right now she'd be considered a solid S-class. Good news, right? Right?

Body horror aside, this room was a perfect copy of the place where Wist had testified against me. At the time, I'd listened to her without taking in a word she said. When she spoke, it had been as if everyone else in the courtroom turned to mannequins, and my own hands became rubbery props in my lap.

The temperature in the windowless room had been calibrated such that, despite the seasonal paintings on all the walls, you couldn't tell if the world outside was winter or summer, clear or stormy, day or night. When she spoke, something inside me seemed to meld with the room and its spotless, unfeeling detachment.

Now here came that same numbness. I barely felt as if I were inside my own body. The nausea, my own high shallow breathing that was all I could hear—it stopped mattering.

I walked unsteadily toward the throne. The mountain of junk, rather. I had to pick my way with care to avoid stepping on any of the Extinguishers or their umbilical cords. The white carpet sucked up the sound of my feet.

The Extinguishers were no threat anymore, and the smoky hands were mere smoke now, clouding the hole in the stories-high ceiling. But I didn't call out to Wist. Conscious or otherwise, she was a berserk mage right now. The last thing I wanted to do was provoke her.

The floor turned black at the edge of the junk heap—the ends of Wist's overgrown hair. I made sure not to touch it as I climbed toward the throne.

My foot slipped.

My breath sputtered.

Debris clattered.

Something had caught me, stopped me from falling. I looked down. An umbilical cord wound around my waist like a climber's rope. I looked up. Wist looked back at me, barely covered by her ruined clothing. There were three small holes in her forehead.

"These?" She pointed at the holes. "They tried to shoot me," she said wryly. "With a gun. Can you imagine?"

For someone missing most of her lungs, she didn't sound that different. Maybe a few notches deeper than usual. Then again, I couldn't tell if I were hearing her voice with my ears or with my magic perception.

That wasn't what disturbed me—it was the look on her face. Not at all expressionless. Bright, curious, with a tiny cat-like curve to her mouth. Berserk mages were supposed to have red eyes, but hers were almost indistinguishable from before. Normally they were such a deep brown they looked black. Now they might perhaps have turned a very dark, dark red, darker than a blood clot. It was hard to tell for sure.

The cord at my waist yanked me closer. I toppled onto Wist and the mass of translucent flesh-cords filling her. They were warm, undulating like worms in a bait bucket. I recoiled. The climber's cord released me, but now her hands caught me, kept me sitting on her, kept me from going any further.

"I missed you," she said.

"We've been apart less than a day."

"I still missed you."

"You got by just fine when I was alone in prison for seven years," I said through my teeth.

"I missed you then, too." She looked at me like she meant it.

I wanted to crawl out of my skin. Most mages—even the kindest and gentlest—became uncontrollably violent when they snapped. Obviously some kind of terrible violence had already taken place here, but why was berserk Wist suddenly acting affectionate? If anything, it would suggest that this neediness was the exact opposite of her true nature.

At first my consternation kept me from noticing what she was up to. Once I realized, I nearly levitated in shock.

"*Wist!*"

"Sorry," she said breezily. "I really love your butt."

"That doesn't give you a license to grope me!"

She stopped, but her hands were still suspiciously low on my waist. I'd almost forgotten why I was here.

"Wist," I said, "you're killing the Extinguishers."

She flicked a glance down at her carved-out torso, at the throng of fleshy cords crushing into it. "They tried to kill me. Now they're working very hard to keep me alive. Seems fair."

This was going to be difficult. "Right. You could call that self-defense. I'm not the morality police." I gestured back at the rest of the room. It was a rather hellish tableau. "But that's a lot of people."

Wist smiled, the very picture of a magnanimous ruler. "They'll live on," she said. "As part of me, or as part of the tower. Don't worry about it."

"You might be happy with that plan right now, sure. I have a feeling you won't be so thrilled with it once I neutralize you out of berserk mode."

Wist considered my face. She lifted a hand and beckoned to me as if she'd lost her voice. I leaned closer. I was wary, of course. As long as she appeared to be in a good mood, though, indulging her whims—within reason—seemed like the safest approach.

She propped herself up. The squirming cords rustled and squeaked between us. Her mouth touched the edge of my ear. Her voice was a whisper.

"Neutralize me?" I felt her laugh without sound. "Oh, Clem. I'd like to see you try."

Fear ripped my senses open. I shoved myself away from Wist hard enough that she actually let go of me. It was pure instinct, nothing planned. I tumbled backward.

Wist was going to reach for me, and there was nothing I could do to stop her.

I didn't fall. Wist didn't catch me. I floated midair like a bird riding an updraft, freed from the chains of gravity and whisked out of Wist's immediate reach.

In short, Fanren's magic had reached out and plucked me to safety. Momentary safety, at any rate. It wouldn't last. Still hovering, buoyed up by his Zero Gravity, I tried to find him. But new umbilical cords were already lashing toward me like whips.

Fanren's magic hurled me backward through the air. My stomach heaved. It heaved again as I came to a sudden halt. The magic lowered me, dropped me on my butt with little fanfare. I nearly sat on a stray Extinguisher. The umbilical cords still followed, faster than ever. Then they smashed into an invisible wall—one of Fanren's barriers—and flinched as if stunned.

I was behind the last row of chairs in the room now, up on a balcony elevated like a choir loft. The chairs on the right side of the loft rippled, then steadied. Now Fanren sat in one of them, ankle on his knee, glasses on his face, clothing and piercings intact.

He looked a bit bruised, but otherwise not much worse for wear. He must've used some configuration of Reflect to make the chair he occupied appear the same as the empty chairs to his left.

I started to say something. So did Fanren. Before either of us had a chance to finish, he jerked to attention, grabbed my wrist, and flung us over the balcony railing. I caught a glimpse of Wist's cords bursting out from the wall at the back of the loft. We hit the white carpet without the force of full gravity, but still none too gently. Lances started materializing at Fanren's back.

"Wait," I said. "What's the plan here?"

"I annoy the Kraken while you try to neutralize her?"

"You'll get yourself killed."

"Got any better ideas?"

"No," I admitted. Damn.

I glanced at the throne on the other end of the room. It was empty. I started to yell for Fanren to move, dodge, block, anything. Instead my voice got wedged sideways in my throat. Someone had tapped me on the shoulder.

Wist leaned on me from behind. She'd ported there silently, still trailing all her cords. "Hard to move with these," she said. She was barefoot, grimacing.

Fanren leapt back lightly, retreating toward the throne at the front of the room. As he moved, his black lances plunged into the waterfall of umbilical cords roiling around Wist's feet, piercing them, pinning them to the floor. The lances poured out of the air like a rain of arrows, seemingly unending. I felt myself tense at the squelching, the thudding. He knew she was drawing life from these cords, didn't he?

The six-foot lances surrounded me and Wist—thump, thump, thump—at first like stalks growing in a bamboo forest, then like the bars of a stereotypical jail cell, then thicker and thicker, no space left between them, a spiky-ended coffin.

"Ow," Wist said softly. "Ow, ow, ow."

She was leaning harder on me now, close to dead weight. I had to brace myself to keep my knees from buckling. She curled her arms around me. I could feel the remnants of her chest move when she spoke. The mass of umbilical cords in her torso twitched against my spine, all up and down the whole length of it. I reached my arm back behind both of us and grabbed at a fistful of her magic.

I missed. Wist had dodged without missing a beat. She shoved me forward into the wall of lances while simultaneously stepping as far back as she could go in the small space the lances allotted us.

"You tricked me," I snapped.

"I never said I couldn't move freely. I could dance around the whole room if I needed to. It hurts terribly, but I could."

I tried to twist around to glare at her. "You're missing a third of your body. Maybe you shouldn't!" She must be reinforcing her arms with magic—in her current physical state, she couldn't possibly possess the strength to hold me down like this unaided.

Fanren had done me a favor, pinning Wist in place and trapping me here beside her. To try neutralizing her, I needed to get as close as possible to her magic core. But once ignited, the reflexive fear made it hard to think of anything but getting away from the berserker. My body wanted to ram itself through the implacable lances.

"I didn't think you'd be afraid of me," Wist said.

"You're the one who's afraid of me," I insisted. My voice sounded thin.

"How so?"

"You wouldn't hold me down like this if you had nothing to fear."

Wist released me. I stumbled, almost hitting my head on the hard wall of lances. I took a breath to pull myself together. I whirled around and lunged for the small of her back. She caught both my wrists and held them up, laughing, as if we were dancing.

I heard footsteps outside the cage of lances. I froze.

The footsteps veered away from us, pounding out a peculiar animal gait. More running. The sound of Fanren catching his breath. A wet puncturing noise like impalement. Crunching blows like bodies flying into walls.

I could sense magic swirling through the room, Fanren's and Wist's, but I couldn't picture what was going on with any clarity.

Fanren made a distant noise, something indecipherable—like the pain was too much. Like he couldn't hold his voice in.

I started to call out to him. Wist's hands tightened on my wrists. The words vanished from my throat as if struck down by lightning. For a moment I thought she'd used magic on me. She hadn't. It was the prey animal instinct shuddering through me again, sewing my mouth shut, sewing me in place.

"Do you really want to distract him?" Wist asked gently.

I shook my head. I fought to swallow. Finally, pathetically, I managed to look her in the eye—a much more obvious red now, a rich unnatural garnet, as if she were only getting worse over time.

"Wist," I said, "Fanren's just doing his job. I'm the one who brought him here. Please don't hurt him."

For the first time, berserk Wist looked back at me without any expression whatsoever. My stomach hurt. If this experience gave me an ulcer—I thought wildly, anything to avoid wondering why she was looking at me like that—I hoped and prayed that the government would send her my medical bills. Surely the Kraken could afford it.

"It's the height of irony," she said, calm and conversational, "to hear you pleading for his life."

"What's that supposed to mean?"

Thudding sounds. A muted cry. Seconds later, the fence of lances around us dissolved like a cloud of gnats scattering.

Fanren was fighting the Extinguishers.

Body parts hurtled through the air at him like missiles. Intact Extinguishers clawed their way out of the walls and floor, ripping through the gracefully painted panels, sending bits of the white carpet flying about like feathers.

They threw themselves at Fanren like wrestlers going for a takedown. They wrenched free bolted-down chairs and ran at him like knights with lances. They unsheathed combat knives. A few carried guns. The bullets stopped whenever they touched one of Fanren's invisible barriers, stayed stuck there in the air like hapless flies on flypaper.

In waking life they might have been mages, or a mix of mages and healers, but none of them used magic now. They flung themselves at

Fanren with brute force, not caring if half their limbs were broken or if shattered bones protruded from shredded skin.

Every single one of them still had an umbilical cord snaking all the way back through the room, leashing them to Wist. New lances danced in the air around Fanren, slashing through cord after cord like the famous living swords of ancient legend. The moment their cords were severed, the Extinguishers collapsed like marionettes. But the cords grew back together almost too fast to see, and the Extinguishers popped up off the ground again, undeterred. And there were so many of them.

"That's enough," I said to Wist. "Call them off."

The room went silent. The Extinguishers paused, some right in the middle of lunging at Fanren. Their eyes followed us wordlessly as Wist went up the aisle toward Fanren, pulling me with her.

Fanren's glasses were cracked. He had smears of blood on his cheeks. He was breathing too hard—hard enough that anyone could see he would begin to struggle if this went on any longer. He wiped his forehead and took a few careful steps away as Wist approached.

"I never liked you," Wist told him.

"That's unfortunate," Fanren said between breaths. "Have I done anything to offend you?"

"Nothing worth bringing up now."

"Is it because people say we look alike?"

Wist blinked. "Ah." She gave him a shark-like smile. "You think I'm jealous because Clematis has a type."

"I do NOT have a type!" I bellowed.

Fanren cricked his neck, swung his arms, stretched his shoulders. "For the record," he said, "I've never been interested in women. Clem knows that."

"And thus, you say, I have nothing to worry about," Wist said evenly.

"Exactly."

Deep red lances started to materialize behind her—one, two, three, four, five. They were a perfect copy of Fanren's black lances, differing only in color.

"I'm sorry," she said. "That isn't quite why I want to kill you."

I grabbed for Wist's magic core. Again she intercepted me, this time without so much as looking at me. "You won't be berserk forever," I said through the panic ringing in my head. I twisted my wrist in her grip and got myself in front of her, between her and Fanren. "Even if I can't neutralize you. It goes away eventually. And then you'll regret what you've done to the Extinguishers. And you'll regret whatever you're about to do to Fanren."

"That's fine," Wist said, almost tender. "Regret is an old friend of mine. A life-long companion. We're very comfortable in each other's company. I don't know what I'd do without her."

A life-long companion.

I didn't know if anything I tried at this point would work, except perhaps to stall her. I'd order Fanren to flee, but I didn't think he would make it. And I didn't think he would leave me.

I stood on tiptoe to block Wist's view of Fanren, to make her look at me. The red lances hovering in a semicircle at her back were the same vicious hue as the berserker light in her eyes.

"Wist," I said. "You wanted something from me. You wanted me to bond you. I'm game now. Let's do it."

That got her attention. "Now?" she said. "Why?"

This was when I knew I'd miscalculated. Wist had only shown an interest in bonding because she was running out of ways to stimulate magic regrowth. She'd only offered to bond with me because she thought anyone who partnered with the Kraken would become another target for the Extinguishers. Better Asa Clematis than some other healer with less blood on their hands.

I remembered the faint scent of her sweat in the dark pool room, her arms crushing the breath out of me. I remembered it so vividly that I'd completely forgotten why bonding came up in the first place. The Wist in front of me right now already had far more magic branches at her disposal than the Wist of just a day ago. She didn't need to resort to desperate measures like bonding with a convict.

Wist's lances swirled in a slick figure eight pattern, as if dancing. As if mocking my silence. *Why?* Why indeed? I had no answer for her, because she had no reason to bond with me anymore.

The red lances vanished. Then reappeared right next to Fanren. My heart lurched. He remained perfectly still, unstartled. Fanren was very good with barriers. But he was also tired from fending off the Extinguishers, and neither of us knew the full extent of exactly what Wist could do with her magic right now.

This was the problem with berserk mages. Usually there would be no point in trying to reason with them. "Wist," I said—mouth so dry it almost hurt to speak—"Wist, I—"

Her lances shot up to impale the ceiling, grazing Fanren as they went. Fresh lines of blood beaded on his arm, the side of his face. He seemed otherwise unharmed. Sprinkles of plaster dust floated slowly down from the ceiling like lonely flakes of snow. Wist was laughing, one hand braced on my shoulder like she needed me to hold herself up.

"I would enjoy killing your friend in front of you," she told me. "But I would also enjoy bonding. It's a toss-up."

"Wow," I said faintly. "Color me flattered."

From the corner of my eye, I watched Fanren move out from underneath the area of the ceiling pierced by Wist's lances. He stepped over a fallen Extinguisher and leaned on the remnants of a wall panel painted with green summer rice fields. He dabbed at the blood on his face and his arm.

"I know bonding will likely neutralize me," Wist remarked. "I assume that's why you suddenly became interested."

I pulled at her till she faced me, her back to Fanren. Constant dread had gilded my hands with cold sweat, but Wist made no comment.

"You'll bond with me anyway?" I said. "You won't harm anyone else?" This wasn't exactly an example of negotiating from a position of strength. I just wanted to make sure I understood what she was really getting at.

"That's right." There was something ironic in her tone, and I had no idea why. "It would be very satisfying to impale your friend back there, but I'll restrain myself."

I swallowed. While I was busy gambling with our lives, might as well up the ante one last time. "Can I ask you one thing first?"

The usual Wist wouldn't tell me much. Berserk Wist might be a different matter.

"Want a kiss?" she said. "Sure."

I didn't dignify that with a reaction. "Which taboo did you break?"

Wist looked down. Her train of black hair trailed across the white carpet at her feet. When she caught my gaze again, it was with a small, knowing smile. "I'll give you one hint."

"Talk about stingy," I blurted—milliseconds before coming to the realization that maybe it'd be smarter not to needle her too hard in berserk mode.

Luckily for me, Wist didn't seem too annoyed. "Would I usually be so generous?"

Yeah, guess she had a point there.

She rested a hand on my head, smoothing my hair. It had probably been sticking out all over the place. "The room with the blue door," she said. "The lantana flowers on the desk. What kind of desk was it?"

"Pardon?"

She put a finger to my lips, shutting me up. "Think back to the last time you saw flowers on a desk like that. Perhaps not in a regular flowerpot. Perhaps in a glass, or a pretty vase."

"That's it? That's the hint?"

Wist didn't answer. All right then.

One of her free magic branches broke itself, soundlessly and without fanfare, snapping on its own as if beneath the weight of too much snow. She scooped the cutting out of the air. It lay across her palms, a golden thread easily hidden from the naked eye. When I regarded it with my magic perception, though, it glowed like a firefly.

I didn't really want to show her my back. I settled for turning sideways, hiking my sweater up to reveal the spot where a mage's magic core would be located. Healers had no magic core, of course. We had the opposite—a kind of magical emptiness. A receptacle.

"I offer my bond," Wist said. There was something strange in her voice, beneath the abrupt formality. The sound of it weighted me in place, rendered me unable to turn and look at her.

You're making a mistake, I thought to myself. But what else was new? What else was I supposed to do?

"I accept your bond," I replied.

It wouldn't work if I didn't mean it. I meant it well enough, didn't I? For the sake of recovering her magic. Well, she'd recovered more than enough of it on her own already—in exchange for scores of Extinguishers and most of her bodily organs.

For the record, I'd had a similar thought days ago. If threatening my own well-being was sufficient to inspire magic regrowth, a genuine threat to Wist's own life might work even better. I'd dismissed that idea as being far too risky. It would be great if it worked, of course, but I'd be left in an extremely awkward position if it just ended up killing her. Should've trusted my instincts, I guess.

Okay, so there was no longer a pressing need to bond simply in hopes of kick-starting Wist's magic regrowth. It was for the sake of getting her mind off killing Fanren, then. For the sake of neutralizing her before she got any bright ideas about leaving the tower and gallivanting off to cause true mayhem. She wasn't anywhere near her former full power as the Kraken, but a berserk S-class mage was still nothing to sneer at. You could even say that bonding her—neutralizing her—was my duty to all of Osmanthian society. Not that Osmanthian society had ever done much for me.

I felt the bond take. Wist's magic cutting settled into the hollow at my center. It took root as if it had always belonged there. Just one small sprout, a little parasite inside me, a snippet of alien magic I could never wield of my own accord. But it was enough.

I felt all of her magic—several hundred individual branches now—reorient toward me like iron filings finding a magnet. I felt her mind settle in next to mine, a heavy warmth like sitting thigh-to-thigh with someone on a long-distance train, like the weight of their head on your bony shoulder as they slept. I felt Wist's hand against the small of my back, fingers curled. Her hand didn't seem quite steady.

I barely had to do anything to neutralize her. Her magic was already untangling on its own. It curved toward me like a plant starving for sunlight.

Wist stumbled as if something had struck her. There was too much of a height difference for me to catch her effectively, but I tried. Her eyes had gone black again. She gripped my elbows. I saw very little blood in her face.

"Don't faint," I said quickly.

Her umbilical cords dragged like prison chains on the floor. Her eyes fell to the mass of them streaming from her torso. I took the opportunity to flap my arms at Fanren. It wasn't any kind of agreed-upon signal, but I trusted him to figure out what I meant.

Sure enough, as Wist raised her head, a hexagonal wall slid into being around us. A combination of Fanren's Barrier and Reflection. It was thin and translucent, mirrored on all sides, ceiling to floor. It reflected the two of us alone, effectively concealing the rest of the replica courtroom from view, leaving just a few low-down gaps to make room for Wist's trailing umbilical cords.

I felt Wist's horror through our bond. Either she remembered at least some of what she'd done while berserk, or she was aghast to return to herself and find us already bonded. Maybe a little bit of both. Either way, I was grateful to Fanren for blocking from view the battered Extinguishers with their gawking white eyes.

"You're in bad shape," I told Wist, not that it wasn't already obvious. "Better focus on staying alive."

I wasn't strong enough to hold up her full weight on my own. When she sank to the floor, I had no choice but to go with her. She slumped sideways against me. She touched the tubes running out of her. Look closely, and you could see tendrils of magic trickling through each of them, sucking—well, something—out of the hidden Extinguishers and diverting it to her incomplete body. She lifted part of her hair, now long enough to cover her entire body like a spare cloak, and stared at it as if she had no idea who it belonged to.

"How many?" Wist asked, indicating her torso full of umbilical cords. I didn't answer. She started counting them, pointing and muttering under her breath.

I slapped her hand away. "Even when you were berserk, this was the best you could do," I said. "If you try to detach now, you'll kill yourself. Or maybe just go berserk again. Can you re-learn all your old medical magic off the top of your head? No? Then you're stuck leeching off them till the cavalry arrives."

I didn't need the bond to tell me she was in pain now, magical and physical and maybe more than that, a pain she hadn't felt at all while berserk. She took my right hand and covered it in both of hers as if to shelter it. She leaned on me without moving.

She said something against my shoulder, too quiet to hear.

"What?"

She didn't repeat it. I didn't ask again. It had sounded like *I missed you*. But it could also have been a wordless noise, a tiny eruption of uncontainable suffering.

Berserk mages were gifted a kind of savant brilliance. They could acquire or even invent new magical skills in an instant. That wasn't possible for any normal mage, not even the Kraken herself. To make matters worse, though Wist's branches had now returned en masse, they seemed to have grown back blank, her past skill set completely erased.

While berserk, she'd forced many of her newborn branches to feed her a kind of makeshift life support, drawing directly on the Extinguishers who'd come to assassinate her. It must have been purely instinctual, magic lashing out with the fury of an animal fighting to survive. It had been just enough to keep her from dying. She'd even been able to pick up a short-distance porting skill, and to imitate Fanren's lances on the spot. But she hadn't attempted to start properly regenerating her lost organs. Now, reduced to a neutral state, she would have to spend hours—weeks—days—months relearning magic skills in order to imprint them on the rest of her new branches. No, it'd take her much longer than that. It'd take years to finish.

In the very short term, there was almost nothing Wist could do to help herself. That was why I let her keep leaning on me. That was why I let her hold my hand.

On the other side of the barrier, I heard Fanren talking to someone. The words were too muffled to make out. Hopefully he'd gotten through to Manatree, or at least Mori. Hopefully we wouldn't be alone down here much longer.

As we waited for medical reinforcements, I mulled over the one hint Wist had deigned to give me. Flowers on a desk. Not just any desk. That specific type of desk.

A school desk.

Now it came back to me. Gauzy curtains. Amber afternoon light. One of the old-fashioned healer classrooms. All of the desks were clean and empty except for the one on my left. In the middle of that one desk rested a clear vase of white chrysanthemums.

The boy who used to sit there had died over the weekend. Our teachers said vorpal beasts had killed him, beasts from an uncharted vorpal hole. My classmates whispered that in truth it had been one of the mage students. Or maybe a whole ring of them.

I don't know if we ever got a final answer, or at least not one that satisfied us. I couldn't even remember the kid's name. All I knew now was that this was the one and only time I'd seen flowers sitting on an unoccupied school desk. A quiet marker of death.

CHAPTER SIXTEEN
20 Days Left

WHEN MANATREE RETURNED to the tower, she brought with her the top medical mages in the country. Wist was apparently the medical conundrum of the century. A patient in her state—missing nearly every vital organ except her brain, and shot three times in the head for good measure—would not normally survive long enough to receive any kind of treatment whatsoever. They had plenty of ideas for what to do with her, but they debated hotly over how to get started.

One clear point of agreement, however, was that she couldn't yet be safely separated from the scores of Extinguishers fueling her. Sending Wist to a medical facility, or even just higher up in the tower, would require porting all the umbilical cords and connected Extinguisher bodies along with her. Instead they decided to apply emergency treatment down in the basement. At least until Wist was stable enough to be detached from her former attackers (and current life support).

All this is to say that I stayed in the basement that night. So did Mori and Fanren. And so did Manatree and her fleet of medical professionals, although unlike me, I don't think any of them planned on trying to sleep.

I didn't bring up the fact that I'd bonded with Wist. Fanren did me the favor of keeping his mouth shut, too. And Wist herself wasn't exactly in a talkative mood, to say the least.

I wouldn't be able to keep it covered up forever, but with everyone else focused first and foremost on doing something about Wist's (admittedly horrendous) physical state, I doubted anyone would look closely enough at her magic to be able to tell we were bonded. Mori, for instance, was far too distressed over Wist's brush with death to pick up on any subtle signs of bonding.

Mori and I couldn't do much for her, frankly. We were healers of magic, not of the corporeal human body. Fanren, for his part, could only offer First Aid—which was extremely basic compared to the specialists' skill sets. Yet in other ways, Fanren turned out to be by far the most helpful among us. He took charge of organizing the Extinguishers and their various body parts, sorting them into neat rows of Alive For Now, Questionable, and Definitely Dead.

At some point well after midnight, I conked out in a pile of blankets on a bare mattress pad. Someone had tossed it down in the loft at the back wall of the courtroom, well out of the way, but I could still hear busy voices wafting up from below.

Mori and Fanren showed no interest in sleeping. That was all very well for them. But I, for one, wasn't young enough to pull an all-nighter just for the sake of sitting there and watching what happened. It would be different if I had some kind of useful way to contribute. And it would be different if they knew Wist and I were bonded. Without admitting that out loud, though, I had no excuse to stay close to her.

Even with my eyes shut and Wist well out of reach, I remained constantly aware of the bond. It wasn't entirely unpleasant, just distracting—a feeling like wearing a new piece of jewelry. Hopefully my usual dreams of violent death wouldn't leak across the bond and disturb her rest.

A dream came, sure enough. But not one of the usual suspects.

I'd never had a dream like this before. For one thing, I stayed alive longer than a few minutes. That alone felt unprecedented.

I found myself in an office suite somewhere in the Palace of Magi, the heart of Osmanthian government. Information flowed down living scrolls on the walls and under the glass lid covering my desk. Dark windows looked out onto courtyard gardens rife with fireflies of every color. I startled when I glimpsed my reflection in the nearest window: tailored black dress, hair to my shoulders. Had I ever been this girly?

There was a bond thread around my neck. Sonorous blue-purple, the color of a morning glory. Or a clematis.

Someone knocked at the office door. I told them to enter.

Fanren walked in and shut the door behind him. But it wasn't the Fanren I knew. His hair was cut shorter, and he wore the formal uniform of a security contractor. His glasses were rimless, his only piercings a few inconspicuous studs in his ears. His eyes flicked around the room as if to confirm we were alone.

"You look familiar," I said. "Do I know you?" I'd meant to say something quite different, but I didn't seem to be in control of the script here.

"Ms. Asa Clematis." So this version of Fanren still knew me on sight. "No, we've never spoken. You might have seen me in the halls before. I've worked here for a few years."

"Perhaps," I conceded.

He inclined his head—perfect manners—and came up to the window beside me. I edged away, putting the full length of the desk between us. Fanren didn't seem to mind. He gazed thoughtfully down at the fireflies dancing in the courtyard.

"I come bearing a message from an honored Board member," he said. "From my employer, rather."

I stared at him. Well beyond the point of rudeness, really. I didn't care. I stared first at his magic core, then at the jagged threads of magic that branched through his body as if to mingle with his physical veins.

"Did your employer tell you to get that looked at?"

Fanren—although the me in the dream didn't seem to know his name yet—seemed taken aback. "Pardon?"

I pointed at his core. "You're going to snap," I said. "I can see it in your magic. In less than a year from now, if you don't get it fixed. Maybe less than six months."

"Is this some sort of healer joke?"

"I'm dead serious. You have a kind of birth defect in your magic. Too tricky for most healers to notice. No fault of your own, really. But at this rate, you're fated to go berserk. Sooner rather than later. People will get hurt."

"So you already know why I'm here," Fanren said slowly.

I realized two things simultaneously.

First—he hadn't believed a word I'd said.

Second—we were inside a barrier now, a gossamer cage of magic. It looked delicate, worthless. It filled nearly the whole room. But it would prevent anyone outside the barrier from hearing or seeing anything we did inside it. Someone standing in the courtyard looking up at the office windows would think they saw nothing but an empty room. They wouldn't notice me even if I leaned over and pressed my face to the glass.

I backed away further, trying to skirt toward the closed door. "I don't know why you're here, actually," I said. "Not to get healed, I guess. But I'm very curious. Which Board member—"

Streaks of shadow pummeled my chest. The side of my head. In one ear and out the other. Silent black lances.

I woke up clutching the blankets as if they were strangling me. For a few moments it was as if I'd forgotten how to breathe. I didn't recognize a single second of that conversation—it wasn't a memory. I'd never worn anyone's bond cord. I'd never met Fanren before prison. But it was the first time in my life that my dreams had featured someone with a distinct human face. Not to mention full-blown dialogue.

I felt Wist send a questioning nudge through the bond, a mental touch like a tentative finger grazing my cheek. I shoved her away. I couldn't tell if she were fully conscious or not, anyhow. For all I knew, she might just be rattling the bond in her sleep without realizing it.

The fake courtroom was still bright as day, the medical mages still busy muttering feverish jargon at each other in the open space down below the loft. Their chatter ran past my ears like a foreign language. The air still reeked of torn-open bodies.

I curled tighter in the blankets. I fought to exhale away the punching sensation of the lances passing clean through me. I fought to exhale away the feeling of my mind falling, falling to a place where nothing existed and no one could catch it.

It had been an extremely quick death. Far less painful than most of my dreams. Yet it lingered. It clung to my body like a raw new layer of skin. As if by waking, I'd pulled it with me into Wist's godforsaken basement. As if by waking, I'd made it reality.

CHAPTER SEVENTEEN

From 17 to 10 Days Left

I HAD QUESTIONS. I had theories. I had plans. But all these questions, theories, and plans of mine centered around someone currently trapped in intensive care. I didn't want to sit around waiting like a dolt. So instead I chose to make myself uncharacteristically useful.

I helped a handful of outpost guards install a ladder stretching from the courtroom floor all the way up to the hole Fanren had carved in the ceiling. Now those of us without porting or anti-gravity magic could go find a bathroom unassisted.

Aboveground, up in the tower's central kitchen, I helped Fanren make dumplings—hundreds of them—to feed the medical team. I got quite good at folding the dumpling wrappers. It was nice to have something to do with my hands. Along the way, I learned how to navigate the grocery store-sized pantry, with its long surreal aisles that gradually disintegrated into a living maze at the back. I managed to avoid getting lost mostly thanks to Mori, who had splashed red paint on the pantry floor to mark the point of no return.

A few days after the attack, the mages in the basement had begun to make serious progress in their efforts to extricate Wist from the Extinguishers. I wasn't privy to the gory details, but it seemed that they were using the umbilical cords as raw material, gradually transmuting them into makeshift replacement bones and marrow and organs and flesh for Wist's torso. Well, good luck with that.

As a result, I managed to pull Mori and Manatree aside for the first time in days. Mori's hair looked limp, unwashed; he'd tugged it back into a tiny braid. Though Manatree's face was more creased than usual, her uniform seemed as fresh and crisp as ever.

Whatever I had to say, she told me I'd better make it quick. She refused to stray any further from the courtroom than the replica dorm room right above it. I'd hinted that I wanted to talk with them in private, preferably somewhere without a giant hole in the floor, but Manatree refused to budge. The dorm room would have to do. At least the courtroom ceiling was high enough to make eavesdropping difficult, hole or no hole.

For safety purposes, outpost guards had covered the hole with a lightweight lid. We still gave it a wide berth, crowding over by the narrow bed. It really did look exactly like Wist's old academy dorm room, right down to the poorly focused photos taped all over the wall.

I saw me with my pixie cut and long-skirted uniform, giving the camerawoman—presumably Wist—an oddly defiant look. I hadn't recognized it at the time, but I'd been awfully cute back then. In other photos I saw Wist in her gym tracksuit, swinging her long braid around like a rope for lassoing cattle.

Those were the days, huh.

Manatree urged me to get on with it. I looked her in the eye and said:

"I told you Wist was full-on berserk when Fanren and I came down here. I also told you I neutralized her."

"Quite an accomplishment," she said dryly.

"I didn't do it the standard way, by healing her. I did it by bonding her."

Manatree was silent.

Mori gasped. "Oh," he said. "Oh!" Suddenly he bounded closer. He threw his arms around me. If he were any less tired, he might've lifted me clean off the floor and spun me in a circle.

I choked a bit—he was in severe need of a bath. "Guess you don't mind, then," I said.

"Of course not! Congratulations! I'm really"—oh, heavens, was he starting to get a bit teary?—"really happy for both of you."

"For the record," I warned him, "it was a purely pragmatic decision. We aren't getting married or anything."

At last he let me go. "Either way, it's something to celebrate."

"Not everyone will be thrilled," I said, watching Manatree.

She'd mastered her reaction quickly, but even a horse could've discerned her displeasure. "I'll take your word for it. For now," she said.

"Aw. I'm touched."

"But I'll need to have your bond certified sooner rather than later."

"Mori can help," I told her. Beside me, Mori nodded vigorously. "His magic perception's good enough to confirm the bond, once he knows what he's looking for."

"Indeed." Manatree's lips contorted ever so slightly. It wasn't quite a grimace, and it wasn't quite a smile. "Well played, Magebreaker."

"So what're my chances of getting parole now?"

"I'll have to discuss it with the Board."

Good enough for me. Manatree would navigate all the proper channels before she made me any promises. But as long as Wist survived her current ordeal, no one would dare ship me—Wist's bondmate—back to the old island prison. She'd already recovered a substantial portion of her raw magic. Though severely weakened, she was still the Kraken. There was no way even the Board of Magi could get away with jailing the Kraken's bonded healer.

Unless Wist herself told them to do it. The more things change, the more they stay the same. Seven years later, Wist herself was once again the biggest risk to my freedom.

Put another way, though, I'd gotten exactly what I wanted. The government had dangled parole in front of me as bait, and I'd seized it, and now I'd all but won it. Made it my own.

But I didn't feel much of anything. Mori seemed more excited about the whole bondmate business than I was, even though it meant he'd no longer be able to work as Wist's dedicated healer. Once bonded, mages lost the ability to be effectively healed by anyone except their bonded healer. Others could try treating them, of course, but it simply wouldn't take.

Maybe it just hadn't sunk in yet. Maybe I needed more time to remember life in the world outside. The Kraken's tower, though vast and extravagant, brimming with countless wonders and annoyances alike, was ultimately just another closed-up space.

Wist's treatment progressed little by little, day by day. So did Public Security's investigation of the attack. From time to time I managed to wring an update or two out of Manatree. I'd explained to her and Mori that I wanted to keep my bond with Wist under wraps, or at least have it disclosed only on a need-to-know basis. Wist wasn't in any kind of shape to defend me or anyone else, and I'd prefer not to draw undue attention.

Perhaps Manatree's knowledge of our bond—and her understanding that it might turn me into a target—made her moderately more willing to keep me in the loop about the Extinguishers. Although one of the first things she told me was that PubSec suspected fewer than half of the attackers had been true-believer Extinguishers. They all wore the same snuffed-candle tattoos on their forearms, but many were known mercenaries who'd never associated with the Extinguishers in the past. And their tattoos were much fresher.

I started to question the implications of this, then caught myself. Instead I asked Manatree if the vorpal hole in the forest had undergone any changes.

As it turned out, the original hole hadn't expanded. But some days ago—mostly likely on the night the Extinguishers (or fake Extinguishers) invaded—hundreds of smaller vorpal holes had manifested in the forest. Most were in the same clearing as the original vorpal hole, clustering around it as if to fashion some kind of nightmare planetarium, a galaxy of holes punched in reality. Others appeared further off, like stray constellations. The new vorpal holes spawned as fist-wide abscesses in tree trunks, sprinkles of lady-bug-sized distortions floating midair, empty pockets of missing ground. It would be easy to walk straight through one and lose part of your face or arm or foot if you weren't careful.

The reason Manatree couldn't tell me exactly when they'd formed was because a separate contingent of Extinguishers had assaulted the forest outpost at the same time that their main division approached the tower. The guards had been too busy fighting for their lives to stop and observe the vorpal holes in the deeper woods.

While the medical team worked to keep Wist alive, Mori and Fanren and I started to work on cleaning up the tower. Some side effects of Wist's wild magic had dissipated on their own. It had long since stopped raining in the kitchen, for instance. And thank goodness for that— otherwise, making all those dumplings would have been quite a chore.

Most of the white snakes haunting the first floor had exited peacefully through various open windows and doors, much to the relief of Turtle the cat. But the fireproof morning glories in the parlor proved remarkably resilient, growing back with increased vigor each time we cut them down. And the tower floor maps were still covered in blobs of black-and-white paint.

Mori and I spent one afternoon walking around to note down all the ruined rooftop staircases that needed repairing. I took it as an opportunity to ask him more about vorpal holes. Since Manatree was at this point far too preoccupied to escort him to the city and back, he'd started combing through Wist's various libraries instead.

"And what'd you learn?" I asked.

"Almost everything we know about them is pure conjuncture." He looked quite dissatisfied. "No one's ever been to the other side of a vorpal hole."

"You mean no one's ever gone through one and then come back."

"Exactly."

"So what's on the other side of vorpal holes?"

"That's the problem," Mori said. "No one knows."

I tugged at the back of his sweater to keep him from getting too close to the edge of the broken stairs. "What's the most popular theory, then?"

"Other worlds," he said. "Either one other world, or many different other worlds. Sometimes vorpal beasts come out through the holes and kill people, right? I guess the thinking is that those beasts have to be coming from somewhere."

"Maybe people who fall through vorpal holes in our world become vorpal beasts in other worlds," I mused. Mori shuddered.

CHAPTER EIGHTEEN

9 Days Left

NEARLY TWO FULL WEEKS after the attack, the medical team finally managed to transport Wist up to her own bedroom. Meanwhile, the Extinguishers—or whatever could be salvaged of their once-living flesh—had all been ported off to morgues or government hospitals or secret prisons or wherever else Public Security decided to put them.

Either way, Wist was no longer tethered to any human beings (except me, in a manner of speaking). A jungle of life-support equipment took root in her room instead: drips and clamps and pumps and filters and all sorts of esoteric instruments I'd never seen before. All I knew was that someone or something had to make sure she didn't soil herself while she slept.

They said Wist wasn't comatose, but she sure looked it. They'd put her to sleep so her body could devote all its feeble efforts to integration and recovery. At least by now she had a body that could reasonably be defined as more or less intact, though the majority of her organs were no longer the organs she'd been born with.

Mori insisted that we watch Wist in shifts. I pointed out that, one, she was unconscious and wouldn't know if we were there or not, so why bother? Why not spend that time doing something more productive, like cleaning up the tower? And, two, even if she did have some kind of physical emergency, there was absolutely nothing either of us magic healers could do about it. Besides, the remnants of the medical team rarely left her side. Why go out of our way to get underfoot?

But Mori remained adamant that Wist needed our company. During his shifts with her, he held onto the earring Fanren had given him. He used it to call us whenever Wist did something particularly exciting, like twitch her shoulder or drool a little extra down the side of her face.

The main benefit of this was that it gave me more chances to speak with Fanren alone. Today, for instance, he used Zero Gravity to buoy the two of us past the broken parts of the stairs, up to the various rooftops.

One broad white roof looked like the summit of a castle tower. It was also covered in colorful dead fish, probably the same type that had been happily swimming through the air in a few of the sunrooms located on lower floors. We'd disposed of those fish over a week ago, blissfully unaware that whole schools of them plastered this poor innocent roof. The smell was incredible.

"Look," I said from the doorway. "I've got a proposal."

"Yeah?"

"Let's forget we saw this. Let's turn back."

"It'll just get worse over time," Fanren said sensibly.

"They're kind of spread out. They're getting lots of sun. Isn't this how dried fish get made? Well, Wist loves fish. It's practically all she eats. We can give them to her as a present once she comes to."

"You'll poison her."

"She's obviously been through worse."

"I'm pretty sure you need salt to make dried fish," Fanren said. "These are just rotting." He pulled on a pair of disposable gloves. "You hold open the trash bag. I'll do the dirty work."

Our conversation soon died off. The stench made it difficult to speak, much less think. But if nothing else, up here I could be confident that no one else was listening. When the first trash bag was about halfway full, I steeled myself to ask him.

"Fanren," I said.

"Hm?" He straightened up, waving flies away from his face. He'd put his glasses in a slim case and tucked the case deep in his pocket, presumably to keep them safe from stray splashes of fish guts or maggot juice. Come to think of it, I hadn't seen Fanren without his trademark glasses since back when we first met in prison. They were still cracked from his battle in the basement, but he claimed it didn't bother him.

"Manatree told me a bit about the investigation."

"Investigation of what?"

"The Extinguishers." No, that was the wrong word. "The assassins. Would-be assassins, I guess. Are you still an assassin if you fail?"

"Beats me," he said.

I wanted to take a breath to steady myself, but if I let the fish-rot penetrate any deeper in my lungs, I'd probably faint.

"Now, she didn't tell me everything," I said. "I'm sure I'm missing some details. But if I were PubSec, I'd be wondering how the assassins knew exactly where to go."

Fanren contemplated the dizzying blue sky all around the tower. Being up here must be what it felt like to stand at the top of a mountain.

"The location of the Kraken's tower is common knowledge," he pointed out.

True enough. "The tower, yes," I agreed. "The guard outpost in the middle of the national forest, maybe not so much. Still, I can buy them knowing that. Maybe they paid poachers to tell them.

"What I can't figure out is how they knew exactly where in the tower to find Wist, and how they knew how to get there without accidentally running into the rest of us. And what I really can't figure out is why PubSec hasn't questioned any of us. Not Mori. Not even you or me. We're ex-cons, and everyone knows I've got a huge grudge against Wist."

Fanren spread his arms. Dark fish essence dripped from the tips of his gloves. "I don't know how PubSec operates. But is it so strange that the Extinguishers managed to avoid us? We were all sleeping quietly. And it's an extremely large tower."

I sighed. "You know what—I don't have the patience for this."

His mouth quirked a bit. "You don't, do you."

"It was you," I said. "You leaked whatever information they needed. The current layout of the tower. Wist's bedroom. Things to watch out for."

"And look where it got me," Fanren said wryly. "Getting up close and personal with about a thousand rotten fish."

Neither of us were smiling. "You aren't going to deny it?" I asked. "Not to undermine my argument here, but I only have circumstantial evidence."

"Tell me about it." He looked genuinely curious.

I raised one finger. "You have family on the Board of Magi."

Another finger. "There are factions of the Board that feel they've ceded far too much influence to the Kraken. Plus, yet other factions feel that her very existence is inherently a threat—too much power concentrated in one human being. They'd love a chance to get rid of her."

Another finger. "You got approval to come join me here at the tower incredibly fast. Your connections helped, of course. But I don't think it was just that. They approved my request for you because they realized they could use you."

Another finger. "I don't buy that you slept through hostile forces breaching the tower. No matter how sneakily they tiptoed in. I just don't buy it. You're one of the top duelists in the country."

"I'm sorry if my warrior instincts let you down," Fanren said lightly.

"Hah. For all I know, you met them at the door and led them right up to Wist like a bunch of little ducklings."

Fanren picked his way over to me, striving not to step on any remaining fish. We faced each other across the open trash bag, now plump and juicy with fish corpses. He peeled off his filthy gloves and chucked them in with the rest of the trash. Then he plucked a hand towel from his back pocket and started wiping the sweat from his face and neck. It was chilly out, and he'd stripped down to his tank top, but I could understand how a combination of light exertion and the suffocating stink might make your skin start to get unpleasantly clammy. Just standing up here was enough to give me the illusion of falling ill.

"It'd just as you say," he said. "It was me. Board pressure will keep PubSec from looking too closely." He stuck the towel back in his pocket. "Are you angry?"

Was I? I had no idea. The assassination attempt had failed. Wist was still alive.

Would I have been angry if she died?

I stared down into the hideous pile of fish. I tried to picture Wist dying. I wouldn't have been angry. Angry wasn't the word for it. I didn't have any words for it. Except—

"If Wist died, I would've told you to kill all of them," I said. "Every last one of them. I'd just be going back to prison anyway."

I looked up. I caught his eye and refused to release it. "Why'd you do it? You don't have anything against Wist, do you? Even if the Board was threatening you, or me, or both of us, you could've led the assassins just a little bit astray. You could've leaked intel with a few more mistakes in it. You could've given Wist more of a fighting chance. The tower's full of mysteries, constantly in flux. No one would be the wiser. No one would realize you sabotaged them on purpose."

"True," said Fanren. "I did think about doing that. And I like the Kraken just fine. I've got nothing personal against her."

"Then why—"

"You stabbed yourself with my knife," he said, "and for the first time, some of her magic came back. It got me thinking. I'm sure you thought the exact same thing."

The death-smell in the air faded. No—the smell was still out there somewhere, as putrid as ever, but it stopped getting through to me. My senses were a wall of ice.

"Uh-huh," I said faintly. "Threatening myself worked out okay. But a direct threat to Wist's life might actually have been the most effective way to awaken her magic."

"The Kraken's magic wouldn't let her die," said Fanren.

"Yeah. I had that same thought. I just didn't act on it. I was saving it to use as my last resort."

He nodded. "We're very alike in some ways, you and I."

"Are you saying you sicced assassins on Wist to—to help me?"

"I was hoping it might help."

"I'm not going to thank you," I told him.

"Of course not. I didn't do it in hopes of being thanked."

I would—and did—trust Fanren with my life. If anyone came after me, Extinguishers or otherwise, Fanren would fulfill his duties as my temporary bodyguard to his last breath. He wouldn't let them lay a finger on me. And not merely because it was his job right now. He'd been unfailingly loyal to me since prison. Ever since I diagnosed and healed the hidden quirk in his magic that had once made him dangerously prone to going berserk.

Was it reasonable to trust him with anyone else's life, though? At this point, probably not. But the assassins—and, by extension, the anti-Kraken factions of the Board—had missed their best chance to dispose of Wist. In any case, they'd know better than to try the same trick twice. And if I explicitly asked Fanren to extend his bodyguard services to Wist as well, I trusted him to respect my wishes.

Even so, a peculiar sensation came over me now when I looked at him, easygoing as ever, waiting patiently for me to give him the okay to start scooping more dead fish off the floor. It was a feeling like walking over to the parapet around the edge of the roof and staring straight down with sick fascination at the inconceivably distant ground.

I was very lucky to have Fanren on my side. I was very lucky to have him as my friend. But what if we'd never met? What if he had no reason to care whether some random person named Asa Clematis lived or died or withered away in prison?

"Remind me, what'd you do before you got arrested?" I asked. "For work, I mean."

He blinked. "Private security contractor," he said. "Mostly worked under my uncle on the Board."

"I used to spend a lot of time in the Palace of Magi, too," I said. "When I was deep into politics. Before—well, you know. Think we ever met?"

Fanren glanced up as if casting his mind back to the long corridors of the Palace. Endless offices, dreamy gardens, self-important bureaucrats, scheming mages, bright-eyed lobbyists. "We might've passed each other in the halls once or twice."

I was opening my mouth to ask more when he put a hand to his right ear. Good thing he wasn't wearing those gloves anymore.

"Mori says to come back." Fanren gave the half-filled sack of dead fish a rueful look as he spoke. "The Kraken woke up."

CHAPTER NINETEEN

9 Days Left

MANATREE, MORI, and the medical staff in attendance all pulled extraordinary faces when Fanren and I stepped into Wist's bedroom.

"What's that smell?" Manatree demanded.

"Dead fish," I said. "Go clean it up yourself if you want to complain."

She flapped her hands to shoo us back out the door. "Get washed and changed first. You'll put the Kraken back in a coma."

We ended up following Manatree's orders. A good hour had passed by the time she deemed us fit to enter the Kraken's majestic presence.

When we shambled back into the room with damp hair, it seemed much quieter than before. The medical mages had vanished, and so had about half of the life-support paraphernalia, with its spindly joints that arced up to the ceiling and its long insectile probes. What remained of the equipment cast a diminished yet complex tangle of shadows across the pale cedar floor.

They'd moved Wist's bed away from its former position over in a corner. Now it sat right in the center of the room, presumably to make it easier for the mages to set up their machinery and maneuver around her. Mori was still perched in a chair by the bed. Manatree stood a little further off, arms folded, casting a critical look over at the curtain-less wall of windows.

Wist sat up in bed, supported by a veritable mountain of pillows. Her hair was short again—shorter than before, even, chopped ruthlessly back to the edge of her jaw. She wore a big heather gray sweatshirt that came right up to her neck, effectively hiding the huge half-moon swathe of her torso that had been ripped out and then replaced. There were dark spots like bruises under her eyes. On the whole, though, she looked uncannily hale for someone who should have been dead weeks ago.

I felt a ripple in the bond when she saw me—incoherent and quickly suppressed. It was as if she'd started to touch a hot pan, then jerked her hand away before it could burn her.

"We brought coffee, tea, liquor, and water," I said to the room. "Also some yogurt. And cheesecake. And rice porridge."

Fanren wheeled a serving cart over to the bed. Manatree accepted a small cup of black coffee. Mori fussed until Wist made a few cursory attempts to swallow spoonfuls of porridge.

I took the tray away from Wist after she put her spoon down for good. She craned her neck, wincing a bit, peering around until she spotted Manatree.

"The people who attacked," she said. Her voice was still very rough. "How many survived?"

"Six," Manatree said coolly.

"Out of how many?"

"I'll have the detailed report sent over later. It isn't quite finished yet."

They eyed each other from across the room, both devoid of expression.

A moment later, Manatree walked over and set her empty cup down on the serving cart. She motioned for me to hold out my right arm.

"Next order of business," she said. "The Board granted tentative approval of your request for parole. Due to your ... unique circumstances, I'm going to transfer authority over your probation thread to the Kraken."

Wist eyed the red string around my wrist as if seeing it for the first time. A fizzle of static brushed my skin as the magic cutting woven into the thread reoriented itself, swinging like the arrow of a compass from Manatree to Wist.

Shortly afterward, Mori popped up out of his seat. He trotted over to Fanren as if to offer his help with pushing the serving cart back to the kitchen. "Well, that's enough of us," he said. "Let's leave this tea and water on the table. The medical team said the Kraken should be mostly fine on her own now, but they'll send someone over to check in every morning. They left a paper with a list of magic skills that ought to help the recovery process. Of course, getting plenty of rest is most important."

Somewhat to my surprise, Manatree seemed perfectly willing to let Mori usher her out of the room along with him. I tugged at her uniform. "Wait," I said. "There's something I want you to tell the Board."

"I'm not a messenger service."

"Just listen. It's good news for them. Tell them I'm still willing to work as the Magebreaker."

Her eyebrows went up.

"But I want to get paid for it. And I want to pick my own hours. Have the government deal with me as an outside consultant. I can form an LLC if they need me to."

Manatree glanced at Wist as if expecting her to object.

Wist said nothing.

Eventually Manatree gave up and said shortly, "I'll let the higher-ups know. That's not a guarantee they'll chose to hire you."

"Fair enough," I said. "I plan to be very expensive."

Fanren was the last to leave the room. He had the nerve to wink at me as he tugged the door shut behind him.

I eyed the empty chair Mori had left for me. I opted to plop myself down on the bed next to Wist instead. The bed was large enough for at least six or seven people, anyway. I studied the contents of her gray sweatshirt, then put a hand on her left shoulder. She only flinched a little—more from surprise, it seemed, then pain. I moved my hand to her left collarbone, then to the soft fold where her underarm met her side. Then to the left half of her chest.

Just as I'd thought. I could feel the reconstructed pectoral muscle. I could feel the slow, faint heartbeat, which hadn't been present at all when she was berserk in the tower basement.

"I was wondering if they'd give you your left breast back," I said. "Guess not, huh?"

Wist looked down at herself a bit mournfully. I'll be honest—if it were me, no one would've noticed a missing breast. Mine are practically invisible to begin with. But Wist had always been very well-endowed. The unevenness was obvious even with her upper half swallowed up in a baggy sweatshirt.

"It's all right," she said. "They're emergency medical specialists. Not breast specialists."

"I'm sure they could've reconstructed it if they tried," I countered. "They transmuted back everything else you had missing. But maybe they thought it would be kind of awkward to spend extra time and effort crafting the Kraken a nice matching breast. They probably figured you could do it yourself once you came to."

"Is it strange?" she asked.

"I like it." I patted the flat side of her chest for emphasis. "And they say asymmetry is trendy right now. Nothing to worry about."

"Is it really?"

I snorted. "I'm a seven-year prisoner. You think I've got any idea what's in style?"

Wist caught at my wrist. "Would you stop that?" Her grip was astonishingly weak.

"Stop what?"

She colored a bit. "Just because it isn't shaped like a breast doesn't mean I can't feel anything."

"Payback," I said. "You groped me all over when you were berserk."

"Not all over!"

"Maybe not all over. But you would've if I'd let you."

Wist released my hand. "Do you usually hold people accountable for what they do when they're berserk?"

"Usually not," I said. "But you seem to remember it well enough. And we're stuck with each other for life now."

Something akin to fear passed through her face. It was gone in a millisecond. I could pretend I'd imagined it. I could get up and leave the room and tell her to keep resting. I'd gotten parole, after all. We were bonded. I had the rest of my life to dig up whatever bones I wanted to pick with Wist. Just for today, I could take pity on her. I could keep my big mouth shut. But the thought of it made my stomach hurt. What would I do instead, go brood alone in my guest room full of prison furnishings?

I turned on my side to face Wist. I leaned up against the hefty pile of pillows. There were no lights on in the room yet; plenty of sun billowed in through the glass wall at the back. Right now it was starting to age to the amber-gold hue of an overripe day.

"You offered me a kiss," I reminded her.

Wist stared. For a second I thought she'd forgotten. Then—"I was berserk," she said.

"So you didn't mean it?"

"You didn't seem interested."

"You weren't yourself," I said. "Not your usual self, anyway. Now you are. How about now?"

She leaned toward me as if she needed to get up close to see me clearly. I caught a whiff of her scent—still purely hers, thankfully. I'd been wondering if her transmuted body parts or weeks on life support might have changed it. She touched my hair, half-wet from my post-fish shower. She touched the edge of my ear with uncertain fingers.

She pulled back. She kept her face perfectly neutral. But I could hear the raw edge of despair in her voice. I could feel its needle-edges pricking the bond between us. "I don't understand," she was saying. "You—"

I kissed her cheek. Wist sucked in a breath. I curled my fingers through the back of her hair to make her hold still. I kissed the corner of her mouth. Her lips parted with a noise like a tiny cry of surrender, guttural, lost swiftly in the back of her throat. It wasn't the first time we'd kissed. Not even close. But it was the first time in a very, very long time.

Next thing I knew, she had me on my back. We both startled at the sound of pillows starting to fall off the bed. I burst out laughing—I couldn't stop myself. It was like being teenagers again, leaping apart in terror at the slightest noise. Wist rolled off me and flopped over on her side with a chastened smile. I took her hand and threaded our fingers together.

She looked—

She looked happy.

My gut twisted.

"My dreams changed lately," I said. "Since right after we bonded."

"What's different?"

"I used to dream of dying, but I could never see who killed me. Now I can see them clearly."

Wist's hand tensed. I didn't let go.

"Who is it?" she asked.

"I think you know."

A long pause. Wist shifted slowly onto her back, eyes moving to the high gray ceiling. "The bond hasn't let me share your dreams," she said. "I don't think I've dreamt at all since the Extinguishers came."

"All right," I said. "Then you tell me. What's your problem with Fanren?"

"He facilitated the attack, didn't he?"

So Wist had come to the same conclusion as me. She must have kept her thoughts to herself, though. Even with parts of the Board determined to protect Fanren, I doubt he'd escape unscathed if the Kraken herself raised an outcry.

"Aside from that," I said.

"That's a pretty serious issue to simply set aside." At last she turned her head back toward me. "Clematis, that hurts."

I'd been digging my fingers into her hand without realizing it. I forced myself to relax.

"Here's the thing," I said. "I haven't forgiven you. I don't think I'll ever forgive you for letting PubSec drag me away without saying anything. I'm not that nice of a person. I'm not built that way."

"I wouldn't forgive me, either," Wist said softly. It sounded more as if she were speaking to herself than to me.

"But I know why I got a life sentence."

"Because I informed on you?"

"Traitors are supposed to get executed." I felt Wist go still beside me. Even the multi-branching magic inside her seemed to freeze, as if holding its breath. "I always wondered why I wasn't," I continued. "After a couple years, I found out from Fanren. He's pretty close to the Board himself. He was probably working for them at the time, actually.

"He told me you came to the Board in confidence. You begged—demanded—ordered them to spare my life. You threw around every ounce of your weight as the Kraken. You forced their hand. That's the only reason they carted me off to prison instead of the execution chamber."

I curled my body closer to Wist. "I didn't get it. You got me arrested, then went to all that trouble to keep me alive. But you never wrote. You never visited. You baffled me."

"You mean I hurt you," Wist said without expression. "I was the worst thing that ever happened to you."

"Don't flatter yourself," I snapped. "But you'd like to think that, wouldn't you? I'm not completely dense, you know."

"I—"

"There must have been a time when you loved me," I said. "Even if you never said so. How about now?"

Those dark eyes widened. A few more thick seconds of silence, and I might very well either vomit off the side of the bed or faint to blackness. I wanted to do to the emotional center of my brain whatever Wist had done to ravage and silence her own magic. I watched her sit up. She put her head in her arms as if she too were about to be sick.

"Wist," I said unsteadily. "I'm not an idiot. I already put most of the pieces together. You can't keep hiding what you did. And even if you could, you shouldn't. We're bonded now. Have a little respect for me, would you? Let me know what I'm bonded with."

She made a choking sound, one very much like laughter. Then she began to unfold herself. She sat up straight and gazed down at me, hands neat in her lap. She moved with care, as if not quite used to how her body fit together.

"So you haven't found the lantana pot yet," she said. "Any idea where I hid it?"

"I could tell you all the places where you didn't hide it," I retorted, irritation rising. "I've been looking all along. It's been an incredible waste of time."

Wist's lips twitched. "I suppose I outdid myself. I didn't think it was that smart of a hiding place." She held her arm out for me to take. "Let me show you."

The short-distance porting skill Wist had acquired while berserk must have carried over. I hooked my arm through hers with a scowl.

In the next breath, we were in the shadows between two elegant streetlights. It seemed as dim as evening. My breath puffed out white. Wist leaned her weight on me, as though unused to standing on her own. Were we even still in the tower?

Out in front of us stretched a path walled off on both sides by deep green hedges twice as tall as Wist. I looked over my shoulder. Behind us stretched green hedges that trailed off to reveal tall shelves stacked with boxes of cereal, bags of chips, sacks of dried pasta, every canned food under the sun.

The living maze at the back of the kitchen pantry.

"You're kidding," I said.

Wist gave an apologetic shrug.

"Mori said the maze was infinite. He said it's always changing. It's a death trap."

"It's more dangerous than I meant it to be," Wist admitted. "Porting doesn't work past this point. Are you okay with walking?"

"Are you?"

By way of answer, she began forging ahead. I made her slow down and keep an arm around my shoulder, so I could at least pretend to offer some semblance of support. I didn't want to get stuck dragging

Wist back through the hedgerows, on the off chance that she lost her strength and suddenly passed out.

With each awkward step, unwanted memories kept rushing back. Things I hadn't thought about in years. The time when Wist got a fever and decided it would be a great idea to sleep it off on the floor of her dorm room. I came in and saw her lying there, and for some reason I immediately thought she was dead. The time when I fell in the lily pond in the Palace courtyard and pulled Wist right down with me. The time when we rode the train all the way to the border just to try a box of the best cinnamon rolls in the country. The first time Wist took me flying for fun. The first time she took me down to explore the ink-dark water at the bottom of Osmanthus Bay.

Wist knew where she was going in the maze. I couldn't see how—the hedges kept shifting on all sides, closing in behind us with a sinister crackling. But clearly there was some kind of trick to it. Well, she'd always had a better sense of direction than me, anyway.

She stopped beneath one of the yellow streetlights. A curly wrought-iron bench sat with its back to the hedge up in front of us. In the middle of the bench rested a small potted lantana in full bloom. It was my first time seeing it in person. It was just as Fanren had described—clusters of tiny flowers, a jumble of colors like a painted sunset.

"You'll have to take it out of the pot," Wist said.

I stole a glance at the side of her face. Impassive as usual. But she sounded strained.

I pushed her over to the bench, made her take a seat. I picked up the lantana in both hands. It was just a simple terracotta pot, nothing more and nothing less. I lifted the pot and slammed it down on the arm of the bench.

"Well, that's one way to do it," Wist muttered.

The pot had shattered. I picked through the crumbling earth, much of it still held together by the lantana plant's intricate roots. I spotted something blue. A stabbing pain hit me in the stomach. I ignored it.

I dug a circular blue cord out of the dirt. It was as thin as the red parole string on my wrist, and long enough to just barely fit around someone's neck. It was the exact color of the bond thread I'd seen myself wearing in recent dreams. The blue-purple bond thread I'd never once seen or touched when awake.

I set the homeless lantana down on the velvety moss at the foot of the bench, surrounded by pot shards. Lantanas were resilient in the wild—to many people, after all, they were weeds. It still had dirt surrounding its roots. It could figure out what to do to survive.

I looked over at Wist, still seated at the other end of the bench. She looked back at me steadily. She had her right arm lying on the armrest, her hand curled down to clench its filigreed ends.

Technically we were in a space connected to the kitchen pantry. Yet above us seemed to stretch an inchoate gray-purple sky. The ground was dark and eternally damp. The air smelled of rain that might never come. My throat ached.

"I know which taboo you broke," I said. "Reviving the dead."

I held out the blue bond thread, forced her to look at it. "I don't remember anything except what I've seen in my dreams. But I've seen enough. There was a world where we bonded quite young, wasn't there? There was a world where you gave me this bond thread. There was a world where Fanren assassinated me, and I didn't even know him yet. You brought me back. You gave me another life."

Wist's eyes lingered on the dirt-smudged bond thread. "Even if that's true," she said slowly, "it happened in a different world. In this life, Fanren would never try to kill you."

"Didn't need you to tell me that." Despite my best efforts, my voice shook. "This is your answer, isn't it?"

I dropped the bond thread in her lap.

Wist jerked as if I'd slapped her. She looked up. "What? What do you mean?"

"The Clematis you loved never went to prison. The Clematis you loved was never called the Magebreaker."

"You're the same person," Wist said. She sounded legitimately bewildered.

"I'm older now than she ever got to be!" I could understand now how someone might have a stroke from sheer rage. "You did love me—in another life. And in this life you told PubSec to throw me in prison. I guess last time I died before you could get tired of me!"

Wist turned white. Her mouth parted. She said nothing. She bowed her head to wind the blue bond thread around her left wrist. Stray clots of black dirt smeared her skin.

"You made me what I am now," I said. "You put me in this life. You owe me the truth about it. What happened when you revived me? It's not like you just restarted everything right after I died. This time around, I never even met Fanren till we were both in prison. How far back in time did you punt all of us?"

"To the beginning," Wist said, little more than a whisper. "We went back to the very beginning. We were born again. We were children. We grew up. This bond thread is the only artifact I brought over from our original lives."

"When did you remember?" I demanded.

"Remember—remember what?"

"The other world. Our other lives."

Wist seemed to shrink in on herself before me.

"I never forgot," she said.

I took an inadvertent step back. "So the entire time I've known you, you already had a lifetime of memories."

My eyes seared. Words clawed their way out before I even knew what I was saying. "When I thought I was meeting you for the first time, you already knew who I was. When we taunted your family by pretending to be bonded, you knew there was another life where we'd already been bonded long ago. When I introduced you to Fanren, you knew he was the man who killed me. My whole life's been one stupid prank. And you're the only one who got to be in on the joke."

Wist covered the bond thread around her wrist with her right hand, as if to protect it. "What was I supposed to do?" she asked tightly. "Should I have told you that you got murdered in another world—but not to worry, I saved your life? Even if you listened to me—even if you believed me, and I don't see why you would—the knowledge would be nothing but a burden."

"You should've erased your own memories if you felt that way," I snarled.

"Then I wouldn't have been able to stop you from getting killed the same way again!"

I laughed. It rang out hollowly under the dark false sky. "Nice excuse. You probably just couldn't bear to forget the first me. Your one true love who died before she could commit any serious crimes. This time you ended up chucking me in prison with a life sentence, and apparently planning to never see me again. Wow, great job! What an incredibly happy ending! I'm sure that was worth breaking taboos for. How many more vorpal holes formed after you revived me? How many more people died because of it?"

"I didn't know what the price would be." Wist's hands curled into fists in her lap. "Breaking the taboo was my mistake. My responsibility." She met my gaze again, her expression newly empty of emotion.

"This is why I didn't want you to know," she said. "Has knowing this made your life better? Has it satisfied you? Has it made you happier?"

It was like being stabbed in the lungs. I couldn't answer. I couldn't look at her. She was close enough to touch and at the same time unforgivably distant.

Wist hadn't tormented me in prison—if only because I'd learned not to think of her. How could I avoid thoughts of her now? We were bonded for life. Worse, now I knew everything was her doing, her fault. Not just my trial and tenure in prison, but the very fact of my birth in this world.

And worst of all, there was a part of me that didn't care about any of that. There was a part of me that wanted to overlook all of it. There was a part of me that keened in misery solely because Wist had loved the wrong Clematis.

CHAPTER TWENTY

7 Years Ago

WIST USED TO BE on the Board of Magi. Does this surprise you? It was my doing, of course. On her own, she would never have been interested. Besides, we were in our early twenties at the time, and no one under forty had ever been anointed a full Board member.

But Wist was the Kraken. They could hardly refuse her a seat. If anything, the rest of the Board must have been relieved that she didn't demand the keys to the whole country. A single Board seat was a small price to pay to appease her. After all, she had more than enough magical power to single-handedly declare and enforce a dictatorship.

So, yes, I maneuvered Wist onto the Board of Magi. It was right after we left university. I dropped out, and she followed me. (For the sake of appearances, Wist's departure ended up being treated as an early graduation. No special treatment for me, though.)

Wist joined the Board as the youngest member ever selected. I was—well, on paper I was her administrative assistant. In reality I was the one telling her which issues to bring to the table, what to say, who to befriend, how to vote.

Wist did exactly as I told her, and to her credit, she did it with aplomb. We were a very effective team.

But we still only had one Board seat between us. At the time there were twenty-six mages on the Board, Wist included. If everyone was in attendance, we'd need a simple majority—fourteen votes—to pass the Healers' Bill of Rights. Wist and I spent a good five years winning over the other Board members one by one. We got thirteen votes locked in, Wist included. One more couldn't be that hard, right?

The other thirteen Board members were deeply suspicious of and deeply averse to anything that might weaken the status of mages. They saw it as a zero-sum game: if healers gained, then mages would lose. Hell, maybe they were right. As far as I was concerned, maybe it was about time for mages to start losing.

Here's an example—under Osmanthian law, healers are legally obligated to service their bonded mages. It doesn't matter what the mage does to them. There's no legal excuse to avoid healing your bondmate.

So what legal obligations does a mage owe their bonded healer? Shelter? Protection? Health insurance? A fair wage? Nope, none of that. Absolutely nothing. And on top of that, if a mage got taken to court for murdering their bonded healer, they could pretty reliably get off with little or no sentence by claiming that the healer failed to adequately discharge their duties.

Wouldn't it be nice, I thought, if we made it just a bit more difficult for bonded mages to abuse or murder their healers and get away with it. Yet because bonded mages can only be healed by their bondmates, most of the Board—even those we ultimately convinced to vote for the

Healers' Bill of Rights—feared the consequences of giving bonded healers the right to refuse.

A mage denied sufficient healing would eventually snap and go berserk. If bonded healers had the right to withhold healing, they could use it as a weapon—a threat—to extort and control their mages. The remaining thirteen Board members said they'd have blood on their hands if healers' rights became enshrined in law. They said they couldn't possibly vote for anything that might lead to more berserk mages. Berserkers are a danger to everyone around them, healers and subliminals included. So they warned us.

That was all very well. It didn't change the fact that a bonded mage could beat the shit out of their healer and still legally demand that the healer come crawling home from the hospital to treat them. Again and again and again. For the rest of their natural lives.

The Healers' Bill of Rights would have been a very small first step. I wasn't asking that they put healers on the Board of Magi—or into any position of power whatsoever. But even that one small step started to seem impossible. Five years on the board, and we'd accomplished exactly nothing. At this rate, it looked like they'd be happy to stonewall us for decades.

But if just one person missed just one meeting, all of that would change.

The Board would vote with whichever members were physically present. Few members ever skipped a meeting. If they did, however, they'd simply lose their chance to vote. Which meant that if even a single person out of the other thirteen missed a single key meeting, we could pass the Healers' Bill of Rights in their absence, with a one-vote majority.

Just one person.

Just one meeting.

As I got deeper into politics, I had plenty of chances to meet people who had frustrations with the same Board members as me. Subliminal activists, anti-magic radicals, Jacian immigrants, you name it. Our goals differed—sometimes drastically—but we shared a common foe.

They offered to help delay one key Board member from one key meeting. Just delay him, you know? He was a mage from one of the great families, wealthy and heavily protected. It wouldn't be easy. But success would be worth the effort.

They didn't just delay him. They took the information I'd fed them, the careful plans I'd drawn up, and they killed him.

Wist resigned from the Board after turning me in. The Healers' Bill of Rights never passed. In the end, it never even came close.

Here's the curious part: I didn't have any real anger for the foreign agents who'd used me. I'd been trying to use them, too. They had their own objectives, and little interest in my pet cause. I'd known that from the start. We were playing the same game. They outplayed me.

I saved my rage for Wist, who had known exactly what I was doing, exactly who I was talking to, exactly how we planned to win the un-winnable vote. She never tried to stop me. She never said a single word hinting that maybe this wasn't the greatest idea in the world. And it wasn't! She would have been justified in pointing that out. But she didn't.

I thought Wist's silence meant that she understood the gamble, understood the line we were crossing and its possible risks. I thought it meant she'd be with me no matter what happened, no matter whether we succeeded or failed. That assumption was perhaps just as big of a mistake as leaking sensitive intel to my Jacian buddies.

The man's full title was Magus Gwindel. The Gwindels are one of the great Osmanthian families, much like the Shiens. We move in very different circles, naturally. Few of the Gwindels have ever ended up in prison. In fact, you'll probably never hear about this family from me again.

He was a haughty man in his sixties with an equally haughty mage wife, and a much younger bonded healer. It was his second bonded healer; the first had died under tragic circumstances. You might wonder if he killed them, but it seems to have been a genuine accident. He treated his healers well enough. He regarded healers in general with an attitude of old-fashioned noblesse oblige.

His greatest problem might have been a lack of imagination. If someone told him stories of a mage mistreating a healer, he'd start looking for reasons why it happened. He couldn't comprehend that sometimes there are no deeper reasons, no understandable provocation, no acceptable excuse. Sometimes people act in horrible ways, and there's no good explanation for it, and anything you do to try to force it to make sense only serves to dilute the awful truth of their actions.

Anyway, I say this because Magus Gwindel had a name. And by all accounts, he suffered a slow and terrible death. Now I wondered anew what Wist was thinking when she heard the news. She brought me back, kept me alive past my original death date—and then what? I killed a Board member. Well done, Wisteria. Well done, Clematis.

CHAPTER TWENTY-ONE

The Day I Left, and 2 Months Later

MY HEAD WAS A MESS. But I knew one thing for sure: I had to get out of that tower.

Everything became easier once I realized what I needed to aim for. All the next steps fell into place in my mind, and then it was just a matter of executing them.

I set aside what I'd learned about myself, about Wist. I had the rest of my life to grapple with that, didn't I? No point in coming to a standstill now, sentencing myself to stay trapped in the Kraken's tower with the Kraken herself.

Parole had once been so far out of reach that I eliminated it from my daydreams, excised the very concept from my awareness. I'm not one to make myself miserable by longing for the impossible.

Yet now, miraculously, I'd earned the very thing I'd given up on from the start. No matter what lay in wait for me, I wouldn't fail to take full advantage of my newfound freedom. I may have been a traitor to the nation, but I wouldn't be a traitor to myself.

First I made sure to win over Mori. I tucked my arm through his and pulled him along with me on a walk through the tower. I led him past all the same rooms he'd shown me on my first grand tour a month ago.

Because Wist and I had bonded, I was now the only healer in the world who could successfully treat her. Normally, this would result in Mori resigning—or being dismissed—from his previous duties as her on-call healer.

"Don't leave," I told him. "You have an even more important job now."

Yes, Wist had recovered vast numbers of magic branches. But with the exception of the few she'd forcibly imprinted with specific skills while berserk, the vast majority were still blank. She couldn't do anything with them. To actually wield her magic, she would need to reinstall her old skill set, one skill at a time.

Even the simplest magic skills would each take at least a few hours to relearn and imprint on a specific branch. She'd only be able to work through two or three per day without exhausting herself. Going through that same process for complex, high-level skills—some of which might require multiple branches—could take days or weeks at a time.

As expected, Mori was still worried about the prospect of me leaving the tower. "That's not what you should be worried about," I said. "I'll heal Wist whenever she needs it. I'll just be a portal away."

"But—"

"The thing is, all I can really do is heal her. I'm not familiar with her current duties as Kraken, much less her latest skill set. The last time we worked closely together—and she still had all her magic—was seven years ago. I have no idea what skills she's picked up since then. You, on the other hand, have been her main healer for at least the past few years.

Right? What she needs right now is someone who can help her get organized and make a plan for which skills to relearn when."

Every mage was required to register a list of their magic skills with the government. Even if you wanted to erase a branch and imprint a different skill on it, you needed to notify them of the planned change and await approval. Being the Kraken, Wist probably bent the rules more than most. But technically she was still supposed to keep a full record of her skills—the ones she'd had most recently, before all her magic got wiped out—stored somewhere.

Once I mentioned this, Mori took me to a shelf in one of the tower's research libraries. He pulled out a binder listing Wist's officially registered magic skills. Based on the thickness, she probably had at least a couple thousand unique skills to recover.

If they were a combination of simple and complex skills, taking varying amounts of time and energy to relearn, she'd need at least a few years of constant work to regain all of them. Or maybe more than half a decade, if she stopped to take breaks and eat and sleep and do other tasks from time to time. I think. Mental math isn't really my strong suit.

"Are these all her skills?" I asked, although I suspected I already knew the answer.

Mori's face clouded. "It's everything she has on file with the government."

"Right." I looked him up and down. "You're very conscientious. I'm sure you did your best to update the list whenever you saw her using a skill not written here."

"Well ... I tried."

"She used to invent loads of new skills and forget to mention them to anyone. Guess that hasn't changed." I patted the binder. "Anyway, this proves my point. Because you've been so close to Wist, you know her skill set better than anyone in the world except Wist herself. You're the best person to advise her on how to triage this list. It'll take years to come anywhere close to finishing it. So deciding what order to relearn her skills in is an incredibly important task—not just for Wist, but for Osmanthus. For the world.

"Should she prioritize regaining the ability to seal vorpal holes, or should she prioritize offensive and defensive magic, in case more Extinguishers pop up again? That's the kind of decision she needs to make now. I can't help her with this. You can. Don't leave her to muddle through on her own."

I knew what I was doing when I looked him in the eye and said this. And it worked. Mori would need a different job title, but he agreed to stay by Wist's side. Just like before she lost her magic.

As for yours truly, all I needed to do was heal her ad hoc. I told Wist I would be leaving. I told her to call me through the bond when she needed me.

One of the perks of being bonded was that I didn't even have to be in the same room with her to heal her—I could do it remotely, using the bond as a conduit. I could perform my legal duties as a bondmate without ever having to look her in the face.

When I told her I was leaving the tower, something in the bond went still. It wasn't an emotion so much as a sensation of lurching to a stop. It felt like she'd forced a wall into the bond to keep her reaction from leaking through.

Well, good for her. That was the one thing I'd worried about—the one huge weakness in my escape plan. I could go far away from the tower. I could heal Wist without ever needing to come back to her. But I couldn't escape the bond. If she strove to give me space, to keep our connection as businesslike as possible, all the better.

To be honest, I'd thought she might try to force me to stay. I'd thought she might bring up arguments about safety. I forestalled any such arguments as best I could, by working with Manatree to plan my reintroduction to Osmanthus City—the best place for me to be based, if the government still wished to engage my services as the so-called Magebreaker.

In this respect, I was highly fortunate that the mageocracy had so heavily censored the news of my trial and conviction. They didn't want me attracting the support of other healer or subliminal activists. Everyone in the country knew that someone called A. Clematis was a terrible traitor, a murderer, but hardly any of them knew my exact age or background or what I looked like. As further insurance, Public Security would put me into a type of modified witness protection.

I explained all of this before Wist had a chance to say a peep.

"You already let me rot in prison for seven years," I said. "Don't tell me you want to keep me prisoner here for the rest of my life."

"I wasn't going to," Wist said quietly, her face controlled. And that was all she said.

It reminded me of how blankly she'd looked back at me when I first came to the tower. It reminded me of seeing her surrounded by the Shien family, gazing into her dinner plate as if it were a scrying glass.

Back then I'd been able to tell when she folded up her emotions over and over as if crafting a tiny perfect paper model—not because of any kind of magic, but simply because I knew her so well. Now we were bonded, and I had no idea what was happening on the other side of the wall.

It was a good thing, though, that Wist didn't try to hold me back. I should've been relieved. I should've been glad. Whatever the case, Manatree helped her expand the range allotted to me by my parole thread. Now I could roam the tower, Osmanthus City, and the island prison—although I would only visit the prison when they hired me to hobble sentenced mages. Manatree or one of her underlings would need to port me back and forth each time.

That was how I found myself in an Osmanthus City apartment, rented under the name Asa Lantana, located on the fourth (and topmost) floor of a squat brown building facing a tree-lined residential street. PubSec gave me all-white hair—apparently the black-and-white skunk look was too distinctive—and helped me with some of the initial procedures to set up my consultancy. I'd need permission if I wanted to take on any clients outside the government. So far, though, they paid well enough for me to make rent and still have plenty left over.

My younger self would have hated this, I thought vaguely—living comfortably off money from the mageocracy, profiting directly from the system and all that. Then again, I'd already had two chances to change Osmanthus. Both times, I blew it. The first time, I got myself killed before accomplishing anything. The second time, I was one vote away from passing a bill that would've granted healers at least some semblance of legal rights, and instead I got Magus Gwindel killed and lost everything.

I was in the middle of breakfast when my doorbell rang: eight am on the dot. I got up to let Mori in. He had on what appeared to be two different jackets, a sky blue scarf, and an orange knit hat with fox ears sticking up out of it.

"Cute," I told him.

He was shivering. I poured him a mug of hot coffee and showed off my magic-heated floors (my biggest splurge to date). He sat at the tiny kitchen table and looked around curiously at the art on the walls, mostly posters and prints I'd scavenged from neighborhood flea markets.

We chatted about my work as the Magebreaker. We chatted about Fanren, who'd rejoined the winter dueling season in top form. He was already rumored to be a contender for next year's international championship. We chatted about the progress of Mori's dissertation and his work with the National Healing Research Institute. We chatted about nearly every topic under the sun except Wist.

At last Mori stopped drinking from his mug. I poured him more coffee, but he sat there with his hands cupped around it, unmoving. A duo of the usual brown-gray neighborhood birds screeched somewhere nearby, noisy even with the windows closed. Farther off, a crow croaked in response. Mori's nose and cheeks were still flushed red from the cold outside.

"You haven't been back to the tower," he said finally.

Yes. This, no doubt, was why he'd insisted on visiting me. I studied the dirty dishtowels hanging on hooks above my sink.

"I've been treating Wist through our bond," I replied. "And I've done an excellent job of it, if I do say so myself. You can't possibly criticize the quality of my healing. Her magic's never been this untangled."

"No," Mori said heavily. "No, I can't fault your healing. It's perfect. It makes me wonder what I was doing all this time. The Kraken has hardly any magical aches and pains nowadays. Before—she was always at least a little stiff, a little cramped. It might've been a lot worse than she used to let on, in fact."

He looked over at me until I relented and returned his gaze. His hair had grown out quite a bit in the past few months. The pale braid he'd taken to wearing now fell to drape over his left shoulder.

"I understand that the government keeps you busy hobbling mages," he said. "But not so busy that you can't decorate your apartment. Not so busy that you can't keep up with Fanren's matches. If you've got time for that, you've got time to come to the tower."

I took a long drink from my own cup to hide my face. Once I set it down, I said, "I know you have good intentions, but Wist is a grown woman. If she requires me to be there in person, she can tell me herself."

"That's not—" Mori stopped, took a breath.

After warming up, he'd taken the fox hat off and stuffed it in a pocket. Now he pulled it out, stretched it in his hands. The hat stared back up at him; it had little black eyes and a black nose sewn on. "She's under the impression that you want as little to do with her as possible." It looked more as if he were talking to the hat than to me. "She's trying to respect your decision to stay away."

"Good for her," I said. "Very mature."

He gave me a startled sidelong glance. He seemed almost wounded. "The Kraken will never ask you to visit. But I see her almost every day now, and there's something—there's something different from before. She isn't in pain because of her magic tangling anymore."

"What's the problem, then?"

"I don't want to make assumptions. I can't speak for her. She never says a word of complaint. But I think she's suffering. I think she's really unhappy. And I don't know exactly what happened between you in the past—"

I cut him off. "What's that got to do with anything?"

Mori raised his head. I saw his fingers tighten on the fox hat's fluffy ears. The heated floor started to feel uncomfortably warm underfoot.

"It might not be any of my business," he began.

"Yeah, that's what I'm thinking."

His face hardened. "I look at you," he said, "and you seem fine. You're thriving."

"What—Wist making herself miserable means I'm not allowed to thrive either? That's no fair."

"That's not what I mean," Mori said, visibly frustrated. "It feels like this is you getting your revenge for when the Kraken put you in prison."

"Hey," I said. I gestured around the small apartment: the meaningless art on the walls, the cheap brown floor mats, the old-fashioned tile backsplash in the kitchen area behind us. "I was locked up on an island for seven years. I'm just trying to live my life here."

"I think you have the Kraken exactly where you want her," he said. "She's tied to you for life now. I think you like holding her away from you, knowing she's stuck there at the other end of the rope, knowing she'll never approach you. I think you like knowing it makes her miserable. I think you like being the one in control now."

I got up and took my cup with me. I went over to do the dishes. It was only about two steps away. "I thought you were researching healing," I told him over my shoulder. "Not psychology."

Mori didn't answer. I finished washing my mug and stuck it upside down on the dish rack.

"Here's the funny thing," I said. "Wist never came to visit me in prison. I never even got so much as a letter. And you want me to feel sorry for her for moping over two measly months apart? When we're bonded? And I heal her through the bond every few weeks anyway?"

"I'm not saying it's right that she didn't visit you," he said with difficulty. "I just—it would be so easy for you to go to the tower now. I just don't understand why you wouldn't."

Because you're such a nice boy, I thought. Inherently good-hearted. And so young. Of course he would try to understand, and of course he would fail.

"Question for you," I said. "I'm sorry if this is too personal." Mori gave a wary nod. "Do you have any personal experience with vorpal holes?"

He didn't seem to know what I meant. I suppose I had brought it up rather suddenly. I tried again. "Have you ever lost anyone to a vorpal hole?"

His eyes went wide. "How'd you know?"

"Lucky guess," I said.

I was about to move on—I certainly hadn't planned on pressing him to elaborate—when he said in a fragile voice, almost vanishing: "It was my brother."

He spoke as if in a trance. The air hung tense between us.

"We were only a year apart. We were eight or nine at the time. I was older, but he was stronger and faster, better at everything. We were playing outside in an abandoned lot. I heard—it must have been the sound of a vorpal hole forming. It was brand new, not marked off or anything. I'd never seen one before, but I must have known what it was. We threw some rocks and cans at it. Then my little brother went to look through it. I—"

He twisted the fox hat in his hands, crushing the shape of its face. "He used to, to make a game of pushing me into things. Off things. He'd push me off the bed, off hillsides. He'd push me into creeks and pools.

"The vorpal hole wasn't that big, but it was bigger than we were. We were just scrawny little kids. I saw him standing there right in front of it, and it was like something made my hands move, and I saw my hands moving and I knew I had to stop, but I was already pushing him.

"It's not a secret," Mori said. "I told everyone. I told our parents I did it. I told the police. I told them I pushed him in. But everyone said I was wrong. They said it was an accident. They said I'd imagined it. They said getting too close to the vorpal hole distorted my memories. But I know what I did. I felt my hands on his back."

I should probably have said something different. I should have expressed—something—other than the first thought that came to mind. But I heard myself saying it anyway. "Did you ever tell Wist about it?" I asked.

"I thought she deserved to know before she took a chance on me." He sat slumped in the little kitchen chair I'd given him, the only one I had to spare. "I don't mean to talk big about what's right or what's wrong. I just think sometimes it would be better if you were the one there with her. Even if you didn't do or say anything special." He looked me in the eye, attempted a strained smile. "It might make a big difference," he said plaintively.

I saw Mori out the door later, orange fox hat pulled down over his ears again, back hunched against the cold. Afterward I stood alone in the silent apartment with an ache in my throat.

Something in me had reared up giddily when he said Wist was suffering, suffering without breathing a word about it. Wasn't it better not to feed that part of myself? Wouldn't it be better for both of us, in the long run, to keep a healthy distance? Then again, since when had I cared about what was better for anyone?

Whether he knew it or not, Mori had read me uncannily well. My heart swelled at the idea of Wist being miserable because of me specifically—at the idea of her being reminded of me every single day because of our inexorable bond. Here I felt safe. I could sense her at the other end of the bond, but I didn't have to look her in the eye. I liked it that way.

It was the first time in my life—maybe the first time in both my lives—I'd had the advantage. Wist had known me before she'd met me. She'd known what I would do in just about every scenario. She'd known how our future would unfold without intervention. She'd intervened subtly, I suppose, to keep me from dying the same way a second time. I'd thought I was so smart. I'd thought I could make the Board of Magi do my bidding, if only I worked hard enough and made a few clever bets. And yet for all those years, I'd had no idea what was really going on.

Now we were in a future she'd never seen before. Now we were bonded again. Now she was bending herself over backwards not to intervene further. Now I could just sit back and relish the knowledge that she was tying herself in knots over my death in my first life, my crimes in my second life, and all the deadly new vorpal holes that had started spawning because she made the fatal mistake of bringing me back.

I drank the rest of the coffee Mori had left behind unfinished. I never throw away food or drink if I can avoid it. The coffee had gone cold and deeply bitter.

I thought of Wist going out of her way to seek out Mori—the young healer prodigy who'd been so afraid of getting forced into a bond match against his will; the boy whose little brother had died in a vorpal hole. I was honestly still surprised that Mori hadn't fallen in love with her. A tall older woman with dark hair and dark eyes and shades of unhappy romance in her past. The most powerful mage in the world, and yet one who swore she would never force him to bond.

You're projecting, I thought, and I almost started laughing at myself right there in the empty apartment. How I wished I were Mori. Life would be so much easier as a sweet-faced, good-natured kid without a criminal record. Well, he might feel that he deserved a criminal record because of what he'd done to his brother, but no one had ever sent him to prison, now had they?

Besides, he could go see Wist every day without fighting his pride over it. He could go see Wist every day without making her feel the weight of the world.

CHAPTER TWENTY-TWO

One Winter Day

My first excuse was that I needed time to process the fact that Wist had brought me back to life. Or, rather, granted me a new life. An apparent fresh start. While desperately hoarding her own memories of my long-lost dead self all the while.

My second excuse was that I needed space to develop my own post-prison life. It was mundane, and from the outside it must have seemed quite lonely. But most importantly, it was mine and mine alone.

My third excuse was that I was afraid. Of what? All sorts of things, most far too pathetic to put down in words.

My fourth excuse was that I was hurt. Heartbroken.

And that, in the end, was the one that got me to put on my jacket and shove my hands in my pockets and stalk down the stairs outside my brown brick apartment. I could prove it was wrong if I refused to believe it.

I could prove it was wrong if I looked it square in the face and re-mained unshaken.

Osmanthus City was technically located on the coast, but the metropolis sprawled so far inland that you could easily spend your entire life here without ever catching a glimpse of the ocean. The housing Public Security found for me was way off to the east, about as far from the bay as you could get while still technically remaining within city borders. Even on the darkest winter nights, the temperature almost never went below freezing. Some roses managed to stay in full bloom right up until the very end of the year.

It was mid-morning now, a few days after Mori's visit, and I only needed earmuffs in the shade. I walked to the park around the corner from my apartment. It wasn't anything fancy—a couple large bare trees, some evergreens, a few bushes with enormous globes of citrus growing all over them. A mix of grass and mulch and moss covered the ground.

I sat on a boulder under a naked cherry tree. Someone's magic cutting wound itself all around the boulder like a net made of invisible vines. The boulder, in other words, was a portal enchanted to respond to me and me alone. I reached down to touch a shallow hollow in its side.

In the next moment, I found myself seated on a similar—yet subtly misshapen—boulder on one of the tower rooftops. It seemed to be part of some kind of rock garden. A red-trunked pine tree soared high overhead.

Going to the tower would always have been this easy. It was quite literally around the block for me. PubSec had set up the portal under the assumption that, as Wist's bonded healer, I would need to visit her frequently. I'd asked them to put it in the park instead of right in my apartment for security reasons. But the truth was that I just didn't want to look at it or think about it. I'd been so sure I'd never use it.

I realized belatedly that just because I'd given myself a day off didn't mean Wist would be sitting around here doing nothing. By this point she must've recovered at least some of her most crucial magic skills. The Kraken's services had always been in high demand—now more than ever, no doubt, since she'd dropped off the face of the earth for a couple of a months.

Come to think of it, Mori had mentioned that the Board of Magi and VorDef (the International Vorpal Defense Council) were arranging for her to tour the entire continent. Osmanthus was hardly the only nation with vorpal holes that needed closing.

If I were smart, I would've asked Mori to tell me about Wist's schedule. If I were smart, I would've given Wist some kind of heads up that I was coming. But if I had to do either of those things, I might never have succeeded in dragging myself here in the first place. Call me a coward, but it only worked because I emptied my head and focused solely on the task right in front of me. Walk a straight line down the block. Step into the neighborhood park. Find the right boulder.

I'll be honest: I was relieved to find the tower empty. I explored it a little bit, just so I could tell myself I hadn't given up and left immediately. I found the guest room where I used to sleep—empty now, all the furnishings sent back either to prison or to the dump. They'd never been mine to begin with, anyway.

I thought about leaving a note in Wist's room before I departed, but that seemed coy to the point of stupidity. I thrust my hands in my pockets and went up the stairs back to the rooftop rock garden. Turtle the cat followed close in my footsteps, perhaps expecting me to feed her.

I was two steps away from the red pine tree when the cat started—well, I guess you could call it meowing. Now it really sounded desperate for food. I looked back. I saw the cat yowling. I saw Wist right behind it, in her puffy outdoor jacket and tinted glasses. I froze.

"Did you come to see the cat?" Wist asked after a moment. With her eyes hidden, it almost felt as if it could have been a genuine question.

"I don't even like cats." I gave Turtle a shrug of apology. "Maybe I'd be tempted if you had a dog."

Wist crouched. The cat ceased its screeching and leapt up onto her shoulder. It stayed balanced there as she stood carefully and held out her hand to me. She had my old blue bond thread wrapped around her wrist. Since she didn't wear it around her neck, no one would recognize it as anything other than a colorful accessory.

"It's cold," she said. "Come inside."

"Not that cold." I didn't move. "Where'd you come from? Did you just ditch work to show up here?"

"I was in a meeting at the Palace of Magi. It just wrapped up. I sensed you at the tower." Wist lowered her hand. "If you want to leave, I won't keep you here."

I could tell she meant it. I gritted my teeth. It would have been infuriating if she acted like she had any right to make me stay, but it was equally infuriating that she didn't make the slightest effort. My own annoyance at this was the most infuriating part of all, of course. I wanted to punch myself in the stomach.

Instead I took a small breath and brushed past Wist, heading for the door down to the rest of the tower. "You owe me a favor," I said. "I'll give you the details downstairs."

Apparently Wist's idea of hospitality involved sitting me down in the piano parlor. At some point in the past two months, it seemed to have acquired a family of self-playing harps.

The morning glory vines now covered every single wall but left the floor and ceiling bare, which I suppose meant she had reached some kind of tentative truce with them. The flames in the fireplace had evolved into a shifting dance of green and violet.

Wist offered me something to drink. I declined. She offered me a seat. I soon sprang up, too restless to stay still.

"That cat," I said, watching it twitch its tail on the damask sofa beside her. "Why wouldn't you give it a name?"

"Her name is Turtle."

"That's what Mori decided to call it. He said you refused to name it."

Wist removed her tinted glasses. With a turn of her wrist, they vanished into thin air. "I thought you said you wanted to ask me a favor?"

"Right now I'm asking about the cat."

"You're asking in a way that makes it seem like you already know the answer."

"Oh? Is this pattern starting to feel kind of familiar?" I shot her a grin devoid of humor.

"Asa," Wist said.

"What?"

"That's what I used to call her."

"You named your stray cat after me? You named a cat Asa and fed it treats and loved it and petted it while I kept laboring away in prison?"

"When Mori asked, I told him I couldn't think of a name."

"That's a fine sight," I said. "A woman in her thirties too embarrassed to admit to the name of a cat."

I threw myself down on Wist's other side. The couch squeaked. The cat made a noise of disapproval. "Got any other humiliating stories to share? I'm all ears."

"I was beginning to think I'd never see you again." There was no emotion in her voice; no judgment. Just a quiet statement of fact.

"Yeah, well, I thought the same thing when I got sentenced for life." I looked at her sideways. "Decided to become an archer?" Her left breast was still missing.

"I'm right-handed," said Wist. "And I believe that's a myth."

"No breast removal for archery? Huh. Then what, just decided you like it this way?"

"Of all the magic skills I need to relearn, cosmetic surgery isn't really a top priority. I don't think I ever knew it in the first place." Wist tilted her head to contemplate me. "I thought you were the one who liked it this way." She put a hand over her heart.

The feeling that jerked through me was almost exactly the same as when you begin to lapse into sleep, and get tricked into thinking you're falling, and then find yourself lying wide awake with helpless adrenaline. My fingers curled in on themselves. Wist was so terribly close.

We watched the cat hop down from the couch and trot silently out of the room. I recalled something about morning glories being poisonous to cats—better be careful, I thought. Not that it was any of my business.

"Wist," I said, looking straight ahead at the empty-seated piano. At least my voice came out evenly. "Do you know where my parents went?"

For a moment she said nothing.

Then: "Did you try to go see them?"

I shook my head. "Officially I'm under a new identity now. Don't want to cause any trouble."

"Do you want me to take you?"

I couldn't answer.

Wist stood up from the couch. "Let me show you something," she said, in the same sort of tone one might use to continue a discussion of gardening techniques. "It's still in the tower. Just deeper."

She held out her hand again. This time I took it, albeit only with the very tips of my clammy fingers. The cord around her wrist was such a perfect unbroken blue.

Wist took me to part of the tower basement I'd never seen before—a place even lower down than the replica courtroom. Like a few other levels of the basement, it had an illusory sky that seemed to arc miles overhead. The air felt like early autumn, well before leaves start falling, too warm and sunny for our coats.

We were outside a small house with a large garden. Not large in the sense that it had a lot of land. But it was absolutely packed with roses and angel's trumpets and hydrangeas and rhododendrons and red spider lilies and bell tree dahlias far taller than Wist; with miniature maple and plum trees and artfully twisted pines; with sweet olive bushes and climbing clematis vines and sprawling rainbow-hued lantanas.

Even in temperate Osmanthus City, there was no one season where you'd find all of these in full bloom at the exact same time. It just wouldn't happen.

Yet somehow the garden looked exactly the way I remembered. Somehow it felt just like it did on that fall day when I first took Wist home with me. I couldn't recall the occasion—it might've been something as simple as a three-day weekend. It was well before the government officially proclaimed her the Kraken, well before I ever saw her palatial mansion or met anyone else from the Shien clan.

We showed up with our school bags and helped my father cook dinner. I introduced Wist as a friend from the academy. My parents were both subliminals, but they still had enough magic perception that they must've been able to tell she was no ordinary mage.

To their credit, they didn't probe about her classification. They asked us perfectly ordinary questions about dorm life, about our studies. My mother brought out a huge stack of board games after dessert, delighted to finally have four players around the table. She insisted that I let Wist have my bed—not because she was a mage, but because she was a guest.

Indignant, I snuck out of my sleeping bag and got into bed with Wist anyway. The two of us could fit if we squeezed, and I wasn't about to surrender my childhood bed to anyone. I kept poking Wist to talk to her, and she listened, but she was very quiet. I figured she was tired from all my parents' delighted bantering. Maybe a bit too full from the ice cream after dinner. Maybe even a little homesick, from lying surrounded by the smells and sounds of someone else's house.

Later on, Wist told me she wanted to stay there forever. At the time I thought she was kidding. Years afterward, when it became my turn to visit the Shien family manor, I finally understood that she'd meant it.

"The real house is gone," Wist said as we looked together into her copy of my parents' overflowing garden.

I'd figured as much, but it made something twist inside me all the same. "What happened?"

"Your parents left the city years ago. The house was torn down soon after. The new owners built over most of the garden. You wouldn't recognize it now."

"Where'd they go?"

"Do you want to know?"

I didn't have an answer for that. Wist tilted her head back to look up into the dangling angel's trumpets, huge yellow-green flowers that grew pointing straight down at the ground.

I elbowed her in the side and pointed my toe at the multicolored lantanas poking out through the fence around the garden. "How'd you know my parents were originally going to name me Lantana? That's why you mourned me with the lantana pot, wasn't it? But none of us ever told you. I'm sure of it."

Wist had tied her puffy coat around her waist. Her black sweatshirt hung partway off one shoulder, fell loose to the middle of her thighs. She'd tried to tuck her hair behind her ears, but it was still a little too short; it kept escaping.

"The very first time I ever went to your house," she said. "In our previous lives. I stopped and looked at the lantanas for a long time. I'd never seen a flower with so many different colors all in one cluster. Or maybe I'd seen them before, but never up close—I'd never actually noticed them.

"Your father saw me lingering over there, and he told me what they were called. He told me you were almost named after them. You were there with me. You were listening."

"But not in this life," I said. I didn't have a perfect memory, but I wouldn't have forgotten that. I was sure of it.

"In this life, I didn't stop to look at them as long. I already knew them. Your father didn't say anything."

"That's the whole story of this life, isn't it?" I said acridly. "You already knew everything."

Wist turned to face me, her back to the closed garden gate. "I didn't know if I'd done the right thing," she said. "I didn't know what else we could do to pass the Healer's Bill of Rights. I didn't know how to keep you safe once we reached a future I'd never seen before. I didn't know if I could live without you."

"Well, isn't that romantic."

Wist gave me a look of—nothing, actually. Of practiced blankness. I could read anything into that expression—exasperation, confusion, dark humor.

"Do you want to go in?" She gestured back at the cottage, a perfect imitation of my parents' old house.

I demurred. "The real thing is long gone, isn't it? Thanks for showing me, though. Did you make this on purpose?"

She shook her head. "I didn't make anything in the basement on purpose."

"Let's go outside," I said.

"Outside," Wist repeated, as if she didn't know what the word meant.

I pointed up at the illusory sky (aka the basement ceiling). "When I was stuck here trying to get your magic back, we hardly spent any time on the ground outside the tower."

That was how we ended up walking side by side through knee-length grass that shimmered blue like a butterfly's wings in the light. It was before noon, but the winter sun already stretched our shadows out at a long angle, as if eager to set. I was in cargo pants, with the ends tucked into sturdy boots, and a small knit turtleneck. Wist didn't seem to be walking particularly fast, but I had to take big strides to keep up with her. I caught her glancing over at my all-white hair as if she wanted to ask about it.

"Did the Board give you shit about us bonding?" I asked.

"Not today."

"Today can't have been the first time you met with them after regaining your magic. How about before?"

"Don't worry about it," Wist said.

"I'd prefer not to," I retorted. "But you know Fanren didn't decide to sic mercenaries on you all on his own. Someone on the Board was using him as a conduit. That's who I'm wondering about. I'm wondering what they'll try to do next."

She stopped in her tracks. All of a sudden she looked downright genial. To be completely honest, it was a tad disturbing. Wind stirred the bluish prairie around the tower. The tall grass swishing made a sound like running water. Wist gave me a munificent smile.

"What'd you do?" I asked.

"Nothing special," she said cheerfully. "There were some questions about where I'd been, doubts about how much of my magic I'd recovered. I gave a little demonstration to reassure them."

"Hah. Sounds fun."

"It was very cathartic," Wist confessed.

"Wish I could've been there." I said it without thinking. We exchanged looks for a moment and then started walking again, without any particular discussion of our destination. The old-growth woods loomed up ahead.

CHAPTER TWENTY-THREE

The Magebreaker and the Kraken

IT WAS MUCH EASIER than the last time I'd traced this path through the woods. My shoes fit better, and this time I hadn't stabbed myself in the leg. Funny how that made a difference.

I put my coat back on and zipped it up as high as it would go. With the colder air now, there were hardly any gnats out. No need for Wist to constantly wave them away from her face.

"I need to explain what I meant," she said. She watched the ground—a slippery mass of rocks and moss and roots—as she spoke. "I told you I didn't know if I could live without you."

"And here I took it as a confession of undying love."

"If you don't want to know—"

I caught at her elbow for balance. "No," I said. "Tell me."

We picked our way past shaggy vines as thick as my wrist, past gargantuan pink slime molds. I kept hanging onto Wist's arm. If I fell, she could either try to do something about it, or she could tumble down with me.

"I didn't bring you back to life right away," Wist said.

"I figured not."

The first Kraken had forbidden resurrection of the dead—but that didn't mean anyone actually knew how to do it. Wist would have needed to first develop the technique from scratch, and then imprint it on one of her magic branches. It would most likely have taken up multiple branches, actually, given the complexity of what she was trying to accomplish.

Anyway, it wasn't something you could just come up with on the spot. Not even if you were mad with grief, and not even if you were a certified genius. For better or for worse, she would've had plenty of chances to take a good hard look at what she was attempting to do. She would've had plenty of chances to reconsider.

"You were cremated," she said. "Your parents kept your ashes. I kept your bond thread. At first I started designing resurrection magic as—as a way to keep busy. A theoretical exercise. I went through the motions of life blindly. I thought of nothing except how to make it work. I thought of it while washing my hands. I thought of it while failing to fall asleep. I thought of it when the Board called me in to tell me your killer had acted alone, that he was just some kind of psychopath who'd gone rogue."

"Don't tell me you bought that."

"Of course not," Wist said. "But I didn't argue. I barely heard a thing they said. My head was too full of resurrection magic. Not that I planned to actually go through with it."

"Because you were afraid of the consequences?"

She made a sound that came up just short of a laugh. "What consequences? The previous Kraken never actually said a word about what would happen if someone broke one of her taboos. Don't use magic for this, she said, and left it at that. And it didn't make sense to think disaster could strike simply as a result of using magic in a certain specific way. People use magic to kill each other all the time, and the continent hasn't shattered yet. Why would using magic to give someone life be any different?"

"Fair," I said, "but then why did you tell yourself you wouldn't do it?"

Wist went silent. The curly ferns in this area came up to my hips. I fervently hoped they weren't sprinkling bugs all over me.

"I thought I understood why the previous Kraken made her list of taboos," she said eventually. "Not because using magic to bring back the dead or change the flow of time would have any special repercussions in and of itself. It's because—if you started to do that, where would you stop? I wanted you alive. But what about parents who just lost a newborn? What about that one classmate of yours who died back when we were still in school? What about everyone else lying in grave and urns? Why not them?"

She still had that one branch of magic that functioned like a long tail, reaching forward to push sheets of hanging vegetable matter out of the way.

"Well, all right," I said. "I get the point. I'm not a philosopher. So what changed your mind?"

"My magic was acting up," she said. "Wild magic started manifesting around me. Nothing that would hurt anyone. Easy enough to cover up. But no amount of healing would stop it.

"Then I started to sense my control slipping. Sometimes I'd black out for a second or two, and when I came to I'd see that I'd used all kinds of magic without realizing it. I asked the top healers at NHRI to take a look at me. No one saw anything wrong."

We had to be close to the clearing now, the one with the vorpal hole. Wist stopped short. I stumbled, still holding her elbow. Her magic curled around me like a third arm—not that it was possible to pull me much closer. Unlike before, it was now far warmer to the touch than human skin. I could feel its heat seeping down through all my layers of clothing. Quite nice to have in winter, actually.

Someone had wound caution tape from tree to tree, blocking the way. Behind the tape, tiny vorpal holes filled the air like all the little shiny bits of an exploding firework frozen in time and space. There were far too many to count, scattered high and low, clustering closer together as they approached the clearing that contained the original vorpal hole, their ancestor. They were every shape and size, some small and irregular like cancerous moles, some sagging like rips in a pair of jeans. It hurt to look at. My eyes tried to focus and failed; kept trying and failing until the strain became too much to bear.

"I thought I was on the verge of going berserk," Wist said. "No—I was sure of it. Without you there to heal me, I would just get worse and worse."

"Wait," I interjected. "We were teenagers when we first met. That means you already spent almost half your life getting healed by other people, and you never snapped. If you got along okay without me all those years when you were growing up, you should've been fine without me once I died."

"I thought the same thing at first."

She took a few steps back from the caution tape, pulling me with her. The clearing—and the misshapen galaxy of vorpal hole shrapnel surrounding it—was extremely quiet, as if the forest birds had by now learned to give it a wide berth.

"Then I started looking at PubSec data," she said. "Mages are statistically most likely to snap within the first few years after losing a bonded healer.

It's not a huge difference, but it's there. And I could feel myself getting worse by the day. I started having hallucinations. I saw vorpal holes where none existed. I saw people at the supermarket trying to use magic on me when in reality they were subliminals or healers or simply mages minding their own business. I almost killed a man on reflex, and all he was trying to do was reach for a bag of grapes.

"I had no choice, I told myself. If I went berserk, there was no one alive capable of stopping me, much less neutralizing me. I couldn't even imagine what I might do. It made me sick to think of it. I couldn't keep any food down. For the sake of the world, I needed to either destroy myself, or bring you back to keep me from going completely berserk. And I thought—at the time I thought I could still do greater good by living on as the Kraken."

I looked up at the side of her face. "So that's why you tried to avoid bonding this time around. You feared you'd go through the whole thing all over if you bonded a healer again and then lost them."

Wist shook her head, a small tight motion. "Reliving everything from birth gave me a lot of time to think," she said. "The more time passed, the more I questioned myself. What if I'd been imagining my symptoms? What if I'd made the whole thing up? Not a single mage or healer or magic perception specialist ever saw any kind of fatal twist in my magic.

"After you went to prison, the questions came back stronger. In the beginning, I thought I'd better go tell the Board I still needed you to heal me. I thought I'd have to tell them it was the only way to keep me from going berserk. But I didn't want to cause unnecessary alarm. So I waited to make sure. I waited and waited."

"But we weren't bonded when I went to prison," I said, perplexed. "In our previous lives, we bonded young, and then I died. Wasn't that what set you off in the first place? So you played it safe in this life. You didn't bond me. It makes perfect sense that you were still fine even after you ditched me."

Wist's magic branch released me. Its heat lingered, but now I could breathe easier. She glanced down at me with the same face she used to wear when surrounded by Shiens, that implacable mask that let nothing in or out.

"I went to look for the same data I saw the last time around," she said. "The Public Security records showing that mages are most prone to going berserk after losing a bondmate. I couldn't find it. It didn't exist. No—the data was there, but all it showed was that the timing of a mage snapping is completely unpredictable. No statistical patterns. Bondmate loss has nothing to do with it."

"Okay," I said. "Maybe the studies had a different outcome in this world. That's not unthinkable."

"But it is," Wist said, almost kindly, as if trying to let me down easy. "This world is exactly the same as the one we were first born in. I heard so many of the same conversations. I went to the same classes and took the same tests with the same answers. I saw the same murders and terrorist attacks reported in the news. The same winter storms came, and the same amount of snow fell, and the same companies surged to the top of the stock market, and the same slate of Board members welcomed me with the same words when I took my seat among them.

"The only differences were in my own actions, and I changed as little as possible. Just enough to see you live past twenty-five."

"There was another difference, wasn't there?" I said. "More vorpal holes forming after you brought me back. Vorpal holes everywhere. The true consequence of breaking the previous Kraken's taboo. If only she'd gone to the trouble of warning us about exactly what would happen. I wonder if she even knew."

I was still holding Wist's arm. She lifted my hand away and retreated another step or two, watching as though to make sure I wouldn't follow her. The air was hushed and cold and full of shadows. No direct sunlight made it all the way down to the forest floor; it poured distorted through layer upon layer of leaves and branches.

Wist said: "I doubt I was ever truly at risk of going berserk, not for a second. I saw what I wanted to see. I convinced myself I couldn't live without you. I concocted a morally justified reason to resurrect you. I pretended I was doing it to save the world.

"In truth I was tricking myself. I was the same as every other person who's ever lost someone they loved. There was nothing deeper or more special or more deserving about my loss or my grief. But I made myself believe I had a legitimate excuse to bring you back, and you alone. After you'd been in prison for two years or so, I finally admitted it. And I—"

She swallowed whatever she'd been about to say next. The vorpal holes' seething presence in my peripheral vision was still more than enough to turn my stomach. Wist gazed at them as if they didn't bother her in the slightest.

"No guards here anymore," I said, if only to make the heavy air do something more than just sit there.

"Observers come by to check up on the holes once a week or so."

"Not a high priority for sealing, are they?" They weren't in a high-traffic area. They weren't spawning deadly vorpal beasts. They weren't actively expanding.

"If the government asked me to close every vorpal hole like this, there'd be no time to eat or sleep."

"Or frolic in the woods with your girlfriend."

Wist gave me a wordless look. I laughed loud and sharp. The sound almost seemed to vanish too fast, as if the vorpal holes were sucking it up.

"What would happen if I tried to go through one of these?" I asked.

"Don't."

"Mori told me his brother fell through a vorpal hole when they were children," I said. "Get what that means? If far fewer vorpal holes spawned in our first world, Mori's brother probably stayed alive. You traded him for me, in a sense. Not just him. Tons of other people we've never met, never heard of." I curled cold fingers into fists in my pockets. Didn't feel like going to the trouble of putting my gloves on. "You had no idea that's what would happen, of course."

"But it happened," Wist said.

"And here we are." I glanced sideways at the jumble of vorpal holes and quickly regretted it. "Let me guess. You lost your magic trying to make it better?"

"...How'd you know?"

"This isn't exactly high-level detective work," I said tartly. "I've never seen or heard of a mage who succeeded at completely ripping up their magic by the roots. Not just that—you salted the fields so nothing grew back. You must've been trying to do something only a Kraken-class would dream of attempting. That sure narrows down the possibilities."

I gestured in the direction of the vorpal holes, this time without looking their way. "You vanished from summer to fall, and then you reappeared without your magic. Or so they told me. What really happened?"

Wist looked down, like she needed to think about it.

"We're bonded," I said.

No response.

"You owe me this." I paused for effect. I wasn't sure if it would have much of an impact on someone who apparently had long since drowned herself in guilt, filled her lungs up to the very top with it. No one could stop me from trying, though.

"I learned how to look through vorpal holes," Wist said to the caution tape stretching along on her right. "It took a few years of trying. I looked through and I saw other worlds. Countless other worlds. Some completely different from ours. But I also found our first world, our original world."

"It's still there?"

"It didn't stop existing just because we abandoned it. It's still there. It's the world where you died at twenty-five. And then the Kraken vanished. And then the largest vorpal hole ever recorded devoured half of Osmanthus City. And then more vorpal holes spawned all over the continent, swallowing entire towns and farms and schools and bridges and factories. They've suffered so much worse than anything that ever happened in this world. And they had no Kraken left to seal any of the holes for them."

Abruptly she turned toward me. "You mentioned Mori's brother," she said. "In our other world, they're both dead now. So is Manatree. Fanren. The entire Shien clan. Your parents. Everyone you ever knew on the Board of Mages. The vorpal holes forming here in this world? They've increased. They're still deadly. But they're nothing in comparison. I took a gamble when I broke the first Kraken's taboo. Our first world is what suffered the consequences. When I saw that...."

"You had to fix it."

"I went over to the other world. I thought if I tore my magic out—if I used it all at once, right down to the core—I could seal all their vorpal holes and stop new ones from forming. It wouldn't bring anyone back to life. But it might at least stop the world from breaking further."

She glanced at her naked hand.

No gloves for Wist. Just cold aching fingers in the open air, I guess. Or maybe she had the strength of mind to disregard it. Maybe she felt nothing.

"I was only there for a few hours," she said. "It seemed to work. I left right away, without anyone seeing me. But when I came back, three months had passed here."

So that was why Wist had been so adamant about avoiding the vorpal hole in the clearing. She'd feared that the magic regrowth it gave her was simply being stolen away from what she'd deliberately left behind in our other world.

I thought of the miniature vorpal holes massing behind the caution tape a scant few meters away from us, thick and numerous as a school of fish. Had Wist truly regrown any of her magic from scratch? Or had she merely taken back what belonged to her, branch after branch after branch, unintentionally ripped it away from the ruined world that lay on the far side of those teeming wounds in reality?

I caught at Wist's hand before she could pull it back out of reach. It was as chilly as expected. "All right," I said. "That's enough of this place. Take me home."

"To your apartment?"

"To the tower."

Wist's room felt strangely empty without all the life support devices rearing up to fill it. When she sat on her bed, I sat next to her without awaiting an invitation. It's not like she had much other furniture to offer me.

"Clematis," she said. It came out rough. She cleared her throat, took a drink of stale-looking water from her nightstand.

"Yeah, what?"

"I won't complain about you being here."

"You better not."

"You have every right to ask whatever you want from me."

"I sure do," I affirmed.

Wist looked at me helplessly. "What do you want from me?" she asked.

I had my knees pulled up to my chest, my arms around my knees, my boots discarded near the door. Our shoulders touched.

I remembered the single moon-shaped window high up on the wall of my prison cell. I remembered hobbling mage after mage after mage until my brain turned to porridge and I almost fainted onto my floor bed. As I fell asleep I'd see visions of the magic of every mage I'd ever touched, their cores and the unique shape of their branches. I never forgot any of them—I remembered them like a palmist remembering hands.

Once I slept, I dreamt of dying a million different ways; the same dreams I'd had all my life. Then more mages the next day. It was incredible to me that so many mages had gone berserk or broken the law or simply fallen out of favor with a Board member. Some weren't Osmanthian. Some seemed like political prisoners, innocent of any real wrongdoing. Whatever the case, the supply never seemed to run dry.

"I spent all my time in prison not missing you," I said to Wist. "I had to learn to live with the knowledge that I would never see you again. I had to learn to live with the knowledge that whatever I'd once meant to you, it wasn't enough for a single token visit."

"I'm—"

"No," I said. "I definitely don't want your apologies. Anyway, I understand now that you had your own suffering to deal with, and your own reasons to stay away. The reasons don't really matter at this point. I spent all those years learning to live with the fact that you were somewhere out there in the world, living your own life, and no matter how much or how little I thought of you, our paths would never cross again. Because you'd decided they shouldn't.

"Me, I had no choice in the matter. I had to wake up every day with that. I had to accept it. It had to become part of me. It's very—it's very difficult to turn around now and try to unwind that."

"You don't have to force yourself," Wist said quietly.

"Well, I don't like the idea of being stuck with what prison made me into, either." I nudged her. "So you found my other self dead. Did you feel me dying through the bond? Did you get there before I died? Or was I already gone when you arrived?"

The blood had left her face. "Clem—"

"Did you call out for me?" I demanded. "Were you crying my name? What'd it sound like? Was it the same as how I cried out for you when they took me away?"

"Clematis." An edge of desperation had crept into her voice. "I truly don't know what you want. What do you want from me?"

"Wrong question," I said. I got up on my knees and glared at her, one hand on the headboard for balance. "'*What do you want from me?*' What do you think you are, some kind of saint? You sent me back to live life fresh and clean from the start. Meanwhile you clung to memories of your previous life—your previous failure—so you could play at being my guardian angel. You must've been bored as hell as a baby. As a toddler."

"There was a lot of sleeping," Wist said. "I didn't have an adult brain. It took a while to even be able to understand what was happening around me. It took longer to be able to articulate myself. But it wasn't hard. All I had to do was blend in."

I snorted. "Go through school all over again? I'd go crazy! Not only that, you didn't even try to change things up at all, did you? You strove to interfere as little as possible. Except in the areas that you thought might improve my chances for survival. Like putting off bonding. You've spent this entire redo of life suppressing yourself, secretly watching over me, being horrified by the consequences of reviving me, and fighting to clean up the aftermath. And you did it all alone, without a single person in the entire world having any idea what you were going through.

"God, it pisses me off! Could you have more of a martyr complex? Did you welcome every second of punishment? Did you congratulate yourself for struggling nobly through the pain? Or were you just miserable and frustrated and confused and frightened, the loneliest woman on the continent?"

There were no lights on in the room, just the sun slanting obliquely past the window-wall. Wist looked at me with wide dark eyes, then looked away. I'd heard her make a noise like I'd punched her, like she had something to say about it. But she said nothing.

"If you're going to ask me anything, you'd better answer first," I said. "You owe me that much." I pointed at her. I pointed at myself. "What do *you* want from *me*?"

Wist started to get up. I caught her shoulder.

"Tell the truth," I said.

The mask slipped for a second. Her face contorted, then went empty again. She took my hand off her shoulder. She took my other wrist. She pushed me down on my back on the colorless bedding.

"There isn't any wanting left in me," she said plainly. "I have my duty to this world. I have my duty to the other world. I have atonement. Nothing else left."

"Tell the truth," I said.

I touched the wall she'd put in the middle of our bond. It was a mental blockade—nothing magical. Two could play that game. The wall had only lasted because I let it stay there, because I'd cooperated. Now it crumbled to dust at my touch. I felt Wist flinch at the other end of the bond. I felt her cower.

She released my wrists and fled. I got up slowly, followed her to the window. She leaned her forehead on the glass. I watched her for a moment, then tugged at her sleeve, made her take a halting step away from the window. I put my arms around her from behind.

I must've looked ridiculous; my head hardly came up to her shoulder blades. I buried my face in her back and took a deep breath of her sweatshirt.

She said my name under her breath. She said it again. She turned in my arms and held me tighter, straining my neck. I quickly went up on tiptoe to spare myself—now wouldn't be the best time to suffer a surprise spinal cord injury. I felt like an idiot for it, like a dumb trained animal, but I really did love her scent.

"I want you to stay with me," Wist said into my hair. Her voice broke and broke again. "I want you to love me."

There were no words in the bond. But the bond told me she was talking to me, the me holding her right now, not the old me who had died a lifetime ago and gone deaf to her cries. Don't leave me, she said. I deserve to be alone for the rest of eternity. But please don't leave me alone again.

I could say the same to you, I told her.

CHAPTER TWENTY-FOUR

13 Years Ago

A MIDSUMMER EVENING, just cool enough to be tolerable. We were twenty-one. The Palace of Magi courtyard was filled with the voices of crickets and frogs and cicadas. I stood there throwing pebbles into a lily pond. Fireflies idled in the bushes and treetops, colorful as tiny lantana flowers, red and green and blue and neon yellow. Dim floating lanterns drifted through the air without any support, seeking out patches of undiluted shadow.

Finally Wist emerged from the building and came over to join me. She was in a dark suit, perfectly tailored. Even in flat shoes, it made her look taller. She wore the suit as if she were used to it, although I knew for a fact that she wasn't. Her thick four-strand braid draped over and around one arm like the long end of a scarf.

I caught at her hand and made her show me the slim ring on her index finger—some kind of shining black material that at first glance looked a bit like hematite. As a piece of jewelry, it wasn't terribly impressive. But only Board members could wear it.

"So this is it," I said. "You're in. You're one of *them*."

Wist watched me poke at the ring, her expression unreadable. "When revolution comes for the mageocracy, I hope you spare me."

"Ha, ha. I'll think about it." I straightened up. "This is the start of how we change the world, or at least Osmanthus. A grand occasion. Time to celebrate!"

I passed her a canned cocktail from my bag. The throngs of fireflies and the occasional passing lantern offered just enough light to read the label. Wist turned it in her hand.

"Time to celebrate," she repeated. "With this? Do they even allow drinking here?"

I took out another silver can for myself—it was just as lukewarm as the twilight summer air around us—cracked it open, and knocked it against hers. "You're Magus Shien now. Who's going to stop us?"

Wist took a reluctant sip. "Classy," she said.

"We can get fancier drinks after we go down in history," I told her. "We've got to earn them first. Here's to the start of the dream."

I made her tell me about all of the other Board members. Everything they'd said to her at the induction ceremony. How they'd looked at and interacted with each other. Who seemed like rivals, allies, ideological enemies. The courtyard garden was excessively spacious. We hardly saw another soul except for the fireflies.

We crossed a walkway to a gazebo right in the middle of the water. It felt a bit cooler here. My drink—something lemony—tasted sour and lingered stickily on my tongue.

I leaned on Wist and told her our plan. First we would pass the Healer's Bill of Rights. That might take three to five years. Then I wanted to take a closer look at international affairs. Osmanthus was extremely insular, and had tense relations with most of its neighbors. But that might start to change if it became known that healer's rights were finally progressing a little more here.

The more exposure Osmanthians had to other cultures, the easier it would be to make them see the flaws in the mageocracy. And anyway, Wist herself—both feared and admired as the Kraken—was potentially the greatest diplomatic tool of all. Every country on the continent could use some form of magical aid, something more than what we already gave them.

"Sounds like a lot of work," Wist said as we looked out at the glimmering pond. Her braid curled around my side the way an affectionate cat might twine about your ankles.

"It'll be worth it," I told her.

"You're the brains," she said. "I'm the muscle."

"Still a team effort."

Without warning, she leaned over and kissed the top of my head. "It's a good dream," she said, muffled. "I hope it comes true."

I squirmed away to get a better look at her. Her eyes were very dark. No fireflies out here in the center of the wide black pond.

"We'll make it happen," I insisted. "Or if we fail at politics, then maybe we'll just have to burn the whole place down."

Some time later, several more empty cocktail cans stood neatly lined up on the gazebo table, and my bag felt infinitely lighter.

I was starting to doze off on Wist's shoulder. Leaning up against her in the darkness like this made me want to curl up in a nest of her clothes to sleep. She hummed quietly—a melody of her own invention, although she still managed to make it sound vaguely off-key. The frogs and crickets at the water's edge began to seem very far away.

Wist's humming stopped. "One thing I noticed," she said. "All the other Board members have bondmates."

I yawned without lifting my head. "And they're all quite old, aren't they? Bet a bunch of them are on their second or third bonded healer. Bet at least a few of them had healers that fell out of windows. Shot themselves in the back. All sorts of unfortunate accidents."

"They asked me about my plans for bonding."

"Want to bond?" I asked sleepily. "I mean, if it'll improve your position as the newest Board member—"

"I didn't come out of that meeting thinking I wanted to be more like the rest of them."

I sat up and grinned at her. "That's the spirit."

Wist took my hand as if to idly examine it. Her black ring felt surprisingly cold now. Drinking changed little about her demeanor, but it made her gestures lazier, more affectionate. She touched my knuckles to her mouth—not really kissing them, just holding them there. No real reason for it. I observed her with amusement.

"Let's bond after we pass the Healer's Bill of Rights, then," I said. "What better way to celebrate?"

"That might take years," Wist said against my hand.

"Well, if you want to elope right this instant, that's fine too," I replied. "I'm not picky."

Wist's expression remained as deathly still as the nighttime pond water all around the gazebo, with its near-perfect reflection of the lanterns floating pensively overhead. But the long rope of her braid briefly tightened around me, a reflexive tensing like a sudden shiver she couldn't completely suppress.

"I like your first suggestion," Wist said.

"Delayed gratification? Sure, that works." I stooped my head and kissed her index finger, right above the precious black ring. "Now we've really got to pass that bill."

We talked about making Osmanthus a better place for healers and subliminals. We talked about traveling the world—at the time I'd never left Osmanthus. We talked about whether anything would change if we bonded. We joked about getting matching bond threads and parading ourselves around the Shien family manor.

I was young and brilliant and arrogant and absolutely certain in my knowledge that Wist needed me and loved me, so sure of myself that I never sought out any words for it. I never imagined getting assassinated, much less resurrected. I never imagined getting a Board member killed—at least not by accident, anyway. I never imagined getting caught and sentenced for treason. More than anything, I never imagined that Wist would be the one to turn me in for it.

I didn't bring revolution to the mageocracy. I didn't pass the Healer's Bill of Rights. But almost everything else we talked about came true in the end, years later. We bonded. Eventually, after wrangling permission from the government, I left Osmanthus for the first time. I went with Wist to every country on the continent. I breathed the air of mountains and river valleys, farmland and desolate beaches, young foreign cities and ancient monuments. And not just that. Together with Wist, I looked into the myriad other worlds that lay on the far side of vorpal holes.

Not even Wist knew what life held for us next. We were already years into a future unknown to her. And whatever happened, no one would be bringing me back to life a second time. The first time had already cost far too much.

So I let my pride go into early retirement. I took Wist's hand even when she didn't reach for me. I wouldn't let either of us suffer alone again, not ever. I stayed with Wist, and I loved her.

A Note from the Author

THANK YOU FOR READING! Loved it? Hated it? All reviews are deeply appreciated.

I've written quite a few novels before, most of which will probably never see the light of day outside my hard drive. But this was the first time since becoming an adult that I dove into a story and simply wrote exactly what I wanted to—without questioning myself, without over-thinking.

I spent several years noodling away at the initial concept and making zero real progress. Then one day, right around the end of 2021, something clicked. I decided to stop worrying and give my id the reins. I decided to write about the complex, indelible, ambiguous—and perhaps a bit tortured—sort of relationship that I myself love to encounter in all forms of fiction, from books to anime to video games. And then it was as if the writing I hadn't been doing during those years of frustrated, circuitous brainstorming (and a whole lot of gaming) came rushing out all at once.

Again, thank you so much for spending your time with *The Lowest Healer and the Highest Mage*. It was a pure joy to write. It might take me a little while, but I definitely plan to publish more novels set in the same world (and perhaps focusing on the same characters).

Follow my Author Page for future updates if you'd like to see more: **amazon.com/author/hiyodori**

Hope to see you next time!

– Hiyodori